Trent looked downright flirtatious.

"Are we done?" Erin managed to squeak out.

Trent's blue eyes sparkled with mischief, and Erin's first instinct was to smile back at him. Thankfully, her common sense kicked in, and she stopped herself. Smiling at Trent struck her as an activity only a tiny bit less dangerous than carrying around a lit stick of dynamite. The man had handsome devil written all over him.

When Erin didn't return his smile, he only grinned more. She could tell he found her amusing, but she didn't care. She wasn't going to flirt with this man no matter how tempting it might be.

Trent continued to stare right at her. "Congratulations. You're no longer a suspect in Pookie's kidnapping," he finally said. "I will have to continue my investigation, though I'll be looking elsewhere for clues...."

"Woosh. Well, that's a relief—"

"But I'd say *we're* far from done."

For more, turn to page 9

"You're rescuing me?" Leigh asked.

"Well, when the band started this slow number I didn't want you to be embarrassed about your dance partner wandering off," Jared explained, swaying her to the soft music.

Annoyed by his attitude, Leigh had a devious idea. She placed her hands on his chest and waited until they got bumped again by other couples. Then she softly undid a few buttons on his vest. He was in for a major surprise when this dance ended.

"I'm glad we've talked, Leigh. For lots of reasons things didn't work out between us before. But I'd like to know you're still my friend."

Maybe a truce was the only logical thing to do, she thought. He skimmed the fingers of one hand slowly down her back to her waist, and she barely managed not to sigh.

"I'd like to think we're friends," he continued. People who help each other out in times of need."

Something in the way he said that made her frown. "When would we ever need to help each other?"

His lips rested right next to her ear, then whispered, "How about now? I'll rezip your dress if you refasten my vest."

For more, turn to page 197

HARLEQUIN DUETS

ISBN 0-373-44153-3

Copyright in the collection:
Copyright © 2002 by Harlequin Books S.A.

The publisher acknowledges the copyright holder
of the individual works as follows:

MEANT FOR TRENT
Copyright © 2002 by Mary E. Lounsbury

LEIGH'S FOR ME
Copyright © 2002 by Mary E. Lounsbury

This edition published by arrangement with Harlequin Books S.A.

® and TM are trademarks of the publisher. Trademarks indicated with ® are registered in the United States Patent and Trademark Office, the Canadian Trade Marks Office and in other countries.

Visit us at www.eHarlequin.com

Printed in U.S.A.

Meant for Trent

Liz Jarrett

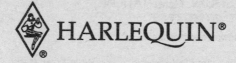

TORONTO • NEW YORK • LONDON
AMSTERDAM • PARIS • SYDNEY • HAMBURG
STOCKHOLM • ATHENS • TOKYO • MILAN • MADRID
PRAGUE • WARSAW • BUDAPEST • AUCKLAND

Dear Reader,

There's nothing like a good plan. It lets you decide what you want to accomplish and helps you see how to make it happen. Leigh Barrett understands the value of a good plan. She created one to help her systematically get all of her meddling brothers married. Once they're married, she'll be a free woman, able to enjoy her independence.

Too bad life likes to mess up the best of plans. Poor Leigh. She no sooner gets her brothers married than Jared Kendrick comes back into town. He's the last man on earth Leigh ever wants to see again...so why can't she stop thinking about him?

I hope you enjoy these last two stories in the HOMETOWN HEARTTHROBS series. I loved writing about the Barrett family, and I hope you love reading about them. They're a fun bunch.

Happy reading,

Liz Jarrett

Books by Liz Jarrett

HARLEQUIN DUETS
  20—DARN NEAR PERFECT
*71—CATCHING CHASE
    NABBING NATHAN

HARLEQUIN TEMPTATION
827—TEMPTING TESS

*Hometown Heartthrobs

To my sister, Barbara, and my brother, Doug.
Thanks for making childhood fun.

And as always, to my editor, Kathryn Lye.
These books wouldn't have happened without you.
Thanks so very much.

1

"TRENT BARRETT, I INSIST you arrest Erin Weber immediately. The woman is a thief and belongs in jail," Delia Haverhill said loudly, her arms crossed under her ample chest. "Arrest her right now."

Trent scratched his jaw and considered the middle-aged woman in front of him. Delia wasn't what you would call the sweetest person in Paxton, Texas. Truth be told, she put the cur in curmudgeon.

But still, as chief of police of Paxton, he couldn't simply ignore Delia's complaint. And the woman hadn't, to his knowledge, ever had anyone arrested before. There very well could be some truth in what she was saying. A least, a little.

"Why don't you tell me what the problem is and who Erin Weber might be," he said in a calm, soft voice, hoping Delia might follow suit and stop hollering at the top of her lungs. "Then we can figure out what's the best course of action to take."

Unfortunately Delia didn't lower her volume one bit. She leaned halfway across his desk and said, "I've already told you what action needs to be

taken. Erin Weber needs to be arrested. Now get up
from behind that desk and come with me. I'll show
you who this woman is and what she did. You
won't believe her nerve. I was nice enough to visit
her store last Saturday with my grandson, and she
rewards me by stealing my Pookie. And to make it
worse, she's displaying Pookie right outside her
store. The woman belongs in jail, I tell you.''

Trent thought he was up-to-date on all the street
names for drugs, but he'd never heard of pookie.

''What in the world is pookie?''

Delia wagged a finger at him. ''Get out of your
chair, and I'll show you.''

Reluctantly Trent stood. ''I'll be happy to get one
of my officers to help you, Delia. But I have a meeting with the mayor in about an hour.''

Delia frowned. ''Did I or did I not change your
diapers when you were too young to know your feet
from your hands?''

His secretary, Ann Seaver, had walked in mid-
way through Delia's comment. She raised one eyebrow and looked precariously close to giggling.

Trent shook his head and sighed. ''Delia, I sure
do hope you're talking about when you used to
baby-sit me years ago. If you mean something else,
then one of us is seriously warped.''

Delia was obviously not amused. She looked at
Trent like he was something stuck on the bottom
of her shoes. ''Of course I'm talking about when I

baby-sat you. And I would think that means you'll be happy to help me now.'' She gave him a squinty-eyed look. ''After all, I never let you cry yourself to sleep like some baby-sitters do. I rocked you to sleep and sang you pretty songs.''

Ann made a spurting sound behind the hand she had across her mouth. Trent was certain she wasn't the only one who would be laughing today about what Delia had said. No doubt Ann would tell most of the officers and by the end of the day, everyone would be quoting Delia Haverhill.

Dang it all.

''Come on, Delia. Show me what this pookie is.'' He circled his desk and stood next to the older woman. ''I think you've already shared enough baby-sitting stories for one day.''

Delia didn't even crack a smile. She simply nodded, and headed toward the door. When they drew even with Ann, his secretary was still laughing.

''What in the world are you laughing about, young lady?'' Delia asked her. ''Seems to me I changed more than a few of your diapers, too.''

Ann turned bright red and Trent chuckled as he trailed after Delia. That was one major advantage of growing up in a small town. Sure, everyone knew embarrassing things about you. But hey, you knew embarrassing things about them as well.

''So, Delia, how long do you expect this to

take?'' he had to ask as they headed for the front door.

''It will take however long you need to read Erin Weber her Melissa rights.''

The bright sunshine hit him once they were outside, so Trent pulled his sunglasses out of his pocket and slipped them on. ''Miranda.''

''What?''

''Not Melissa. Miranda.''

Delia waved one hand and started down the street. ''Melissa. Miranda. What difference does it make? Just read her the rights and toss her in jail. Now come on.''

Reluctantly Trent followed. He sure didn't like being ordered around, but as the chief of police, he had to keep the people of Paxton happy.

''Tell me, what is this pookie stuff you think some woman stole from you?'' he asked, once they were headed down Main Street.

''First off, it isn't pookie stuff. His name is Pookie. Pay attention, Trent.''

He thought he had been, but reading smoke signals would be easier than understanding Delia Haverhill. ''Sorry if I misunderstood.''

''Second off, it isn't just some woman who stole my Pookie. It's Erin Weber, the woman who opened the pet shop over on Collier Street. Naturally I suspected her as soon as Pookie disappeared.''

By now, he and Delia had turned off Main Street and were halfway down Collier. Delia pointed to the front door of a store.

"There's Pookie. Big as life. On display for the whole town to see. Erin certainly has some nerve."

Trent looked where she was pointing and bit back a grin. Pookie was a plastic statue of a rabbit, the kind you might put in your garden or flowerbed. The statue was old and well-worn and couldn't be worth more than a couple of bucks.

But Delia was cooing and fussing over the blasted thing like it was real.

"Now go on inside and arrest her," Delia said.

Trent slipped off his sunglasses and glanced around. As he could have predicted, he and Delia were starting to draw a crowd. Paxton didn't offer a lot of diversions, so anytime anything even moderately interesting happened, everyone rushed out to see what was going on. He better head on in and talk to this Erin Weber before he found himself knee-deep in nosy citizens.

"Arrest her, arrest her, arrest her," Delia said loudly. Then she folded her arms under her ample chest once more and took on the expression of one who believes herself incapable of error.

Damn, what a way to start the day.

With about as much enthusiasm as a ten-year-old boy stuck at a Girl Scout meeting, Trent shoved open the door of Precious Pets and walked inside.

He'd only made it a few steps when a woman yelled, "Freeze!"

Trent froze as instructed and started to go for his gun, when a petite, brown-haired dynamo rushed at him from the back of the store.

"Don't move or you'll frighten Brutus," the woman said. "You almost stepped on him. He's right by your left foot." She tipped her head, her expression more than a little accusatory. "Didn't you see Brutus when you came in?"

Obviously not or he wouldn't have almost stepped on him. Trent glanced around and didn't immediately see anything. But after learning what Pookie was, Trent wasn't certain he wanted to know what a Brutus might be. Probably a big ol' ugly snake. Or maybe a tarantula.

But curiosity got to him, so he looked down anyway, then breathed a sigh of relief.

Brutus was a little, bitty fluff ball.

"What kind of animal is that?" he had to ask.

The woman frowned. "A puppy, of course. What in the world did you think he was?"

Trent studied the round, white ball of fur with two black specks for eyes. "He kinda looks like a dust bunny."

The woman moved forward and picked up the puppy off the floor. "A dust bunny. Sheesh. He's a sweetheart, aren't you, baby?"

Obviously knowing he was being praised, Brutus

let out a series of yips and yaps. Trent would give the puppy credit—he had an impressive bark for something that looked like a ball of dust. No wonder the dog had a tough name like Brutus. He needed every advantage he could get.

"Is there something I can help you with?" the woman asked, still cradling the dog.

"I'm Trent Barrett, chief of police here in Paxton." He extended his hand, which the woman shook in a firm, no-nonsense handshake. Just like the pup, the woman might look small and fragile, but she was stronger than she appeared. Her grip would do a lumberjack proud.

"I'm Erin Weber. I own Precious Pets." Brutus started squirming, so Erin put the puppy down. The furball immediately trotted over and tugged on Trent's shoelaces.

"Hey, mutt, cut it out," he said.

"Brutus might not be a pedigree, but he's hardly a mutt," Erin defended.

"I didn't mean it in a negative way."

"Mutt is a word that has no positive connotations," she countered. "Even though he's from the animal shelter, Brutus has a great deal of dignity."

Trent grinned as he watched the pup chew on the shoelaces of his best boots. "Is that a fact? He has dignity?"

Erin frowned. "Of course."

Trent tried to wipe the grin off his face but the

dang thing refused to budge. "I'll keep that in mind."

There was a loud rapping on the front door, then Delia hollered, "Have you arrested her yet?"

Erin frowned. "Who's that?"

"Delia Haverhill. Do you know her?"

"Yes. I met her last weekend. Who does she want you to arrest?"

Brutus had settled down on one of Trent's shoes, apparently to take a nap, so Trent bent down and scooped him up. The dog panted and yipped at him and looked like he might leak from either end, so Trent handed Brutus back to Erin.

"Arrest her, Trent. Do it right now," Delia continued hollering through the door. "How dare she take Pookie!"

Erin was staring at the door to her shop, obviously befuddled. "Um, what does she—"

Trent blew out a sigh. "I'm afraid Delia wants me to arrest you for stealing her Pookie."

ERIN COULDN'T HAVE HEARD this man correctly. There was absolutely no way she could have heard him correctly. No one had a reason to want her arrested.

Pushing away her initial panic, she politely asked, "Excuse me? Did you say you're arresting me?"

Trent Barrett smiled, a slow, sexy, lady-killer

smile. Erin absolutely refused to react to his smile. Her days of falling for handsome but unreliable men were over. So what if he was tall, with deep black hair and the most amazing blue eyes. He wasn't her type. Nope. Not at all.

And even if he were her type—which he wasn't—she could hardly be attracted to a man who might arrest her.

"I said Delia wants me to arrest you, but I'm only here to ask a couple of questions," he explained.

The woman outside the front door banged on the glass again. "I'm serious, Trent, I expect results."

Confrontation in any form always made Erin uncomfortable—at least, it used to. But since her wedding day fiasco, she'd worked hard at becoming more assertive. These days, she really tried to stand up for herself. She couldn't imagine what she had done to Delia Haverhill that had made her so angry, but Erin wasn't about to be intimidated either by the handsome chief of police or the irate woman outside.

"Look, Chief Barrett—"

"Trent," he said.

Erin shook her head. "No, I'll call you Chief Barrett, if you don't mind."

Once again, he flashed a flirty grin that Erin suspected usually reduced any female within a two-mile radius into a fluttery mass of jelly. Too bad for the chief that she was now flutter-proof. Okay, not one hundred percent flutter-proof, but close to it.

"So, Chief Barrett, whatever Delia thinks I've done, I haven't. I have never broken the law."

"I appreciate that, Ms. Weber. Delia is upset about Pookie."

Erin took a deep, calming breath and tried again. "You said that pookie thing before. What in the world is a pookie?"

He chuckled, the sound deep and inviting, but Erin ignored it. Well, tried to, and came pretty darn close.

"Pookie is the name of Delia's plastic rabbit, which used to reside in her garden and is now sitting in front of your store. Delia seems to think you had something to do with Pookie's relocation."

"That's the silliest thing I've ever heard. I have no idea what you're talking about. Let me put Brutus in his carrier, then I want to see this Pookie."

Trent nodded. "Seems like the best approach, but I'll warn you, Delia's a trifle hot under the collar. I'm going to head on outside and give her a couple of pointers on police protocol."

Erin had to ask, "Such as?"

"Mostly that she's not allowed to scream and yell while you and I are chatting."

"I don't think you should call interrogating me about a plastic rabbit chatting, Chief."

"I don't think you should call what I'm going to be doing interrogating, Ms. Weber."

Erin didn't want to soften toward Trent Barrett, for a lot of reasons, but she had to admit, he hadn't done anything too terrible. At least not so far.

"I'll put Brutus in his carrier and be outside in a sec," she repeated, not as nervous as she'd been before.

"I'll go talk to Delia."

Although Brutus didn't appreciate being put into his dog carrier, he accepted his fate with as much good grace as a feisty puppy could manage. Then Erin smoothed her green T-shirt that read Precious Pets and her beige slacks.

She took a series of calming breaths following the techniques she'd read about to reduce tension and said the affirmations the book had advised: "You're powerful. You're strong. You're filled with energy."

Then she headed to the front door, her steps decisive, her head held high. She'd just moved to this town and opened her business. Sure, the people of Paxton didn't know her. But she wasn't a thief, and Delia Haverhill was about to learn that fact.

Feeling ready, Erin stepped outside and noticed two things—first, that Trent must have had a really intense talking to with Delia, because the older woman had her mouth clamped shut and looked about to explode.

And second, she noticed that Pookie was one sad and sorry-looking plastic bunny rabbit.

Going on the offensive, Erin said to Delia, "I'm so sorry about what happened to you, but I didn't take your rabbit. I have no idea how it came to be in front of my store. But I'm glad you found it and can put it back in your garden."

Delia continued to glare. "If you didn't put it there, who did?"

"Ah, but if I'd stolen it, why would I display it in front of my store where you'd readily see it? Wouldn't I hide Pookie so I could keep him?"

A tiny fragment of doubt crossed the older woman's face. Erin knew Delia was now a little less sure.

"Delia," Trent said softly. "Remember what we talked about before you say anything."

Delia eventually made a noise that sounded like *"hmmrrphfft"* but didn't say anything else. Erin frankly couldn't tell if that was a good *hmmrrphfft* or a bad *hmmrrphfft*, but at least Delia had stopped demanding that Erin be arrested.

Now Erin turned her attention to Trent, needing his help to solve this mystery. "Honestly, I have no idea how that statue—"

"Pookie," Delia said. "His name is Pookie."

Erin nodded. "Right. Pookie. Well anyway, I have no idea how Pookie came to be in front of my store."

"You have to know something," Delia said. "Did you see anyone lurking around?"

"Delia," Trent said again, raising one eyebrow and giving the woman a look that Erin could only call marginally polite. "I'm sure if Ms. Weber had seen anyone lurking, she would have called the police whether of not they'd been carrying a pookie."

"Hmmrrphfft," Delia said again.

"You didn't notice Pookie outside when you came to work this morning?" Trent asked.

Erin only wished she had. Although, truthfully, even if she had seen Pookie, she probably wouldn't have called the police to report a plastic bunny. "I didn't see it because I live in the apartment above my shop. I don't come in through the front door. I come down the back stairs."

While Trent wrote a few things in a small notebook, Erin looked at Delia. She felt sorry for the older woman. Delia was obviously very upset. "Delia, I want you to know I would never steal Pookie. I know what it's like to have people take things that belong to you. I can imagine how upset you were when you discovered Pookie missing. He's such an…er…um, attractive rabbit. He must bring you a great deal of joy."

Delia's expression softened, but just a minuscule amount. She still pretty much looked like she wanted Erin beheaded.

"Yes, Pookie is dear to me," Delia said.

Erin reached out and patted the battered plastic animal. "He's sweet. You must have missed him."

Delia held the statue close. "He is sweet, which is why someone stole him."

Erin deliberately ignored the baiting tone in the woman's voice. Instead she said, "I'm so glad you got him back. When I was in first grade, one of the boys stole my lunch box. I was devastated. I ran home and cried and cried."

Delia's expression softened a little more around the edges. "What kind of lunch box was it?"

"Scooby-Doo. And I loved that lunch box. I was so proud of it. I couldn't believe it was gone."

Delia nodded. "Scooby-Doo is a good choice. So did you get the lunch box back?"

"No. Although I knew who took it no one would believe me. My parents said I'd probably lost it on the bus and wouldn't buy me another because they felt I'd been careless. My teacher said I'd probably lost it at home somewhere and didn't believe me when I said Billy Porter had stolen it."

"You poor thing," Delia said, patting her on the arm.

"The worse part was that a couple of months later, Billy started coming to school carrying the Scooby-Doo lunch box. I could even see where he'd marked out my name and written his own. I was so upset, but no one would do anything, so I had to ignore it. But it was hard to ignore since

Billy liked to tease me by saying 'Don't you wish you had a lunch box as nice as mine?'''

"That rat," Delia huffed. "Someone should have taught that boy a lesson."

Erin looked Delia directly in the eye. "I agree. What Billy did was horrible. That's why I would never, ever take something that didn't belong to me. As you can tell, I still to this day remember the Scooby-Doo lunch box incident."

Delia patted her arm again. "You poor thing."

Trent cleared his throat. "Excuse me but, Ms. Weber, do you have any idea who might have left Pookie outside your store?"

Delia spun around and glared at him, her hands on her wide hips. "Trent Barrett, have you no manners?"

Both Trent and Erin looked at each other. He seemed as baffled by Delia's comment as she was.

Trent explained. "Delia, I'm trying to find out about Pookie. I thought that was what you wanted me to do."

Delia pointed one finger at him. "You should have sympathized about the lunch box first. Then you can ask about Pookie."

Trent turned to Erin, his deep blue eyes sparkling with humor. She could tell he was trying hard not to smile. To his credit, he managed to look sincere when he said, "My deepest apologies," he said. "I'm so sorry to hear about your loss."

"Thank you." Now Erin had to keep from smiling at the mischievous look in Trent's eyes. The man was a flirt, plain and simple. She could tell from the way he was looking at her that he found her attractive.

"Now that I've paid my respects to your lost Scooby-Doo lunch box, do you have any idea how Pookie came to be outside your store?" he asked.

"None at all," she admitted and glanced at Delia. "I really am sorry this happened to you."

Delia patted her arm yet again. "I appreciate your concern. And I realize now that you couldn't possibly have had anything to do with Pookie's disappearance. Not when you've suffered yourself. Trent will have to figure out who really did it."

Erin was relieved the other woman believed her. Not only would she hate to think someone blamed her for a theft, but it wouldn't do Precious Pets any good if everyone started thinking badly of her.

"I'm not done asking questions," Trent said to Delia.

Delia shook her head. "No more questions. She didn't do it. Enough said. Go on back to your office and arrest someone else. I'm going to visit with Erin for a bit." She glanced at the store. "Do you sell dogs and cats? I didn't pay that much attention when I was here with my grandson last Saturday. You remember Zach, don't you?"

Erin smiled. It would be difficult to forget the

eight-year-old. He'd asked a million questions while Delia had visited with the mayor and his wife.

"Yes, I remember Zach. And no. I don't sell dogs and cats. What I do is help the local animal shelter find homes for the strays. A couple times a month, they bring a few of their pets here to see if my customers are interested in adopting. And then sometimes, I act as a foster home to a kitten or a puppy. Right now, I'm taking care of a puppy named Brutus. He's a sweetie and needs a good home."

"Let me take a look at him. Also, do you sell birdseed? I have a new bird feeder that looks like the Tower of Pisa. I need to stock it."

Erin smiled, relaxing for the first time since this whole mess had started. Even though she knew all along that she hadn't done a thing wrong, just the threat of being arrested made her jittery and jumpy. She was used to always being the good girl. The good daughter. The good student. The good fiancée.

She wouldn't know how to be bad if someone gave her lessons.

"I have several types of birdseed," Erin told Delia, thrilled the woman was now being friendly. "I'm certain I have something that will work for you."

She turned to look at the handsome chief of police. Her pulse rate picked up, but she ignored it. Even Pookie, the plastic bunny rabbit statue, was smart enough to know a man like Trent Barrett was trouble.

"Are we done?" she asked him.

He grinned, his look downright flirtatious. His blue eyes sparkled once again with mischief, and Erin's first instinct was to smile back at him. Thankfully her common sense kicked in, and she stopped herself. Smiling at Trent struck her as an activity only a tiny bit less dangerous than carrying around a lit stick of dynamite. The man had lady-killer written all over him.

When she didn't return his smile, he only grinned bigger. She could tell he found her amusing, but she didn't care. She wasn't going to flirt with this man no matter how tempting it might be.

"You're no longer a suspect in Pookie's kidnapping," Trent finally said. "But I'd say we're far from done."

With that and a goodbye to Delia, he walked away. Erin frowned. What did he mean by that crack that they were far from done?

"Woo-wee, that boy is a handsome devil. All of those Barrett boys are," Delia said as they watched Trent Barrett leave. "But that one, he's a flirt through and through. A mighty fine-looking man, but a flirt, that's for sure."

"Mmm." Erin didn't want to discuss Trent Barrett. The man made her...pensive. And pensive could be bad for her emotional health.

Delia yanked open the door to the shop and headed straight for the birdseed. "You have a wonderful selection."

"Thanks." Erin helped her pick just the right type for the birds she wanted to attract. Then after introducing Delia to Brutus, she rang up the older woman's order.

"Sure you don't want to adopt this puppy? He's a great little fellow," Erin tried, even though Delia had already made it clear she thought Brutus was way too active.

"Brutus isn't right for me. Does he have any sisters?"

Erin hid her disappointment. Delia wasn't the first person to ask that. So far, Erin had sent three people to the county animal shelter to see Brutus's sisters.

Well, an adopted animal was one more with a home, so Erin told Delia, "Yes. The shelter has several females left from the litter."

Delia eyed Brutus, who was now gnawing on Erin's sneaker. "Yes, I think one of the girls might suit me better. I'll go over there this afternoon."

Erin reached down and detached Brutus from her shoe, telling him firmly, "No, Brutus." Then she said to Delia, "I'm sure you'll find a wonderful dog to love."

"I'm sure I will, too." Just as the older woman was about to leave, she said, "Hon, before I go, I wanted to say I'm so sorry about the mix-up this morning. I only hope Trent finds the people who stole Pookie. They deserve to be in jail.''

"I'm sure the chief will do a thorough investigation," Erin assured her.

"You're probably right. Even though he's something of a rogue, Trent's good at his job. He keeps this town running smoothly." She leaned forward a little and added, "But just so you know, be very careful if you decide to go out with him. That man breaks hearts as easily as I crack eggs."

Erin handed Delia the bag with the birdseed, and said as much to herself as to the other woman, "I'm not worried. *My* heart is unbreakable."

2

"DANG IT, LEIGH, STOP yanking on my arm. I told you, I already met Erin Weber. Last week."

Trent's sister made a snorting noise and kept tugging. "You tried to arrest her. That doesn't count. Now come on and meet her the right way, without the threat of imprisonment hanging over her head. You'll love Erin. She's in my pottery class."

Trent stopped and refused to let his sister tow him any farther. "You're in a pottery class?"

Leigh rolled her eyes. "Jeez, you're easily distracted. Okay, yes, I'm taking a pottery class."

Trent shuddered. "Just the thought of you around all that fragile stuff makes me cringe."

"Very funny, bozo. Now come on. I want you to meet Erin the right way."

Trent groaned. He and his brothers had developed almost a sixth sense over the years when it came to Leigh and her evil plans. This little visit to meet Erin Weber had "Leigh plot" written all over it. She was up to something as sure as snakes liked to slither.

"Don't even think about it," he told her.

"Don't even think about what?"

"Whatever scheme you've got cooking in your devious mind. I'm not falling for it."

"I have no idea what you're talking about. I'm not up to anything. I just want you to meet a friend of mine." Leigh tried to look innocent but he didn't buy it for a second.

"You're guilty all right."

Leigh put her hands on her hips. "I am not guilty. Besides, you can't prove a thing."

"Now there's a comment seldom made by an innocent person."

Leigh snorted again and started walking toward the pet shop. "You know, Chase and Nathan aren't nearly as suspicious as you are. They believe me when I tell them things."

"Well, that's only because they're not paying attention these days." Boy, that was the understatement of the year. Chase had recently married the town's librarian, and he and Megan were blissful honeymooners. And Nathan was engaged to Hailey, a woman Leigh knew from college.

Suddenly, like a whack to the head, Trent understood Leigh's plan.

"You're trying to fix me up," he accused.

Leigh laughed. "As if. I like Erin. Why would I want to ruin her life by getting her mixed up with you?"

Even though he didn't care for her tone, his sister

had a point. Not about the ruining this woman's life stuff, but the thought behind it. Leigh, like everyone else in town, knew he wasn't the type to settle down. He liked to enjoy life and as far as he was concerned, love was for saps.

If Erin really was a friend of Leigh's, she wouldn't try to fix them up. Leigh had never tried to fix any of her friends up with him.

Even Leigh wasn't that evil.

They'd reached Precious Pets, so Trent held the door for his sister. She rewarded him by leaning up and giving him a quick kiss on the cheek.

"You're my favorite brother," she said. "Now be nice, or I'll kick your butt."

He made the snorting noise Leigh was so fond of and said her favorite phrase, "As if."

"It's true."

"Oops, watch out for Brutus," Erin called from inside.

Trent looked down just in time to see the furball making a break. He scooped up the dog seconds before the rascal made it out the open door. Giving the pup his most serious look, he said, "Hold it, mister. You're under arrest."

"Better Brutus than me," said Erin, coming over to take the puppy from Trent.

As he handed over Brutus, their hands brushed. He couldn't resist prolonging the contact a little longer than necessary. She gave him a startled look, then took the puppy and stepped back. He smiled. Dang. The woman might not like him, but she sure wasn't immune to him.

"Trent's here to tell you how sorry he is for trying to arrest you," Leigh said.

Trent frowned at his sister. "No, I'm not. I'm here because you dragged me here." He glanced at Erin. "Not that it isn't a pleasure to see you again, Ms. Weber."

"You can call me Erin now that you're no longer threatening to arrest me."

"Erin. And for the record, I didn't threaten to arrest you. I said Delia *wanted* me to arrest you. I only intended on asking you a few questions."

"Have you found out who stole Pookie yet?" she asked.

Leigh hooted a laugh. "Pookie. I still can't get over that Delia names those plastic statues in her yard. What does she call the armadillo she's got out by the tree?"

"His name is Stanley. And the turtle statue she's got in her flowerbed is Dazzle," Erin said.

"You and Delia seem to have hit it off despite her wanting to arrest you," Trent pointed out.

"Delia has stopped by a couple times in the last week. We've had a chance to talk. She's very nice. She adopted one of Brutus's sisters and has been coming in for supplies," Erin said, placing Brutus on the floor.

Trent raised an eyebrow when Brutus came over and started chewing on the side of his shoe. "Hey, cut that out."

When the dog didn't stop, Trent looked at Erin. "What's with the furball and shoes?"

Erin sighed. "His chewing fascination isn't limited to shoes. He'll pretty much chomp on anything that slows down. I'm working on breaking his bad habits, but he's a scallywag and isn't coming around easily."

"Sounds like a male I'd be related to." Leigh reached down and scratched Brutus. "What this guy needs is a home with someone who's as much a rascal as he is, don't you, fella?"

Brutus yapped, almost as if he were agreeing with Leigh. His sister laughed. "See, he thinks I'm right."

"Unfortunately I haven't had any luck finding him a home. The people at the shelter suggested I bring Brutus back and see if I can place a different animal, but I can't give up on Brutus. Not yet."

As soon as Leigh stopped scratching Brutus, he returned to chewing on one of Trent's shoes.

"Dang it, dog," Trent said. "I mean it. Cut it out."

Brutus yapped again and resumed chewing.

"He obviously thinks your shoe is a bark-o-lounger," Leigh teased.

Trent groaned. "Bad joke."

"Brutus liked it, didn't you, sweetie?" Leigh leaned over and picked up the puppy. "You need a wonderful home with someone who understands the male mind. Someone who's had a lot of experience with wild impulses." She grinned at Trent over the top of the puppy's head. "Someone like my brother."

ERIN HADN'T REALIZED Leigh's brother liked dogs. In fact, looking at the frown on his face at this very moment, she still wasn't sure he liked dogs. He was staring at his sister like she'd just announced he should adopt a rattlesnake.

But before he could protest, Erin gave him her best smile and pushed her advantage. "Would you really consider adopting Brutus? That would be wonderful. I don't want to take him back to the shelter, and I live in the small apartment over the store, so I can't adopt him."

Trent sighed and shook his head. "Leigh was joking. I can't adopt him."

Disappointment flooded through Erin. Something awful could happen to Brutus if he didn't find a home. "Are you sure? He's actually a sweet little guy."

At that moment, Brutus started gnawing on the collar of Leigh's blouse.

"Seems to me he's more like a one-man demolition team," Trent said dryly.

"Oh, come on, Trent," Leigh said. "He's no worse than you were when you were young. And look how you've settled down." She totally undermined her statement by laughing when she finished. "Well, sort of settled down. At least now you're less likely to be caught."

Normally Erin wouldn't press someone on a decision like this, but despite his teasing of Brutus, Trent had been kind to the puppy, and she was frantic. The animal shelter might put Brutus to sleep.

She scanned her mind for some way to convince Trent to take the puppy. The best she could come up with was "He's young, yet. He'll calm down with age."

Trent was frowning. Frowning a lot. "I'm not the sort for a puppy. I'm not home much."

"I'll help you take care of him," Leigh offered. "I can stop by while you're at work and play with him and walk him."

Rather than looking pleased by his sister's offer, Trent continued frowning. "I'm not interested in adopting a puppy. Thanks for asking, Leigh."

"I'll buy the food," Leigh said, upping her offer.

"No," Trent said.

"I'll pay for all the shots."

"No."

Since Leigh was striking out, Erin made the only other offer that came to mind.

"I'll help you train him," she said. "I'll throw

in free puppy-training lessons. A class starts in a few days, and there's room for you to join.''

Leigh tapped him on the arm. "Now how can you pass up free puppy-training lessons given by Erin? By the time she's done, Brutus will be better behaved than a choirboy. And who knows? Maybe you'll learn a thing or two about behaving.''

Trent continued frowning at his sister.

Erin quickly pressed on. "Yes, Brutus will learn how to behave. And after you have him neutered, he'll—''

"Whoa, whoa. Hold it right there," Trent said. "Neutered?''

Erin mentally crossed her fingers, hoping Trent wasn't going to be difficult about this. She gave him a reassuring smile, but he looked positively horrified.

"The shelter won't let you adopt Brutus unless you agree to have him neutered," Erin explained. "They'll do the operation there at a discount, or you can take him to your own vet and have it done.''

As she watched, Trent seemed to pale beneath his tan. "Neutered?'' he repeated.

Leigh snorted and cuddled Brutus. "Stop acting like someone is trying to do it to you. Of course you have to have the puppy neutered. You can't contribute to animal overpopulation. But look at it this way, Brutus is going to live a long and happy life in the comfort of your home. Isn't that a fair trade-off?''

Erin thought so, too, but Trent turned his head and glared at his sister. ''Not in my book, it isn't,'' he said. When Leigh snorted again, he added defensively, ''It's a male thing. You wouldn't understand.''

''Oh, let it go,'' Leigh said. ''We're talking about the dog, not you. And *you* have to save this poor dog's life. If he goes back to the shelter, he may be put to sleep.''

Erin took a step closer to Trent. He turned and looked at her. Wow. His eyes were so incredibly blue. Amazingly blue.

For a second, she just stood there looking at Trent. Then Leigh nudged her. Hard.

''Isn't that true, Erin? Couldn't poor, unfortunate Brutus end up being put to sleep if no brave person steps forward and adopts him?''

Erin nodded. ''Yes. But Trent, if you really don't want to adopt Brutus, then you shouldn't. You should adopt a pet because you want to love them, not because you're forced into it.''

Leigh dismissed her comment with the wave of one hand. ''Trent, don't listen to Erin. She's trying to be nice. But I'm telling you right now, it's your moral duty to adopt this puppy.''

Trent raised one eyebrow. ''My *moral* duty? I don't think so.''

"Sure it is. If you don't save him from the puppy gallows, how will you sleep?"

Now that was laying it on a bit thick. Erin figured Leigh had pushed her brother about as far as a person could be pushed. She wasn't surprised when Trent made a sound that was almost a growl. "Stop talking, Leigh."

Leigh held Brutus out in front of Trent. "Look at his face. Look at his sweet puppy eyes. Can't you see he's begging you to adopt him?" When Trent continued to frown at her, Leigh said in a high, squeaky voice, "Please, Mr. Trent, please adopt me and give me a home. I'll be a good puppy. Every morning, I'll fetch your paper—"

"I don't subscribe to the paper," Trent said flatly.

"Then I'll bring you your slippers—"

"I don't wear slippers."

Now Leigh was frowning right back at Trent. "Fine. Then I'll answer your phone."

Trent sighed.

"Leigh, if he doesn't want to—" Erin said at the same time that Trent said, "Okay."

Erin froze and looked at him. "What did you say?"

Trent reached out and patted Brutus. "I said okay. I've been convinced. I'll adopt the furball."

With a loud, "Wahoo," Leigh danced around with Brutus, singing him an off-tune song and making up words to rhyme with his name. "Brutus is the Cutest" was okay. "Brutus is the Rootest" didn't make much sense. And "Brutus is the Dooest" sounded totally bizarre.

Trent looked at Leigh, then glanced at Erin. "You don't by any chance know someone who wants to adopt a sister, do you? She's almost house-broken."

With another snort, Leigh leaned over and gave Trent a loud, smacking kiss on the cheek. "Har-de-har-har. You're so funny. I can't stop laughing."

"I'm serious," he told her, but even Erin didn't believe him for one second. For starters, he was smiling at his sister. And then there was the fact that he took Brutus from Leigh and carefully cradled the dog as he walked over to the pet food section of the store.

"What does the furball eat?"

Erin studied the man before her. Trent Barrett might be a world-class flirt, but he was also one heck of a nice guy. The flirt part was easy to resist. The nice guy part made her nervous. Very, very nervous. A nice guy who loved his sister and was sweet enough to adopt an admittedly rowdy puppy could prove tempting, especially to a woman who'd been on her own for a very long time.

"So what does he eat?" Trent repeated, turning to look at Erin.

She cleared her suddenly tight throat, and a slow,

lazy grin crossed Trent's face. He knew she'd been thinking nice things about him. She frowned, and he laughed.

"Come on over here, Erin. I won't bite," he said in a deep, beguiling voice.

"Don't count on it." Leigh walked over and rapped her brother on the arm. "I wouldn't put much past this yahoo."

Rather than appearing offended, Trent continued to grin at Erin. "Maybe the lady would like to find out for herself what I'm capable of doing."

Oh, no. No, no, no. The lady was most definitely not interested in anything this flirt had in mind. Erin mentally erased every single nice thing she'd thought about Trent. He wasn't a sweet guy. He was a flirt.

"Thanks, but no thanks," she said coolly.

A nice guy might have tempted her, but a flirt she could resist.

TRENT EYED HIS NEW PUPPY, who was happily chasing his own tail on the floor of the family room. He'd brought the dog home yesterday and he still couldn't get Brutus to do a single thing he told him to do.

"That's one dumb dog," Trent said. "What does he think is going to happen when he catches his tail?"

"He's not dumb," Leigh maintained, nudging

the pup so he'd leave his tail alone. "First off, he's only a puppy. Second off, he's your puppy, so a little pity wouldn't be out of place."

"Real cute," Trent said, settling back in his chair. "It's your fault he's my puppy."

"You always said you wanted a dog." Leigh patted Brutus.

"A dog, Leigh. I wanted a dog. Not something that looks like it should be vacuumed up."

Leigh laughed and looked at Brutus. "Mean old Trent. He's saying bad things about you. But you ignore him. He's just grumpy because Erin didn't like it when he flirted with her."

Trent groaned. "I didn't flirt with her. I was only being nice."

"As if. You flirted with her and she didn't melt like butter on a hot sidewalk and you're not used to that so now you're in a bad mood. I took Intro to Psychology. I know how people work."

Trent would give anything to tell Leigh she was wrong, but dang it, she was right. At least sort of right. He was annoyed that Erin had blown him off. And the lady had. Big time. After his remark about not biting, she'd treated him like he had some highly contagious disease.

Not that he was vain, but ladies usually liked him. A lot. But even though he could tell Erin was attracted to him, he could also tell she didn't like him. And that bothered the hell out of him.

"Knock, knock," called a feminine voice from the front hall. Trent groaned. Great. Now his brother Chase and his new wife, Megan, were here. He could just imagine what Leigh was going to tell them.

"You won't guess what's been happening," Leigh said the second Megan and Chase entered the family room.

Chase grinned. "I'll take a shot in the dark. One of you got a dog."

"How did you ever guess?" Trent asked dryly.

"I'm psychic about some things," Chase said. When Brutus scurried over and flopped on one of his boots, he leaned down and scratched the puppy behind the ears. "This sure is a bitty thing." He tipped his head and looked at Trent. "Can't be your dog because it's way too girlie."

"Hey." Leigh came over and picked Brutus up. "Brutus is not a girlie dog. He weighs almost five pounds. He'll be over ten when he's fully grown."

Chase leaned down and eyed the dog cuddled in his sister's arms. "Oh, yeah? Then I take back what I said. He's a terrifying monster."

Megan moved over and patted Brutus. "I think he's adorable. Is he yours, Leigh?"

"Nope. Trent adopted him."

"Had he seen the dog before he adopted it?" Chase asked. When Leigh bobbed her head, he laughed. "Now why do I get the feeling an attractive lady appears somewhere in this story."

"Stop teasing poor Trent," Megan said kindly. Trent knew he liked his brother's wife. She was nothing like the members of his family.

Chase kissed his wife and told her, "Not possible, sweetheart. Teasing him is my job as his big brother."

Trent decided he'd had enough. He walked over to Leigh, taking Brutus out of her arms. "I think I'll let the furball run in the backyard."

"Make sure the Conners's cat isn't out. Fluffy could make a meal out of Brutus," Chase said with a chuckle.

"Funny. You and Leigh are such comedians." Trent opened the back door and let Brutus scamper out. "For your information, I adopted Brutus because I like him."

Chase came over and dropped his arm around Trent's shoulders. "I've been to the pet shop. I've met Erin Weber. She's very nice and very pretty. And you, well, you are you."

Trent shoved away from his brother, not wanting to talk about this. "I adopted Brutus because I like him," he repeated.

Megan walked over to stand next to him. "Of course you do. Brutus is a very…" Her voice drifted off, and Trent followed the direction of her gaze. As he watched, Brutus attacked a blade of grass. The annoying part was that in this battle of brains and brawn, the grass seemed to be winning.

After a couple of seconds watching the dog and the grass, Megan said, "Brutus is a very interesting puppy. I can see why you adopted him."

"It had nothing to do with Erin," Trent maintained, wishing there were even a sliver of truth in that statement.

"Of course it didn't," Megan said sweetly, but Trent was fairly sure even she didn't believe him. "I think it was a wonderful thing you did. Especially since you threatened to arrest the poor woman."

"What?" How in the world did the truth get so twisted? "I didn't threaten to arrest her. I went to her store to ask her some questions."

Chase hooted a laugh. "I can imagine what sort of questions."

"Don't be ridiculous," Trent said, throwing open the back door. He might as well go play with the furball since his family was more aggravating than a rash. They weren't going to stop teasing until they left to go home. "Erin's a nice woman, but not my type."

"I thought your type was breathing," Chase said.

Trent sighed and headed on outside. His family was wrong. Dead wrong. He hadn't adopted Brutus because he found Erin attractive. She had nothing to do with this decision. He'd adopted Brutus because he liked dogs. Dogs offered you companion-ship. Dogs offered you affection. Dogs offered you protection.

A loud commotion by the fence drew his atten-tion.

"Dang it, Fluffy. Put Brutus down."

Jeez, what kind of dog couldn't hold his own against a skinny, eighteen-year-old cat?

TRENT LOOKED AT THE WOODEN birdhouse sitting next to the back door of Precious Pets.

"It looks like the Leaning Tower of Pisa," he said.

"When I saw it, I couldn't believe someone would leave it out in plain sight," said Joe Rafton, one of his newer officers. "You'd think the thief would have more sense. When Delia reported it sto-len, I figured we'd never find it. But there it is. Big as life."

Trent nodded. Yeah, he'd figured they'd never find the birdhouse. But here it was. Outside Erin's shop. Just like Pookie had been. Only this time, the stolen article was outside the back door rather than the front. Still, it was in plain sight for anyone to see.

Of course, he didn't for a second believe that Erin was responsible for this. He couldn't say why, but he trusted her. Not to mention, a person would have to be phenomenally stupid to leave a purloined article sitting outside in plain view.

No, someone was up to something.

"You want me to question the owner of the pet shop?" Joe asked.

Trent should. He definitely should let Joe talk to Erin. But Joe's wife was going to deliver their first child any day now and his shift was almost over.

"I'll talk to her," Trent said.

Joe didn't even try to cover his surprise. "Gee, Chief, isn't this kind of below you?"

"Course not. Besides, Delia Haverhill got me started on this case when she insisted I arres—question Erin when the first stolen item appeared outside the pet store."

Joe scratched his jaw, obviously hiding a smile. "Do you think *Erin* knows who is doing this?"

Trent ignored the bait. "No. She'd tell me if she did." He was positive about that.

"What I can't figure out is, who in Paxton would do such a thing? We've never had this kind of trouble before."

Joe was right. Something like this had never happened in Paxton. But it sure was happening now, and Trent needed to let Erin know what was going on.

He knocked loudly on the back door of the shop and waited for her to answer. As soon as she opened the door, she frowned.

"You have that chief-of-police look on your face. Are you here to arrest me again?"

Boy, that really fried his bacon. What had he ever done to this woman that would make her think so badly of him? After all, he hadn't *actually* arrested her. Didn't that count for something?

He took a great deal of pleasure in explaining, "Of course I'm not here to arrest you."

Her expression brightened. "Good. So why are you here? Is it about Brutus?"

"No. I need to ask you a couple of questions about this birdhouse." He nodded to the lopsided structure next to the door.

Erin came outside and looked at the birdhouse. "I don't believe it. That birdhouse belongs to Delia."

He hadn't been expecting her to know who the owner was. "How do you know that?"

She maintained eye contact as she said, "Delia told us about it the last time you were here in an official capacity. She said it looks like the Leaning Tower of Pisa, so that has to be hers. How many people in town have one shaped like that?"

Hopefully only one. "I haven't spoken to Delia yet, so I don't know for a fact that it's hers," he said. "But it sounds like the item she reported stolen this morning. Let me get her over here to take a look at it."

Erin sighed loudly. "Fine. But I'm sure it's hers.

What I can't figure out is why someone is doing this.''

''The things people do often don't make sense,'' Joe tossed out. ''Look at Pet Rocks. No one ever understood them.''

Trent let Joe's example slide. ''Don't worry about it, Erin. We'll figure out who's doing this and why.''

''This really bothers me,'' she said. ''Everyone in town is going to hate me.''

''Naw,'' said Joe. ''Paxton is a nice town. We rarely hate anyone. We sometimes dislike a few. Like if they consistently litter. Or maybe don't mow their lawn very often. Or take up too many parking spaces at the grocery store. But other than things like that, we're nice to everyone.''

Erin didn't seem a bit comforted by Joe's assurance. She looked at Trent. ''Will you figure it out before an angry mob shows up on my doorstep?''

''We don't have a lot of torch-bearing villagers around here,'' Trent told her.

Joe rocked back and forth on the balls of his feet. ''Too bad we can't get a mob together. They could watch your store and find out who's responsible.''

In his own way, Joe was on to something. Trent planned on keeping a close watch on Erin's store. Sooner or later, he'd catch the culprit.

''I only hope Delia doesn't go back to wanting

me arrested,'' Erin said, her tone and posture dejected.

"She won't," Trent assured her. "You're still getting a lot of mileage out of the lunch box story. There's nothing like a good Scooby-Doo story to get a town into your cheering section. So don't worry about it. I'll take care of you."

Erin fixed him with an unwavering gaze. "No. *You* take care of whoever is stealing these things. *I'll* take care of myself."

3

"I WANT TO THANK everyone for coming to tonight's Dog Behavior Class. I hope you're enjoying your new family members," Erin said.

Trent glanced down at Brutus. Mostly he'd been cleaning up after the furball. Brutus might be tiny, but he had the disposition of a tornado. He'd gnawed on every shoe he'd managed to find, done a terrific job taking bites out of the living-room drapes and chewed the end of the leather sofa until it was mush.

All in all, Brutus had made himself a little too much at home.

Glancing at the other members of the class, though, Trent hoped his pet wouldn't be the worst one there. Delia had come to the class, bringing along a sister of Brutus's that seemed pretty calm and respectful. Trent was glad the older woman had come. Her presence proved to everyone in town that she didn't believe Erin had stolen her birdhouse. She, like Trent and his officers, had no idea what was going on. But Delia firmly maintained Erin wasn't at fault. And now that Trent had people watching Erin's store most nights, it probably wouldn't be long before they caught the thief.

Besides Delia, there were three more people in the class. The other two women both had puppies that looked like they might be frisky. Karla Ashmore had a spaniel that seemed full of spunk. And Lynn Claude had a boxer who seemed pretty spry as well. No way would Brutus be the worst dog here.

Best of all, the other guy in the class had a German shepherd puppy—a *male* German shepherd puppy. Trent was positive that bad boy had more than a few behavior problems to iron out. He kept giving the other dogs a nasty look that Brutus apparently took to mean he was about to become an appetizer. One look from the German shepherd and Brutus had hidden behind Trent's legs.

"Calm down, furball," Trent said, as Brutus continued to hide. Not that he could really blame the puppy. The German shepherd was a big dog. A tough dog.

Trent looked at Brutus, who yipped and sounded like a perfect little princess. Great. Now the mutt even sounded like a girlie dog.

"How is everyone doing with housebreaking? Any problems?" Erin smiled at Delia. "Is Muffin getting the hang of it?"

Delia patted her puppy. "Oh, yes. She caught on right away. I followed the instructions in that brochure you gave me, and I didn't have a single problem.''

Little Muffin must have known she was being praised, because she practically pranced in place. Trent rolled his eyes. He'd believe Muffin was completely housebroken the day he believed Santa Claus had a cholesterol level under 200.

Trent squatted and gave Brutus a pat. "Like I believe that," he said softly.

Brutus made a doggy snorting noise that Trent took as agreement.

Erin looked at them. "How is Brutus doing with his training?"

In a word? *Failing*.

But both for his own pride and for Brutus's, Trent said, "Good. He's doing good."

Doubt crossed Erin's face. "You're sure? Because Brutus might take a little longer to catch on."

Hey, what did she mean by that crack? Brutus might not be as prissy as Muffin, but he wasn't the dumbest dog at the pound. Sure he was having more accidents than successes, but there was no way Trent was going to admit that to this group. A man had to have some loyalty to his dog, even if it was a furball.

"Brutus is doing just fine," Trent assured her.

Erin smiled. "Good. I'm glad to hear he's doing well. I knew you two would hit it off."

Yeah, like either one of them had had a choice

in the matter. Trent looked at the German shepherd again, then at the dog's owner. The man had moved to town a couple of months ago to work at Nathan's company. What was his name? Sam? Stan? Something that started with an *S*.

Erin looked at the man. ''So Sean—''

''Sean. That's it.''

Both Sean and Erin looked at him. Trent grinned. ''Sorry. Go on.''

For several seconds, Erin continued to look at Trent. Obviously his behavior had her puzzled. He grinned and winked at her, which made her frown and look away.

''So, Sean, how are things going?'' Erin asked the other man, but Trent didn't miss the slightly breathless hitch to her voice. Now that was interesting.

''Good,'' Sean said.

''No problems with Scamp?''

''Scamp?'' Trent chuckled, looking at the German shepherd. ''Jeez, who names these dogs? Mine should be named Scamp, and the shepherd should be Brutus.''

Sean frowned at him. ''I picked the name Scamp. I think it suits him.''

The German shepherd sat perfectly still next to his owner. There wasn't anything remotely scamp-like about the puppy. Brutus, however, had latched on to the hem of Trent's pants and was playing tug-of-war.

"Cut it out, furball," Trent said absently.

Brutus wagged his tail and continued chewing.

Erin walked over to look at Brutus. "The secret to training your puppy is to be firm and consistent."

Hey, he might not be the best pet parent, but he knew how to follow directions. He was following every blasted rule in that booklet Erin had given him.

"Excuse me, Erin, but I'm consistently firm," Trent said.

The second the words left his mouth, he realized what he'd said. Dang it. As he expected, Delia laughed, as did Karla and Lynn. Karla even winked at him.

Erin neither laughed nor winked at him. She blushed. Bright red. Really bright red. Her reaction made the other ladies laugh even more.

Erin cleared her throat. Then she cleared it again. She briefly glanced at Trent, then quickly looked away. See, that was doubly interesting. For a lady who seemed to have no interest in him, she sure was acting suspicious.

"Let's get started with the lessons," Erin finally said, but her voice was almost as squeaky as Brutus's yip.

Trent would give her credit, though. Over the next hour, she tried to be professional. She did a good job, too, at least when she was talking to the other members of the class. But every single time she came to help him with Brutus, Erin became noticeably flustered. She always kept her gaze focused completely on Brutus. Not once did she make eye contact with him.

He took that as a really encouraging sign. Sean didn't fluster Erin, but he sure did. Good. He wanted to fluster Erin. He liked her. He liked the way her eyes sparkled when she patted Brutus, the way she laughed when the puppy rolled over for her to rub his belly, the way she tried to be so stern when she told him not to lick her face.

"Trent, please tell Brutus to leave Muffin alone," Erin said, interrupting his thoughts.

Trent looked at Brutus, who was chewing on Muffin's collar. He sighed and pulled the dog away from his sister.

"Cut it out, Brutus," Trent said.

Erin shook her head. "You need to tell him no."

"I did tell him no."

Again, she shook her head. "You said cut it out. Brutus needs one word to associate with negative actions."

Trent shrugged. "Fine. No."

Erin finally looked him directly in the face. "Say 'No, Brutus' when you want to correct him."

Trent started to follow her directions, but Erin

grabbed his arm. "Not now. You only say that when he's doing something you want him to stop."

"That's pretty much all the time," Trent admitted. He looked at her hand on his arm, then glanced back at her face. She pulled her hand back so fast she almost lost her balance.

Trent smiled. He liked the way things were going tonight. He liked it very much. And he especially liked it when after class was over, Erin requested he stay.

Oh, yeah. He liked this a lot.

WHILE SHE SAW THE OTHER students out, Erin tried to formulate what she was going to say to Trent. He and Brutus had done badly tonight. Very badly. Horribly in fact. At this rate, poor Brutus would never develop even the most basic behavior skills. The puppy simply didn't listen to Trent.

And for his part, Trent wasn't learning a heck of a lot either. These two males needed a good talking-to, and she was just the lady to do it.

"Brutus and I are being kept after school, huh?" Trent teased when Erin returned after seeing the others out.

"Trent, do you think Brutus did well tonight?"

Trent chuckled and pointed at the dog. Brutus was chewing happily on Trent's right shoe. "The whole concept of good behavior seems lost on this fellow."

"I refuse to believe that. Brutus can be trained to behave, just like any animal can be trained."

Trent slowly shook his head. "I'm not sure I agree with you, Erin. Not all animals take to training. Some like staying wild and free. I think Brutus may be a fellow who refuses to settle down."

Erin studied Trent. From what Delia and the other ladies in town had told her, Trent also was one of those animals who refused to settle down. He probably wasn't the best person to train Brutus. Trent had a life's-short-have-fun attitude. For all she knew, he wasn't doing much to try to train Brutus. Heck, maybe he didn't even want to train the puppy.

"Brutus could be a very nice dog if you train him," she said, wanting Trent and the puppy to be happy together. To prove her point, she looked at Brutus. "No, Brutus."

Brutus stopped chewing on Trent's shoe, and Erin smiled. "See? Just a little training is all he needs."

Before she could truly savor the thrill of victory, Brutus trotted over and started chewing on her right shoe instead. Trent laughed loudly.

"Oh, yeah, I can see how trainable he is. You have the boy firmly under control."

Erin reached down and extricated the dog from her shoe. Or rather her shoe from the dog. Then she placed Brutus on the floor and sat next to him.

"Brutus," she said, wanting the puppy to focus on her.

The dog wagged his tail. That was a good sign. He definitely knew his name. When he looked at her, she said firmly, "Sit, Brutus."

Brutus wagged his tail some more.

Erin sighed. This wasn't going to be easy. Some dogs took to training readily. Others needed a little extra help.

And in Brutus's case, he might need a lot of extra help.

"Brutus kinda barks to a different drummer," Trent said, sitting next to Erin. Brutus immediately scurried over and flopped on Trent's lap. When the dog rolled over on his back, Trent good-naturedly scratched his stomach.

"Any ideas what I might try with the furball here?" Trent asked, smiling at Erin. "Believe it or not, I do want the boy to have at least a few manners. How's he going to impress the ladies if he's uncouth?"

Wow. This close up, she could see how amazingly blue Trent's eyes were. He certainly was one gorgeous man. Good thing she was immune to gorgeous, flirtatious men because she'd probably be falling under his spell right now if she weren't.

Of course, her heart was racing, but that had nothing to do with Trent being so close. Sure, her breathing was on the rapid side, but that also had nothing to do with Trent. Not a single thing.

"Hello? Erin? You still with me?" Trent teased.

Erin mentally shook herself and said, "Of course. I was thinking about your question. I'm trying to decide what's the best way to train Brutus."

Trent's expression made it clear he didn't believe a word she was saying. But at least he had the decency not to comment.

"Oh, and remember, Brutus won't need to impress the ladies. You promised to have him fixed."

Trent winced, but didn't disagree. Instead he said, "I have an idea. Why don't I pay you to give Brutus a little extra training? He may do better one-on-one."

Erin had to admit, Trent might be right. Brutus might respond better if he had her complete attention. "Perhaps I can work with him a couple of extra days this week."

Trent was still scratching the dog's belly. "Thanks, because I don't know what I'm doing wrong. I mean, I'm used to training people. Heck, growing up on a ranch, I'm used to training horses, too. But this dog has me baffled."

Erin found Trent's admission endearing. He really was trying to help the puppy.

"Some puppies take a little longer," Erin said. Then because of Trent's admission, she had to make one of her own. "And it's not like I had much luck with Brutus before you adopted him. I hadn't gotten very far with his training.''

"Unless you were teaching him to chew on shoes. He's really good at that.''

Erin laughed. "Um, no, that wasn't something I taught him. I'm pretty sure Brutus is what you'd call a natural-born chewer.''

"I think you're right,'' Trent said dryly as he removed the cuff of his shirt from Brutus's mouth. "The furball definitely likes to chew.''

"I'm sure we can break him of his bad habits,'' Erin assured Trent, wanting to make certain he didn't become discouraged by Brutus's lack of progress.

"I'll have to take your word on that one.''

"Brutus is a smart dog. He'll learn.''

"Oh, I'm not denying he's smart,'' Trent said, moving Brutus when the puppy tried to chew on the pocket of his shirt. "I think he's downright ornery. In my experience, it takes a lot of incentive to get the ornery out of any creature.''

"Did it take a lot of incentive for you?'' Erin found herself asking without really meaning to do so. But now that she'd asked the question, she discovered she really wanted to know the answer.

Trent's smile turned into a full-fledged lady-killer grin. "Some folks say I still have ornery left in me, but I deny it. I'm about as good as a man can get these days.'' He patted Brutus's head. "Dang, I even have a furball for a dog. A man can't have much ornery left in him if he lets himself be talked into adopting a puppy like Brutus.''

"Maybe not ornery," she conceded, "but I think you definitely have a lot of..."

When she didn't immediately go on, Trent chuckled. "Yes? I have a lot of what?"

"Flirt," she finally said. "You have a lot of flirt in you."

Trent tried to look offended, but Erin ended up laughing at his goofy expression.

"Come on, admit it, you're a flirt. You were flirting with Karla tonight."

"I was not."

"Sure you were."

Trent shook his head. "Nope. Not true. She was flirting with me, but I didn't flirt back. The lady recently left her husband. Personally I'm hoping they work out their problems and stay together. I would never flirt with a woman who was married, even if she's separated."

Erin could hear sincerity in his voice, see it in his expression. She'd never admit it, but she was glad to hear Trent had rules about these sorts of things. The more time she spent with him, the more she liked Trent. She'd hate to think he'd run around with any woman, regardless of her marital status.

"A rogue with a heart," she murmured.

"Naw. I just figure no one has the right to meddle with a married couple. They have to work through any problems on their own. I'm not about to hop into a snake pit like that.''

"You consider marriage a snake pit?"

Trent shrugged. "More or less. Some of them I've seen make a snake pit look good."

"You can't be serious."

"Excuse me, but I don't see a wedding ring on your left hand. You must agree with me somewhat," he pointed out.

But she didn't agree with him. Not at all. "I'm not married because I haven't found the right person yet. But that doesn't mean I think marriage is a snake pit."

"And yet you haven't gotten married."

"I almost did."

Her admission obviously surprised him. "How close is almost?"

Even now, she couldn't believe she'd been so foolish as to trust Don. Everyone had told her Don was a flirt and a player. Her family had told her. Her friends had told her. Heck, even the man catering the reception had told her. But she'd refused to see the truth.

"I was stood up at the altar," she said, then clarified, "well, not actually stood up. Don did show up at the church. We even made it to the altar. But after that, things didn't work out."

Trent scooted closer to her. "Hey, you can't stop

there. I'm hooked now. So tell me what happened. You were standing at the altar with what's-his-name, and then?''

Although Erin rarely discussed her wedding fiasco, it no longer bothered her to talk about it. In fact, she firmly believed things had turned out for the best. Don hadn't been the right man for her. He'd been far too wild and immature to get married.

''When the minister got to the part where he asked Don if he 'took this woman,' Don looked at me, said 'Sorry, babe,' grabbed my maid of honor's hand, and they ran out of the church.''

Trent stared at her. ''You're kidding, right? He ran off with your maid of honor?''

Erin nodded. ''Yes. They even left in the car with Just Married painted on the back.''

Trent let out a long, low whistle. ''Wow. That stinks. So you had no idea he was in love with your maid of honor?''

Erin reached over and idly patted Brutus. ''Hadn't a clue.''

''Man, I'm sorry. That must have been tough. On behalf of my gender, I apologize.''

''Thanks, but it's not necessary. Don and I weren't meant to be together. It's good we didn't go through with the wedding.''

She looked at the man sitting next to her. From the way Delia described him, it sounded like Trent was a lot like Don. The handsome chief supposedly didn't date anyone for very long, either.

"There he goes again," Trent said, nodding at Brutus, who was chasing his tail. "He does that all the time. Sometimes he gets going so fast it's hard to tell where one end of him stops and the other starts."

Erin smiled as she watched the puppy play. "He likes to have fun." She couldn't help adding, "From what I hear, so does his owner."

"Ouch." Trent slapped his chest. "Got me with that one."

"You know what I mean." She reached out and patted Brutus, knowing she shouldn't be sitting here talking to Trent. She should tell him to head on home. She had a long day tomorrow and should be in bed by now.

But she was enjoying Trent's company. He was a nice guy, even if he was a flirt. Besides, she'd learned her lesson with Don. Flirts were fine as long as you didn't take them seriously.

And she certainly didn't take Trent Barrett seriously.

"Come on, let me show you a couple of things you can try with Brutus to get him to behave," she offered.

Before she made a move, Trent stood and held out one hand to her. "Allow me."

Without thinking, Erin took his hand and let him

pull her up. What she hadn't counted on was the reaction she'd have as soon as her skin touched his. Desire flashed between them, and she couldn't seem to get it through her thick head that touching Trent was a bad thing. In fact, her entire body seemed to find the idea utterly delightful.

Trent also seemed to find the contact between them enticing. Erin could clearly see a healthy dose of male lust in his gaze.

"Tell me what you want me to do," he said.

Oh, now there was a loaded question. Her gaze dropped to his mouth. She could think of several things she'd like him to do.

"You should use positive reinforcement whenever possible," she said, not surprised that her voice sounded breathless and excited. Trent still held her hand, and she did nothing to break the contact.

"Positive reinforcement," he repeated softly. His thumb lightly caressed the back of her hand.

"Um, yes. Whenever he does something you like, praise him," Erin said.

A wicked grin grew on Trent's face, and he moved closer to her.

"Praise seems like a good way to go," he said.

Her gaze was fixed on his lips. She'd bet anything that Trent was a world-class kisser. He probably could make a woman forget everything with only one kiss. Heck, she was having trouble remembering what she was talking about, and he hadn't even kissed her.

"When he does something you like, say 'Good boy' so he'll know to do it again," she said absently, her attention still focused on Trent's mouth and the seductive caress of his thumb on her hand.

Trent slowly leaned forward and lightly brushed his lips across hers.

Oh. My. Erin sighed with pure bliss as tingles ran through her.

"Good boy," she said immediately.

Trent chuckled and kissed her again.

4

WHILE TRENT GATHERED ERIN closer and deepened the kiss, he couldn't help thinking that maybe he was the one who needed a couple of behavior lessons. Dang, he hadn't come here tonight intending on kissing Erin, but yet here he was, kissing her like there was no tomorrow.

And having one heck of a good time. Man, Erin could kiss, so he didn't waste a lot of time analyzing the situation. He just accepted his good fortune.

Things were humming right along when the *yip-yip-yapping* sound of Brutus tugged them both back to reality.

"Let's ignore him," Trent murmured against Erin's soft lips. "Brutus will be fine."

"What if he needs to answer the call of nature?"

For a split second, Trent almost said "who cares." After all, it was the strongest rule of the male species—you didn't interrupt when your friend was kissing a pretty lady. Brutus was male. He should know this stuff.

But leave it to the furball to decide he couldn't

wait a couple of minutes to answer that call of nature.

Blasted dog.

"That was a surprise," Erin said as she backed away from him like he was a big ol' pile of nuclear waste.

Uh-oh. Sounded like she had regrets.

"A nice surprise," Trent said, hoping to salvage the situation.

But he was obviously too late, because Erin's expression had taken on a determined cast that he just knew didn't bode well. At least not if he were hoping there'd be more kissing between them anytime in the near future. And he had been hoping for more kissing.

Trent glared down at Brutus, who was once again happily chasing his own tail. Dang furball.

"We shouldn't have done that," Erin said, although her voice was soft, her tone was firm. The lady meant business. "I'm not interested in a relationship at this particular moment."

Hell, he wasn't interested in a relationship at *any* particular moment. But if Erin didn't want a relationship, he sure-as-shootin' would bet she really wouldn't be interested in what he had in mind.

"Okay," he said, leaning down and scooping up Brutus.

Erin eyed him closely. "I don't mean to offend you. The kiss was lovely."

She was downright cute. She was giving him the brush-off big time but still concerned about his feelings.

"I'm fine, Erin. No broken heart. No trampled feelings." He took a step closer to her, then added with a grin, "To tell you the honest truth, I don't go in for relationships myself. Short flings, sure, I'm on board with that. We all can use a little fun. But that whole 'till-death-do-us-part' thing gives me the chills."

As he watched, Erin's expression hardened like cement. "I see. It's nice to know what your feelings are on this subject."

For a split second, he considered back pedaling, but then he decided it was best if Erin knew what kind of guy he was from the start. Still, it wouldn't hurt to soften the news a tad.

"Don't get me wrong. I'm not exactly Brutus here when it comes to the ladies, but I'm not the tied-down type, either."

Erin nodded at Brutus. "I sure hope you're not like Brutus, especially since you've agreed to have him neutered."

Talk about giving a man the chills. Yeow. He literally shivered at the thought. "I still haven't figured out a way to tell Brutus about that."

Apparently switching the subject to Brutus and his impending alteration was enough to soften

Erin's mood. She stepped over and patted Brutus on the head.

"You're a good boy and everything's going to be all right," she cooed.

"Just which one of us are you talking to?" Trent teased.

"Go home, Trent Barrett," Erin said with a laugh. "And take your dog with you."

"Yes, ma'am." Trent looked at Brutus. "Looks like we men have worn out our welcome. But I'm pretty sure if we mind our manners, she'll let us come back on Wednesday for more obedience lessons."

"Yes, you can come back on Wednesday," she said. "But next time, I want both of you to behave."

Trent nodded his head and helped Brutus nod, too. "You bet. We boys promise we'll be absolute angels."

Erin sighed and started walking toward the front door again. "Brutus might behave like an angel on Wednesday, but even though I haven't known you long, Trent, I'm positive you haven't got a single angelic bone in your body."

Trent chuckled as he scooted out the front door. "You may have a point."

Erin patted Brutus's head. "You take care of this dumb animal, okay?"

Trent looked at Brutus. "This time, I'm certain she's talking to you."

ERIN TIPPED HER HEAD and studied the bunch of flowers sitting on the doorstep to her store. They looked liked they'd been yanked out of the ground, not picked gently.

"Nice collection of weeds," Leigh Barrett said as she came to stand next to Erin. "Did you grow them yourself?"

"I think it's a bouquet of flowers left by some-one," Erin told the younger woman. "Maybe by the same person who left Pookie here."

Leigh made a loud snorting noise. "First off, those aren't flowers, they're weeds. Second off—" She pointed down the sidewalk. "They're every-where. It looks like someone was carrying a bundle and dropped a bunch on the way."

"On the way to putting the bouquet in front of the door to my store?" Erin didn't like this a bit. It was strange. Who would do such a thing?

Leigh put her hands on Erin's shoulders and turned her so she was looking down the sidewalk. "Look at that, Erin. Whoever was carrying those weeds dropped them everywhere. Yeah, you may have the majority in front of your door, but if you think a secret admirer did this, then how do you explain the weeds in front of the Slurp and Burp?"

What in the world was Leigh talking about? "The Slurp and Burp?"

"Roy's Café. Great chicken fried steak, by the way. Anywho, as you can see, Roy's got a lot of weeds in front of his door, too. Now what kind of secret admirer do you suppose would leave both you and Roy weeds? Roy's a great guy, but he's in his sixties and married to boot."

Erin felt the panic inside her slowly seep away. Leigh was right. There were flowers, or er, weeds, in front of Roy's Café, too. This didn't seem to be a deliberate gesture.

"Thanks," she told Leigh, meaning it more than she could explain.

"No problem. But to make you feel a million times better, let's have Trent tell you what I just said in his official chief-of-police voice. Things always sound more impressive when a person in uniform says them. I mean, would you let someone wearing a thong and sunscreen take out your appendix?" She tugged on Erin's arm, and they started down the sidewalk toward the police station. "Well, maybe you would if he looked really hot in that thong, but for the most part, you wouldn't."

Erin blinked. Leigh certainly was full of zest. "I don't need Trent to reassure me." In fact, Trent was the last person she wanted to see right now. She still couldn't believe she'd actually let him kiss her last night. What had she been thinking?

Her own personal code of honesty set off an alarm. She was lying and she knew it. She hadn't *let* Trent kiss her. Nope. She'd been a very active participant throughout the entire process.

You'd think being jilted at your wedding would teach a woman a thing or two about men. Apparently all it had taught her was to wrap her arms around Trent's neck when she wanted him to deepen the kiss. The experience sure hadn't taught her anything useful, like how to say, "No, thank you. I'd rather you not kiss me."

But no siree, she hadn't said a thing to stop Trent. She'd fallen right in line with the plan and kissed the man back like a crazy woman.

"I don't want to see Trent," Erin blurted. "Thanks anyway, but I have to open my store."

"Erin, Trent's not going to arrest you," Leigh said, and then she laughed.

Erin didn't like the sound of that laugh one bit. Boy, this young woman was headstrong. She didn't seem to even have the ability to hear the word no. But Erin had been raised in a family of headstrong people, so Leigh didn't intimidate her.

"I do *not* want to see Trent," Erin said firmly and slowly.

"Why not?"

At the sound of Trent's voice, Erin yelped. Then hoped the ground would open up and swallow her.

She'd yelped? She never yelped. She wasn't the startled, easily scared type.

But there was no denying the obvious—she'd yelped when she'd heard Trent's voice.

Knowing he stood directly behind her, Erin shot a frown at Leigh, who only laughed, then turned to face the man who had stared in her dreams last night.

"Hi," he said. He had a definite twinkle in his deep blue eyes. "It's nice to see you today."

"Hi," she said, inwardly cringing when the word came out breathless and more than a little flirtatious. Oh, for pity's sake. First she'd yelped, now she was doing a Marilyn Monroe impersonation? Her hormones were getting way out of control. So he was good-looking. So what. And so he was without a doubt the best kisser she'd ever kissed. Again, so what. None of that excused her behavior. When she got back to the store later, she intended on giving her libido a stern talking-to.

"Since Erin seems to have temporarily lost the ability to speak, I'll tell you why we're here. Erin has weeds in front of her store," Leigh said, looking at Erin for confirmation.

"I thought they might be flowers someone had left for me. Like someone left Pookie and the birdhouse," Erin explained, thrilled that her voice finally sounded normal. Or close to it, anyway. Trent was standing right next to her, and she was only human after all.

"Someone left you flowers?" he asked.

"Weeds," Leigh explained once again. "They left her weeds. But there are weeds in front of Roy's, too, and I'm sure no one's trying to woo him."

Trent turned his attention to his sister. "Why exactly are you here?"

"I was going to Precious Pets to buy a toy for Brutus," she said.

Trent raised one eyebrow. "A toy? The furball's got all the toys he needs. He's got my living-room sofa to chew on, and my shoelaces to play tug-of-war with. Seems to me he's all set."

"Ha, ha." Leigh looked at Erin. "It's hard to believe we're related, isn't it?"

"Um, let me think," Erin managed to say with a moderately straight face.

"I know, we look so much alike, how could you not know we're related," Leigh said.

"Leigh, truthfully, your personalities are similar," Erin admitted.

Not laughing at the offended expressions both Trent and Leigh got was one of the toughest things Erin ever did. She couldn't say offhand which of them looked more upset.

Trent was the first one to speak. "I realize we

don't know each other very well, but my personality is *nothing* like Leigh's.''

Leigh bobbed her head. ''That's right. Trent's more like Chase, and Nathan's more like…well, he doesn't really fit in with Trent and Chase. Come to think of it, Chase isn't really like Trent because—''

''Stop. Leigh, that's enough. I think we've shared enough family history with poor Erin.'' Trent leaned closer to his sister and added, ''And I'm nothing like Chase.''

Leigh snorted and looked at Erin. ''See, this is the problem with growing up with three brothers. They drive you nuts, but what can you do? It's not like you can send them back. I mean, come on, what are you going to use for a receipt?''

Okay, now Erin was confused, but at least Leigh had taken her mind off how flustered she was at seeing Trent again. ''What?''

Trent draped one arm around Leigh's shoulders. ''Let me translate. Leigh thinks I, and her other two brothers Chase and Nathan, meddle too much in her life. But she loves us anyway. Now what about those weeds?''

Erin looked from one Barrett to the other. Wow. There were four of these people? Both Trent and Leigh had personality and zest to spare. Were they all like this?

"The weeds?" Leigh prompted again. "Tell Trent about the weeds."

Like a derailed train, it took Erin a couple of minutes to get back on track. Finally she said, "I believe they might be flowers. Or at least whoever left them might have thought they were leaving flowers."

Leigh tugged on her brother's arm. "Come on. We'll show you. You'll see that they're weeds, not flowers, and they've been dropped all along the sidewalk, not left intentionally in front of Erin's store." She gave Erin a sympathetic look. "But don't worry, I'm sure someday you'll meet a nice man who will bring you flowers."

Erin's mouth dropped open. "This isn't about me secretly wanting someone to give me flowers. I'm concerned that someone is leaving things in front of my store."

Thankfully Trent was on her side. "I understand completely. Now let's go take a look at these flowering weeds."

The three of them headed toward Precious Pets, but long before they reached it, Erin realized something was wrong. The flowers were gone. All the ones that had been scattered on the sidewalk were missing. When they got close enough to Precious Pets for her to see, she could tell they were gone from outside her store as well.

"Hey, where'd they go?" Leigh asked, scanning

up and down the sidewalk. "Someone stole the weeds." She shook her head. "It's a sorry day when you can't even leave weeds lying around without some bonehead stealing them."

Trent sighed loudly and pointed at a trash can just beyond Precious Pets. "Looks like someone picked them up and tossed them."

Erin walked over to one of the dark green trash cans the city had placed along each sidewalk in the business district. Sure enough, the flowers had been thrown away. Now, looking at the pile in the trash can, they did look more like weeds than flowers.

When Trent came over to stand next to her, Erin said, "I guess I was overreacting. These are weeds."

"Weeds someone sent to their final resting place in weed heaven," Leigh said as she looked into the trash can. "Oh, well. I'm sure they lived long and happy lives."

This time, Erin was the one to sigh. She headed over and unlocked her store. She'd spent way too much time this morning worrying about these weeds. That whole thing with Pookie and the birdhouse had made her jumpy.

"Thanks for stopping by," Erin said to Trent.

Before Trent could answer, Leigh shoved past both of them and walked inside the store. "You two go ahead and talk while I find a toy for Brutus. I'm in a hurry and need to...um, hurry."

With that, Leigh shut the door to Precious Pets in Erin's face.

"You'll have to excuse Leigh," Trent said dryly. "She was raised by a pack of wild, unruly brothers and has the manners of a Barrett boy."

Erin laughed. "She certainly does have her own approach to life."

"Yes, she does." His gaze held hers, and suddenly, Erin relived every single thing that had happened between them last night. The talk. The fun. The kiss.

"This is kind of awkward," she admitted.

He frowned. "What is? I didn't mind stopping by to look at the flowers. But I have to agree with Leigh on this one. I think someone probably dropped them. Maybe they had weeded that planter down by the hardware store and were just carting the weeds up here to the trash can."

Erin looked at the hardware store that sat kitty-corner across the street from Precious Pets. The planter out front was indeed weed-free. And the trash can near her store was the closest. Trent's theory made a lot of sense.

"I guess you're right. But that isn't what I meant when I said this was awkward." She looked directly at him. "I meant the kiss."

"You guys kissed?"

This muffled question came from inside the store.

Erin spun around and realized Leigh stood in front of the display window right by the front door.

Horrified, she turned back to look at Trent. Rather than being upset, he chuckled. "Well, now that Leigh knows, it won't be long before the whole town does. Don't let it bother you. When folks ask about us kissing—"

"People are going to ask me about it? Why would they care?"

This time, Leigh was the one to laugh from inside the store, but Erin ignored her.

"Seriously, Trent. It was only a kiss. I'm sure no one will care in the slightest," Erin said, but she wasn't sure which of them she was trying to convince.

Obviously herself, since Trent looked like he was struggling to keep from laughing again. "Maybe you're right, Erin. Maybe Leigh won't tell everyone in town that we kissed." He looked over Erin's shoulder, apparently at Leigh, and added, "At least she won't if she knows what's good for her."

Behind her, Erin could hear Leigh muttering, but she couldn't make out what the younger woman was saying. It didn't matter anyway. Even if people in town did hear about the kiss, she couldn't believe they would care. And even if they did care, she could tell them politely that it was none of their business. After all, she and Trent weren't going to get involved. They weren't going to show up around town on dates.

Trent must have read her mind, because he teased, "If anyone asks about us, say in your best cop voice, 'there's nothing to see here, so move along.' That should take care of the problem."

Erin smiled at his nonsense. What was it about Trent Barrett that could make her weak in the knees one second and laughing the next? The man certainly was fun to be around, but Erin had the scarred heart to prove that fun men were the most dangerous kind. They'd break your heart, usually without meaning to, but they'd break it just the same.

"I think I'm going to go inside now," Erin told him, her smile long since gone. "Again, thank you."

Behind her, she heard Leigh ask, "For what? The kiss?" Then Leigh laughed again.

"I don't suppose there's any way you could arrest her, is there?" Erin asked Trent.

Trent scratched his jaw and said, "Man, if I could, I would. Have a nice day."

With that, he headed back toward the police station. Erin watched him go, at least she did until she realized that two ladies outside of Roy's Café were checking him out as he walked by. One of them even let out a wolf whistle that made Trent laugh.

Behind her, Erin could hear Leigh sputtering with laughter, too.

What kind of town was this? What made the people here act this way?

And what was she going to do if it was contagious?

5

"NOW THAT'S A HEARTWARMING sight, a man and his dog."

Trent was walking Brutus to the Friday night dog obedience course, and so far, every person he'd met in town had felt obligated to comment on his dog. He glanced up, not a bit surprised to see his brother Nathan was the doofus this time.

"Yeah, well, at least dogs like me," Trent shot back. He smiled at Nathan's fiancée, Hailey Montgomery. Hailey leaned down and petted Brutus.

"He's a cute dog," she said.

Brutus, sensing praise, launched into a series of flips, hops, yips and yaps. Way to be dignified.

Hoping to distract his brother from Brutus's behavior, Trent asked, "What brings you two downtown tonight?"

They shared a grin, and Trent's internal antenna went up.

"We're out for a stroll. You know, take in the sights," Nathan said, the grin still lurking around his mouth.

"Dang it all, Nathan, what are you up to? I already have more trouble with Leigh than ten men and a saint could handle. I sure don't need you messing with me.''

Nathan laughed. "I said we were out for a stroll. That's all. Ease off, there, Chief.''

Trent looked at Hailey, hoping that since the woman wasn't part of his lamebrain family yet, that she was maintaining some sort of control over the man she intended on marrying. "Is that true, Hailey? Are you two simply taking a walk?''

Hailey looked from Trent to Nathan then back to Trent. Ah, hell, something really was up.

"We are walking,'' was all she said.

Trent turned to his brother. "Where? Where are you walking to?''

Nathan's grin grew. "Oh, you know, here and there. *Here* to the ice-cream parlor for a cone. Then maybe later, we'll go *there*.''

Trent gave his brother his meanest, most effective narrowed-eyed look. As usual, Nathan didn't bat an eye. "Where's *there*, Nathan?''

"Hailey and I thought we might stop by Precious Pets to see how your puppy training lessons were going. Leigh says your dog is having some problems keeping up with the rest of the class. Maybe after Hailey and I watch for a while, we can give you some pointers. Purely in the interest of helping Brutus, of course.''

Trent would rather be dipped in honey and

strapped to an ant pile. And he didn't believe for a second that Nathan's interest was in the dog. His brother wanted to meet Erin. No doubt Leigh had been spinning all sorts of tales about the two of them. She'd probably told most of the town already about the kiss.

Great. Just what he needed. An audience.

"You're wasting your time, Nathan," he said as he steered Brutus toward Precious Pets. "Erin's helping me with Brutus. There's nothing going on between us so there's no reason for you to stop by to meet her."

Once again, Hailey and Nathan shared a look that spoke volumes. They didn't believe for a second that there wasn't something going on.

"I like to meet new people," Hailey said. "Erin sounds like an interesting person."

Trent liked his soon-to-be sister-in-law, but she wasn't a very good liar. The two of them were taking a stroll all right, a stroll right to Erin's shop.

"You're wasting your time," he said. "For starters, Brutus isn't doing that badly, so there's nothing interesting to watch."

"I think I'd like to take a look at the shop," Nathan said. "I'm always interested in new businesses coming to Paxton."

Nathan owned Barrett Software, the largest employer in town. Although Trent knew Nathan encouraged and helped other businesses, he also knew his brother's visit this evening had nothing to do with chamber of commerce goodwill and everything to do with the Barrett ornery streak. He and his brothers and sister had a history of butting into each other's lives. Most of the time, he thought it was a good idea. After all, they loved each other enough to care.

But being on the receiving end of that ornery streak was pretty damn annoying.

Trent had reached the outside of Precious Pets. Hoping to get this over with quickly, he shoved open the door and waved at the interior of the store. "This is Precious Pets. That's the owner, Erin. The other people standing there staring at us are the members of Brutus's obedience class. Now you've seen everything there is to see. You might as well head on over to the ice-cream shop."

But naturally, it wasn't that easy. Nathan and Hailey insisted on going inside to meet Erin. Left with no choice, Trent followed them inside and introduced them to the petite brunette.

Erin shook their hands. "It's really nice to meet both of you. Leigh mentioned your wedding is in a few weeks. You must be busy."

"Yes. But it's wonderful." Hailey snuggled against Nathan, who proceeded to get a goofy look on his face.

Trent tried to resist the urge to roll his eyes but

failed. At least he did manage to keep his mouth shut, but it wasn't easy.

"We hear you're helping Trent," Nathan said, cutting a devious look in Trent's direction.

Trent frowned at his brother. "Don't you have someplace you need to be?"

A lazy grin crossed Nathan's face. "Nope. I'm all clear. Thanks for thinking of me, though." He turned back to Erin. "I know you're new in town, so Hailey and I would love it if you would come to our wedding. You can get Trent to show you where the church is, and the reception is going to be at our house. And if Trent minds his manners, he can come to the wedding, too."

"Cute, real cute," he said, shooting Nathan a narrow-eyed look.

After first making a mental note to disown Nathan, Trent decided if he couldn't get rid of his meddling brother, then Brutus sure could. With a nudge of his foot, he got Brutus to shift toward Nathan. Spotting shoelaces, Brutus pounced on Nathan's running shoes and set to work gnawing his little heart out.

Good dog.

"Whoa, fella, you've got as bad manners as your old dad here." Nathan leaned down and scooped the puppy up. "Looks like you've got your work cut out for you," he said to Erin. "Think you can handle these two or should we call in some zoo-keepers for reinforcements?''

"I'll manage," Erin said with a laugh, and Trent would have resented it if the sound of her laughter hadn't been silky and sexy and enticing. He found himself hoping she'd laugh some more because he found it as appealing as Brutus found shoelaces.

"I think Erin has everything under control," Hailey said, pulling Trent's attention back to the conversation.

Deciding he was tired of this game, Trent snagged his puppy away from Nathan. "I think y'all have enjoyed yourself enough for one evening. Now excuse us, because Brutus and I have a class to attend."

He set Brutus down. "Come on, furball." Then he headed toward the back of the shop to the area where Erin held the lessons. Miracle of miracles, Brutus actually trotted after him for once.

Behind him, he heard his brother laugh, but shoot, he didn't care. Just because Nathan had gone sappy and fallen in love didn't give him the right to go meddling in other people's lives. And Chase and Leigh were just as bad. Yeah, Erin was cute. And smart. And funny. That didn't mean he was going to fall in love with her. Heck, he wasn't go-ing to fall in love with anyone. Like it or not, his family needed to jettison their plan and soon. Because if this kept up, he was going to find himself a new family.

And next time, he'd pick one that wasn't insane.

"WOW, YOU CERTAINLY HAVE a sweet tooth. If I ate that much candy, I'd get so big, I'd form my own gravitational pull. You must have one heck of a metabolism."

Erin recognized the voice immediately. Turning, she found Leigh Barrett standing behind her in line.

"Hi, Leigh. How are you?"

Leigh grinned. "Great. So what's up with all the candy?"

Erin wasn't sure what they were talking about, which was a fairly common situation for her since coming to Paxton. "Candy?"

The younger woman pointed at Erin's grocery cart. "You've got quite a selection there."

What in the world was she—

Erin glanced at her cart, then stared in stunned silence at the contents. Leigh hadn't been kidding. Seven or eight bags of chocolate candy sat on the top.

Erin scooted the candy aside to see if this really was her cart. Maybe she'd grabbed the wrong one. She'd stopped for a couple of minutes to talk to Delia, then she'd come right here to the checkout line. Maybe she'd gotten mixed up when she'd returned to her cart.

A quick glance at the other contents proved that she hadn't. This was her cart, but someone had put several bags of candy in it.

How weird.

"My favorites are the ones with caramel centers. But I like the peanut butter ones, too." Leigh leaned past Erin and said, "Ooooh, I like those nut clusters as well. Are you in a major funk and that's why you're buying so much chocolate? I always eat chocolate when I'm down."

Erin pulled her attention away from the contents of her cart and looked at Leigh. "You get depressed? When? It doesn't seem possible."

Leigh laughed. "You're right. I don't get down too often. I'm an upbeat person by nature."

Upbeat. Offbeat. Both described Leigh. "I don't tend to get down too often, either," Erin said.

"So what's with all the chocolate, then?"

That's what Erin was trying to figure out. "I didn't put this candy in my cart," she said, lifting it out. "I think someone else did."

Erin surveyed the store. No one was watching her, but she couldn't help wondering if the candy had been deliberately put in her cart. Was this another little gift like Pookie, the birdhouse and the flowers? Or was she simply letting her imagination run away with her?

She honestly didn't know.

But the more she thought about it, the more

doubtful it seemed that someone had done it deliberately. For starters, the store was crowded, so mixing up carts would be easy. It had to be an innocent mistake.

Didn't it?

"Don't worry about the candy. Just set it here on the side. They'll put it back on the shelf."

"Thanks." Erin set the candy aside, still puzzled. "It just seems odd."

"I wouldn't think anything of it. This sort of thing happens to me all the time," Leigh said. "I once found a pregnancy test kit in my cart. The cashier was a friend from high school, and she noticed the box before I did. She told the carryout, who told the store manager, and before I could say 'are you out of your mind?' the whole store knew. Thankfully Elsie VanDerHauffen was still in the store and quickly explained that the kit was hers." Leigh rolled her eyes. "Boy, did that cause a stir because Elsie's husband was away working on an oil rig in the Gulf and hadn't been home in four months. I mean, come on, how could she be pregnant, right?"

Leigh paused, and Erin stared at her. What in the world was she talking about? But since Leigh seemed to expect some sort of response, the best Erin could manage was, "Huh?"

With a laugh, Leigh continued. "Lost you there, didn't I? Anyway, turns out Elsie and Bernie, that's her husband, had gone on a second honeymoon at some motel near Galveston, and she hadn't breathed a word to anyone. But now everyone knew. So you see my point.''

''Not even remotely,'' Erin admitted.

''Someone put the candy in your cart by mistake,'' Leigh said. ''Just like Elsie put her stuff in my cart by mistake. Just consider yourself lucky you won't have to worry about three brothers having simultaneous strokes like I had to. For a second there when I couldn't convince anyone the pregnancy test kit wasn't mine, well let's just say things looked bleak. All you have is a few bags of candy. No one's going to start any rumors about you. Well, not exciting ones. Having a sweet tooth is nothing compared to having a love child, so consider yourself lucky.''

When Leigh put it like that, Erin had to admit the candy didn't seem suspicious at all. ''I'm sure that's what happened. Someone put it there by mistake.''

After putting the rest of her groceries on the counter, she told Leigh, ''For a second there, I thought someone might have put the candy in my cart deliberately.''

Leigh frowned. ''Now why would someone want to make you fat?'' Suddenly, her expression brightened. ''You mean this could be some sort of revenge thing. Wow. Wouldn't that be something?

Nothing exciting ever happens in Paxton, and boy, don't I know it. Most days this town is about as exciting as watching dirt age. Maybe you'll bring some excitement to this town. First there was Pookie. Then the birdhouse. And finally, the weeds thing—but to tell you the truth, I'm still not sure that meant anything. And now the candy.'' She grinned. "You haven't stolen anyone's husband lately by any chance? Maybe someone's trying to get back at you.''

"Of course I haven't.'' Erin drew a deep, calming breath into her lungs when Leigh looked disappointed. There was no way that Erin believed for a second that any town in which the Barrett family lived would be boring. "I just thought the candy might be—''

"A present from a secret admirer.'' Leigh studied the bags of candy Erin had set aside. "They could be, I guess. But knowing how boring this place is, I think a mix-up is the more likely scenario. Still, you should tell Trent.''

Yes, telling Trent sounded like the most reasonable thing to do. And ever since Nathan and Hailey had stopped by the store over a week ago, Trent had been a complete gentleman in class. Well, at least as much of a gentleman as a man like Trent could be. He still had that rogue's gleam in his eyes whenever he looked at her, but he'd kept his hands and his lips to himself.

For Trent, that was excellent behavior.

"I think I'll stop by the station on my way home and talk this over with Trent," Erin told Leigh. "Just to let him know."

"Sounds good. But Trent isn't at the station. He's already left for the day. Why don't you swing by his house and tell him?"

"I couldn't simply drop by. That would be rude." More than that, she might end up interrupting something like a dinner party or worse, a date. "I'll stop by his office tomorrow or the next day and tell him."

Leigh seemed perplexed by Erin's answer. "Why would stopping by his house be rude? This is Paxton. People stop by to say hi all the time." She opened her gargantuan purse and started digging through it. "Hold on a sec."

Erin hadn't a clue why, but Leigh seemed so deep in thought that she hated to interrupt her. Still, once the other young woman finally found whatever it was she was searching for, Erin intended on explaining that even though the residents of Paxton might drop in on each other unannounced all the time, it wasn't the sort of thing she was used to doing. Having grown up in a family with three sisters, she valued her privacy and figured other people valued theirs as well.

Even people who lived in Paxton.

With a flourish, Leigh yanked her cell phone out

of her purse, and before Erin could do much to protest, she called Trent.

"Heads up. Erin's on her way over to your house," Leigh said. Then she hung up. "There you go. All set."

Erin barely managed to keep her mouth from falling open. At no point in the brief conversation were the words "can Erin stop by" or "would you mind" used.

Flat-out amazed by the other woman's approach, Erin pointed out, "You didn't ask him if I could come over. You told him. What if he'd rather I not stop by?"

"Why wouldn't he want you to stop by? No offense, Erin, but you're thinking way too much about this. Folks around here expect people to stop by at all times. Else they wouldn't live in Paxton. They'd live someplace like Dallas or Houston where people only come over when invited."

Leigh said the last sentence with so much distaste in her voice that Erin clearly understood that impromptu visits were considered a definite perk to small-town living. At least they were to Trent's sister. Always a firm believer in fitting in with the natives, Erin made a mental note to not be surprised if people started showing up unannounced on her doorstep.

And as far as going to Trent's house went, well, he had been informed, so her visit would no longer be a surprise. "I guess I can stop by for a couple of minutes," Erin relented. "I'm sure he won't mind."

"Of course he won't," Leigh said, bobbing her head. "And if he's got a girl or two over there, you tell them to take a hike. You're there on official business, so they can chase after him some other time."

Erin froze. Surely Leigh was kidding. But from the look on the young woman's face, she realized Leigh was serious. She honestly thought Erin might run into young women at Trent's house.

Maybe going to see him wasn't such a good idea after all. "On second thought, why don't I just call Trent when I get home? I can tell him everything over the phone."

"Have you always been so timid about things?" Leigh asked.

Timid? No one had ever called Erin timid in her entire life. "Just because I don't want to interrupt his evening doesn't mean I'm timid."

"If you say so," Leigh said with a shrug. "It sure seems timid to me. Maybe you could go through some sort of self-help thing with twelve steps and get over your timidness."

That got to Erin. She wasn't timid. Never had been. And especially now, since starting her new life, she'd made a point of being brave and independent. So what if Trent had someone over at his house? Did that mean she couldn't stop by and tell him what had happened?

"I am *not* timid," Erin said firmly to Leigh.

"Okeydokey," Leigh said. "So you're going over to Trent's house, then?"

"You bet I am," Erin said.

"Good for you." Leigh's smile turned downright smug. "You have a nice time."

Suspicion trickled over Erin. There was something about Leigh's smile that made her more than a little uncomfortable.

"I'm only going over there to tell him about the candy," Erin felt compelled to say. "There's nothing to smile about."

Leigh's smile only grew wider. "Of course that's why you're going. I'm only smiling because I'm happy that Trent will know what's going on."

Yeah, well, if Trent knew what was going on in this town, then Erin sure hoped he'd tell her. Because frankly, she hadn't a clue.

TRENT OPENED HIS FRONT DOOR and smiled. Now this was a pleasant surprise—Erin on his doorstep.

"Hi," she said. Then before he could say a word, she hurried on. "I hope I haven't disturbed you, but Leigh said I should stop by. Actually it was more like Leigh insisted I stop by." She peered beyond him to the inside of the house. Since Brutus was yapping at their feet, he couldn't help wondering what she was looking for.

With a glance over his shoulder, he asked, "Is something sneaking up behind me? 'Cause if it is, I'd appreciate a little warning."

When Erin looked at him, she frowned. "What? Oh, no. I was just making sure I wasn't interrupting anything."

Trent chuckled. "Well, I did have a bunch of naked dancing girls over, but when Leigh called, I decided I best send them on home. Figured you'd disapprove. Of course, I can't promise you that Brutus doesn't have a lady friend over. The guy's a real animal."

Erin gave him a wan smile, so Trent knew immediately that something was up.

"You're not disturbing me. What's going on?" He pushed his front door open. Brutus scampered over and did his best to escape before Trent picked him up.

"Nothing, I guess," she said.

But when Erin only gave the pup a halfhearted pat, Trent knew she was lying.

"Come on. Fess up. As much as I'd like to think you stopped by because you were drawn by my sheer charm, I know that isn't the case. So what happened?" he asked.

"Nothing, really." When he continued to give

her a dubious look, she added, "It's just that I found some candy in my cart at the grocery store."

"And?"

She blew out a breath of disgust. "I didn't put it there. I can't help thinking it has something to do with Pookie, the birdhouse and the flowers."

Trent nodded. She might be right. Or it could simply be a mix-up. But either way, Erin was upset, and it seemed like the best idea was to spend some time talking this over with her.

"What did you buy at the grocery store?" he asked.

She frowned, but she still answered him. "I picked up a few things for dinner. Why? Are you thinking that my cart looked like someone else's and that it's all a case of mistaken cart identity?"

"Yeah, sure. Plus I was wondering if you had anything in your grocery bags we might cook up for dinner. I'm starving."

For a priceless minute, Erin simply stared at him. Then she asked slowly, "You're inviting me to dinner if I supply the food?"

"Hey, I'll cook. Unless, of course, you bought liver. Then I withdraw the offer." He gave a mock shudder. "I can't stand liver."

"I bought the ingredients for spaghetti," she said flatly.

Trent grinned and tugged at her arm. "Good, then by all means, stay for dinner. I'll cook, and you tell me more about what happened at the store.''

He could tell Erin was torn. She obviously didn't know what to say, so Trent played his trump card, ''Please stay. Look at Brutus's sad face. He wants you to stay. He's so upset at the mere thought that you might leave.''

His argument would have carried more weight if Brutus hadn't been panting and looking about as happy as a puppy could be.

Finally Erin shrugged. ''Fine. I'll stay. But I want it on the record that I think you're as devious as your sister.''

He nodded. ''Duly noted. Now where are those groceries?''

Before she could argue, he headed toward her car to grab the food. She might think he was devious, but he really did want to talk over what had happened. And sure, he'd like to spend some time with Erin as well. Dinner seemed like the natural solution.

And after all, a guy had to grab every opportunity that came his way.

6

TRENT TOOK A GREAT DEAL of satisfaction watching Erin be amazed by his culinary skill. Why was it that women thought men knew everything about cars and nothing about cooking? Well, he was one rancher's son who knew his way around a kitchen.

And he didn't mind showing off for a pretty lady.

"Tada," he said when he set the bowl of perfectly cooked pasta next to the savory sauce he'd created from the ingredients she'd bought and a few of his own thrown in.

"I'm really impressed," Erin said and he chuckled at her surprised tone.

"Did you honestly think I couldn't cook?" he asked, sitting after she had.

"No. Yes. I guess I didn't picture you as the domestic type."

He handed the bowl of pasta to her and waited while she served herself. "Oh, I'm not domestic. Not in the sense a lot of people mean it. But I can cook. And I clean my own house. Doesn't mean I'm the type to start picking out china patterns, but I can tend to myself."

Erin laughed, and Trent had to admit, he surely loved that sound.

"Calm down," she said. "I wasn't asking you to marry me. I just meant that it's nice when people surprise you with talents you hadn't yet discovered they have."

Okay, now there was no way as a self-respecting male that he could let that comment go without a response.

"I have a lot of talents you haven't discovered yet."

This time when Erin laughed, he was less than enchanted. Especially when she said, "I can't believe you used a line on me."

"Hey, it's not a line," he told her, knowing full well it was a line and not a very good one. But he wasn't about to admit that to her.

She was still laughing when she countered, "Oh, yes, it most certainly was a line. You were intimating something, probably something like what you said in class a couple of weeks ago."

A light flush colored her face, and Trent leaned forward. "Gee, Erin, I have no idea what you're talking about. What line in class?"

He expected her to get flustered or glance away, but she didn't. Instead she stopped laughing and looked him dead in the eye as she said, "You know exactly what I'm talking about."

He pretended to consider what she'd said. "I'm

racking my brain here, and I still don't remember a thing,'' he teased.

"Liar," she said softly.

"For the record, that definitely wasn't a line. And also, you were the one who started it with all that talk about consistency and firmness.'' He took a long sip of iced tea before he added, "I was being a perfect gentleman at the time.''

"To quote your sister——" she said, then she snorted.

Laughter burst out of Trent, and Erin laughed, too. Brutus joined in, yapping and chasing his own tail. By the time Trent finally got himself under control, he realized he hadn't laughed that much in a long, long time.

For a second, they sat looking at each other, humor still in their gazes. But along with the humor was attraction. Strong, vibrant attraction that made Trent want to kiss her again.

"Do you want more?" she asked.

Oh, yeah, did he ever.

He could picture it now. He'd give her a grin, then circle around to her side of the table, take her in his arms, pull her soft, warm body close and——

"No!"

Trent froze. "Excuse me?"

Thankfully Erin indicated Brutus. "He's thinking about making a move.''

Yeah, well, Brutus wasn't the only guy in the

room thinking along those lines. The idea had a lot of appeal to Trent as well.

With effort, he reined in his libido and asked, "What's the furball up to now?"

"He's definitely eyeing your shoelaces. I swear, I'm starting to worry about Brutus. He seems to have a one-track mind."

Trent knew exactly how the puppy felt. Whenever he was around Erin, he seemed to have a one-track mind as well. He gave the pup a stern look. Sure enough, Brutus was slowly creeping toward Trent's feet.

"Furball, what is it with you and shoelaces? Do you need more roughage in your diet?"

"He likes being around you," Erin said. "Dogs are pack animals. You're part of his pack."

"And chewing on my shoelaces would be a sign of what?"

"He wants to play with you."

"After dinner. Right now I'm playing with you." As soon as the words left Trent's mouth, he knew what Erin's response would be. She didn't disappoint him, either. She immediately frowned.

"There you go with the pickup lines again," she said, then turned her attention back to her dinner.

"That's not a pickup line," he protested. "A double entendre, maybe. But not a line. You've got it all confused. A line is something like 'Hey baby,

Heaven's missing an angel since you're here on Earth.'''

She crinkled her nose. "Yuck. Tell me you've never said anything so lame before. No woman would ever fall for something that dumb."

Trent decided not to enlighten Erin and risk ending up with a plateful of spaghetti in his lap. He hated to admit it, but he'd used that line and several like it before with great results.

"Okay, that's a bad example," he admitted. "A good line doesn't sound a thing like a line."

For a few minutes, they ate in silence. Trent knew Erin was dying to ask him what a good line was, but he also could tell she was trying her hardest not to ask. Finally she dropped her fork on her plate and looked at him.

"Okay, I can't stand it. Give me an example of a good line."

Trent barely refrained from smiling. Instead he shook his head. "A good line is no line at all. It's taking the time to really understand the lady you're interested in and being honest with her." He leaned forward a little, then said, "For instance, do you know you have the most amazing laugh? I love the way it sounds. So free. So wild. I've never met anyone who laughs as great as you do."

Erin stared at him, her brown eyes filled with doubt. She didn't know if what he'd just told her was a line he'd used a million times before or the truth. With any other woman, he'd flash a grin and assure her that he was telling the honest truth.

But the funny thing was, this time, he really was telling the truth. He loved the way Erin laughed. And he needed her to know it wasn't a line.

The problem became how to convince her. He knew Erin thought he was a player. Heck, he was. He made no secret of the fact that he liked his single lifestyle.

"I mean it," he said. "You have a great laugh."

Erin rolled her eyes. "You proved your point. The best lines don't sound like lines at all."

"I guess there's no way for me to convince you that wasn't a line, is there?"

She pretended to consider his question, then said, "Nope."

"Okay. So then why don't you tell me what happened at the grocery store? If I can't convince you of my sincerity, maybe I can impress you with my razor-sharp deductive abilities."

Erin quickly explained what had happened at the store. When she finished, Trent wasn't sure what to make of the candy. More than likely, it had been a mix-up.

"Don't you think it's odd that all of these things keep happening? The flowers, okay, maybe Leigh was right. Maybe they'd been dropped by accident. And sure, maybe the candy was an accident, too."

She shrugged. "It just strikes me as an awful lot of accidents."

"Strikes me that way, too." He took another sip of his iced tea and considered her. "Anything else odd happen lately?"

"You mean besides you asking me to stay to dinner so you could use up all of my groceries?"

He grinned. "Yeah, besides that."

"No. And when I stop to think about it all, it seems silly to be upset." She ran one finger up and down the side of her glass. "It was only a few bags of candy in my cart."

"Still, I'll look into it. A person can't be too careful."

Erin nodded, and then her glance met his. For a second, the attraction level between them zoomed.

Then she said, "You're absolutely right. A person can't be too careful…about a lot of things."

ERIN TIPPED HER HEAD and studied Brutus. "I think he's getting worse rather than better."

Trent nodded. "Yeah, I think so, too. But dang if I can figure out why. I keep doing everything you've shown us in class. But each day, the boy seems to get rowdier."

"He definitely fits into your family," she couldn't resist saying.

Rather than being offended, Trent laughed. "He does at that, doesn't he?"

He scooped up the puppy. ''At least, he's definitely related to Leigh. Furball here no more finishes making one mess before he's off making another. Keeps a man busy.''

Erin smiled, watching Trent hold Brutus at eye-level. No matter what the sexy chief of police said, Erin could tell he really liked the puppy. The two males were cute to watch together, although Erin would prefer it if Brutus took to the lessons a little better.

''Since he just ate, I'm going to take your advice and let him run in the backyard for a bit,'' Trent said.

''That's a good idea since you're trying to train him.''

''*Trying* is the operative word in that sentence.'' He glanced at the clock. ''Can you stick around for a while longer? I have to go stand outside with Brutus or else he won't take care of business.''

That seemed odd. ''Why on earth not?''

Trent gave her a rueful grin. ''He's afraid of the neighbor's cat. Scares the bejeepers out of him.''

Erin laughed. ''This I've got to see. Mind if I come with you two?''

With a wave toward the back door, Trent let her precede him outside. Sure enough, as soon as they got out, Trent had to shoo a cat away before Brutus would step off the patio.

"Yep. That's my dog. Afraid of a cat," Trent said dryly.

"In Brutus's defense, it is a big cat."

Trent snorted. "He's also not too keen on birds, and yesterday he ran back inside after encountering a cricket. Face it, my dog is a coward."

"He's still a puppy. Give him a chance. Besides, Brutus is more of a lover than a fighter."

"Is that a fact? Well, since you're making me get the boy fixed, he won't be a lover for much longer."

"He'll still be sweet and cuddly."

Trent groaned. "Great. I'm going to have a cuddly dog. Just what every chief of police needs. Maybe I should stock up on pink bows in case he feels like dressing up."

Erin laughed. "You are so predictable."

"Why?"

"Why? Look at you. You're taking this personally that your dog isn't some man-eating killer." She couldn't help adding, "You know, women like guys who aren't he-men all the time. It's nice to show a softer side of your personality now and then."

Trent turned to face her, and he had pure mischief in his eyes. "Oh, really? Is that all women?"

Oops. She should have thought that comment through before she'd made it. Now he was giving her one of his bona fide sure-to-melt-the-toughest-heart looks.

Her gaze drifted to his lips. Just like that. Wham. She was staring at his lips like she had no self-control at all.

Now this was why she shouldn't have stayed to dinner. Sure, visiting with Trent and Brutus had been a lot of fun. And talking to Trent had made her worries about the cart mix-up fade. She now was convinced it had been an accident.

But being around Trent hadn't done a thing to squash the out-of-control attraction she felt toward him. Nope. That was still thriving. Big time. In fact, the attraction factor had gotten a whole lot worse while she'd been here. Not only had he cooked a great dinner for them, he'd been a wonderful host.

Now how was she supposed to resist a man who insisted on being terrific? It simply wasn't fair.

He took a deliberate step closer to her. "So are you one of those women who likes men to have a softer side?"

"I was speaking in general terms," she said, although her words would have carried more weight if they hadn't come out all breathless and husky. "I didn't mean me."

"So you just like tough he-man types, then?"

"No."

He chuckled, the sound deep and masculine. "I'm confused, Erin. You don't like strong Alpha guys. You don't like tender Beta guys. What else is left?''

''No guys.'' When he raised one eyebrow, she hurriedly added, ''I mean, I like men. I'm just not interested in men at the moment.''

''Ah.'' He glanced over at Brutus, who was happily chasing his tail, then looked back at her. ''That whole 'left at the altar thing,' right?''

''Yes.''

He nodded, then slowly smiled. ''Tell me, when you are interested in men, which kind do you prefer?''

They were on dangerous ground, and she knew it. Flirting with Trent wasn't smart, but she didn't seem to be able to stop herself. The man had charm to spare.

''I'm not sure. I don't think I have a preference,'' she said, her gaze tangled up with his.

''Sure you do. Alpha guys are way different from Beta guys. They talk differently. Act differently.'' His gaze dropped to her lips. ''Kiss differently.''

Uh-oh. Danger. Warning. Erin sternly told herself to tell Trent this conversation was over. She needed to head home and was through flirting with him.

Unfortunately, even though that was what she told herself to say, what she actually said was, ''They do?''

He nodded. ''Oh, yeah.'' Before she could react,

he slipped his arms around her waist. "Alpha guys just go for it. Like this."

Even though she was braced for the kiss, she was in no way prepared for it. Because this was one heck of a kiss. Firm, thorough and completely devastating. Erin quickly found herself slipping her arms around Trent's neck and kissing him back.

When he finally shifted his lips away from hers, she barely resisted the impulse to protest.

"Now see a Beta guy wouldn't act like that," he said, and Erin was thrilled to note his voice was raspy with desire.

"He wouldn't?"

"No. He'd ask first. Something like, 'mind if I kiss you?'"

"Not at all," she said, even though his question hadn't truly been directed to her. But Trent didn't quibble. Instead he kissed her. Slowly. Gently. Tenderly.

It was every bit as amazing as the first kiss had been, and once again, Erin slipped her arms around his neck and kissed him back.

This time, when he ended the kiss they were both breathless. He leaned his forehead against hers.

"So which did you like better?" he asked.

She no more could choose than she could say which leg she liked better. And speaking of legs, both of hers were more than a little wobbly at the moment.

"They were both..." Amazing. Wonderful. Arousing.

She cleared her throat. "Fine."

He chuckled again, obviously knowing she was lying. But he didn't call her on the lie. Instead he said, "Glad you liked them."

Then before she could muster even a faint argument about how they shouldn't have kissed at all, Trent dropped his arms and stepped back.

He whistled, and Brutus slowly trotted over to join them. "Guess it's getting late."

"It is?" She blinked, mentally shook herself, then said firmly, "It is. I need to head home." She took a couple of steps toward the house, then reality forced her to turn to face him. "I guess we should talk about those kisses."

"Decided which one you liked best?" He grinned. "Personally I thought they both had their own advantages."

"That's not what I mean," she said. "I mean we should talk about why we shouldn't have kissed at all, not which kiss was the best."

"Oh, that. Yeah, well since our kissing this time was simply a research project, I wouldn't worry about it. There was nothing personal involved."

He was so full of hooey Erin didn't know how he could stand himself. But then, his plan of calling the kisses a research project offered her the perfect out. They could skip the whole "you shouldn't have kissed me" thing and go on with their lives.

Worked for her.

"Fine. I guess I'll see you tomorrow night at Brutus's lesson."

He nodded. "You bet."

Figuring there wasn't a thing left to say, she opened the back door and was all set to go inside to get her purse when Trent said, "Hey, Erin."

She stopped but didn't look at him. "Yes?"

"Whoever said research is tedious never met you."

Erin laughed and kept on walking. The sooner she put some distance between herself and Trent Barrett, the better. She was not going to fall for that flirt no matter what he did.

TRENT GLANCED AROUND the Wednesday night dog obedience class. Man, these pups had come a long way. Almost all of them were sitting nicely in front of their owners, patiently waiting for the class to begin. Even Delia's dog, who was one of Brutus's sisters, was acting like an absolute angel for the older woman and her grandson.

All the dogs were well behaved. Except Brutus. As usual, he was flopped half on one of Trent's shoes, chomping away at the laces.

Dang furball. For the record, he was *not* Trent's best friend.

"Cut it out," Trent growled at the dog, nudging him with his foot. Brutus wagged his tail and went back to chewing.

"Good behavior is about a lot more than knowing what to do when," Erin told the class as she walked by each dog and rewarded them with a pat on the head. "Good behavior is also about withstanding temptation."

She stopped in front of Brutus, and Trent couldn't help smiling. Yeah, neither he nor his dog seemed any good at withstanding temptation. Brutus couldn't give up chewing shoelaces, and he couldn't give up kissing Erin.

"Brutus, no," Erin said in a firm, no nonsense voice. "Sit and be still."

To Trent's amazement, Brutus did what she asked. He stopped chewing on the shoelace and sat.

"Well I'll be damned," Trent said, and then without thinking, let out a whistle.

Pandemonium broke out. All of the dogs responded to the whistle by yapping and yipping and chasing each other. Erin shot him a look of pure frustration before clapping her hands and saying, "Sit."

All the puppies settled down. Except for Brutus, who once more returned to eating Trent's shoelaces.

"Guess it was a short-lived victory," Trent said.

"You shouldn't whistle when you're in dog school," Delia's nine-year-old grandson, Zach, said in that stern tone kids love to use when correcting an adult. "Whistling makes the dogs go crazy."

Trent winked at the kid. "Thanks for the tip."

After first frowning at Trent, Erin smiled at Zach. "You're right. Whistling does get the dogs riled up. I'm sure Chief Barrett won't do it again."

Zach beamed at her compliment, and Trent bit back a chuckle. Fine, the kid was right and he was wrong. He was man enough to own up to his mistakes, even if they were dumb ones.

"Yeah, I've learned my lesson. No more whistling in class."

This time, he was the one rewarded with one of Erin's smiles. Man, it felt like a punch to the solar plexus. As soon as she smiled at him, the air seemed to whoosh from his lungs, and he found himself unable to look away. She must have felt the same wallop of attraction because she simply stood still, looking at him.

The memory of the kisses they'd shared the night before burned between them. Both kisses had been amazing. Trent couldn't ever remember kissing a woman who got his blood as fired up as Erin did. Moreover, not only did he have the major hots for her, but he liked her. She was a blast to talk to, lots of fun to share a joke with, and a good sport when it came to taking guff from his family.

Yep, Erin Weber was one special lady.

"So is class over? Can we leave?"

The question came from Delia and made Erin blink and look away from Trent.

"The class?" She blinked again. "Oh, no. Class isn't over. Not at all. As I mentioned before, tonight we're going to work with training your dogs to resist temptation. Your puppies will see a lot of things in life that they'll want but cannot have. You need to train them to bypass the things that are bad for them."

"For instance?" Zach asked.

Erin glanced at Trent and he knew without a doubt she'd just put him in the category of things she wanted but shouldn't have. Hey, how fair was that? He wasn't a bad guy. He worked a regular job. Knew how to make spaghetti. Why couldn't she have him if she wanted to?

Someone needed to have a talk with her.

Almost as if she heard him, she frowned and looked away from him. "Things that puppies need to resist are eating bugs, chasing cars, chewing on shoes."

Trent glanced down. Sure enough, the furball was happily slobbering all over his shoelaces.

"Okay, so how do you teach temptation resistance? It's difficult not to give in to the things you want." Trent waited until Erin looked at him, then he added, "And sometimes, things that may seem bad aren't at all. Sometimes they're good. Very, very good."

A light flush colored Erin's face as she stared at him. He knew she completely understood what he was talking about.

"Sometimes things that seem good turn out to be very, very bad," she countered slowly, her words heavy with meaning.

"Sometimes you don't know what's good or bad until you try it." Trent knew the entire class was baffled by their conversation, but he couldn't help using this chance to try to change her mind. Erin couldn't simply blow him off when she had a room full of students. And he was absolutely certain that was what she intended on doing. She intended on telling him that the kisses shouldn't have happened and that they were all wrong for each other.

His way of looking at the situation was a lot simpler—what was the harm in having a little fun? They were adults. No one would get hurt. Why make this complicated?

More importantly, why not give in to temptation?

Erin obviously didn't share his sentiment. She took a step closer to him and said slowly, "I don't need to get hit by a freight train to know it would hurt. Therefore, I avoid things I know are dangerous for me."

"So we also need to teach our dogs to avoid trains, right?" Delia asked. "I think that's a good idea. The train comes fairly close to my house, and I couldn't stand for a tragedy to happen."

"Yes." Erin's gaze never moved from Trent. "Definitely avoid trains. And anything else that might cause serious harm. Better safe than sorry is a great motto to live by."

"But a very boring way to live," Trent couldn't help pointing out. "Very, very boring."

"But a whole lot less messy," Erin countered.

He chuckled. "Yeah, but messy done right can be a whole lot of fun."

7

ERIN SMILED AT DELIA as she and her grandson said goodnight. They were the last to leave following the lesson. Well, almost the last. Trent and Brutus had stayed behind, which didn't surprise Erin. She and Trent needed to talk, not only about the kisses last night, but also his "a mess done right can be fun" attitude.

As soon as she shut the door to the shop, she turned to face him. "I don't agree with your opinion when it comes to messes."

He tipped his head. "Sure? I think the two of us messing around would be a lot of fun."

"Very cute." She started to walk closer to him, and then thought better of the idea. Every time she got too close to Trent, she ended up in his arms. So in an attempt to resist temptation, she decided to keep the distance of the room between them.

Seeing no reason not to be honest, she said, "I don't want to end up hurt."

"Then I'm the perfect guy for you. No one gets hurt in my love life 'cause no one takes it seriously. Life's short, Erin. Why not let yourself have a little fun?'' He took a couple of steps closer, so Erin moved back two steps.

"I'm not sure I can have a relationship where—''

He held up both hands. "Whoa. See that's your first mistake. It wouldn't be a relationship. I don't do relationships. I was talking about dating.''

"Dating?'' Had she really misunderstood his intentions that much? "Oh. I thought you were interested in…'' She shrugged, feeling very self-conscious. "Other things than dating.''

He chuckled, and once again took two steps forward. Again, she took two steps back. Actually one and a half because she bumped into the front door. Still, she was far away from him.

"Erin, hon, if the dating goes well, then those other things happen, too. But no one gets all weepy and clingy. And no one leaves the other one standing in front of the alter holding a broken heart.'' He grinned and looked like the perfect picture of a lady-killer. "See how much nicer my way is? No promises. No heartaches. Clean. Simple.''

The most ridiculous thing suddenly happened to Erin. She agreed with Trent. To her complete and absolute amazement, she saw his point. She didn't want to date a man who made her promises, ones she'd take seriously. Her heart was still healing and needed more time.

In which case, Trent really was the right guy for her at this point in her life.

What a wonderful discovery.

"I agree," she said, returning his grin. "I can't believe it, but you're right. If I don't want a man who will break my heart, then you're perfect for me. You keep your dealings with women strictly on a shallow level. There's no love involved. No emotion."

"I don't know if I'd call it shallow so much as uncomplicated. If you dated me, you'd know from the get-go that we weren't heading to the chapel. That way you wouldn't get all wrapped up in the why-isn't-he-calling-me syndrome. My way is simple. We'd date for however long the two of us agreed it was fun, then we'd say adios and still remain friends."

Erin felt like laughing. She couldn't believe she was actually contemplating having a no-strings relationship—oops, make that a nonrelationship—with Trent. But she couldn't see the downside. They were both incredibly attracted to each other, while at the same time, they had absolutely no intention of spending the rest of their lives together. No strings definitely seemed the way to go.

"Sounds good to me," Erin said.

This time when he took two deliberate steps forward, so did she. Grinning at each other, they each took two more steps closer. Finally they took two more, and ended up standing toe-to-toe.

"Why, Ms. Weber, I'm so glad I bumped into you," he said in that deep, silky voice she loved so much. "I've been wanting to ask you to dinner. Are you free tomorrow night?"

Anticipation hummed through Erin's veins. "We could consider the dinner we shared last night to be our first date," she pointed out.

His grin turned wicked. "I'm shocked. Here I thought you were the shy, retiring type when all along, you've been plotting to take advantage of me."

His silliness made her smile as she slipped her arms around his shoulders. "Do you mind?"

"Not one bit," he said. "You take advantage of me whenever you want."

"Good. Because now seems like the perfect time."

Trent must have agreed because he leaned down and kissed her.

TRENT HADN'T EXPECTED ERIN to come around to his way of thinking, but hey, he was downright thrilled. He kissed her again and again until she practically hopped on him.

"Let's go upstairs," she said. "Right now."

Looked like once the lady made up her mind, she saw no reason to waste time.

He was all set to follow her upstairs to her apartment when he realized he'd forgotten something. He nodded toward Brutus. "What do I do with the furball? I can't tell him to leave us alone for a few hours."

Erin turned to look at the puppy. "Good point. Oh, I know. He stayed with me for a couple of weeks before you adopted him—"

"Technically I didn't adopt him. The furball was forced on me."

With a smile, Erin leaned up and kissed him lightly. "You're so sexy when you pout."

"Hey, I'm not pouting. Just pointing out a fact."

She tipped her head. "Do you want to debate how you came to own Brutus or do you want to go upstairs to my apartment?"

"I definitely want to go upstairs," he told her. "I only hope you're right about him remembering being here before. The furball likes company, and is apt to drive us crazy all night if he's unhappy."

The dimpled smile she gave him made it clear he'd divulged too much.

"Trent Barrett, do you let this puppy sleep with you?"

"Of course not. He sleeps..."

"In your room," she said, finishing the sentence for him.

"No. He doesn't."

"Right outside your room, then," she teased.

Actually that was what he and Brutus had finally settled on. The furball had first jumped up on Trent's bed and made himself comfy. He'd vetoed that idea, setting the pup up on a doggy bed in the family room instead. But as soon as he'd walked away, Brutus had calmly picked up his mattress and carried it into the master bedroom.

No matter how many times he'd moved the puppy out, Brutus had come trotting back. Finally they'd settled on Brutus sleeping by the door to his room.

"To quote you, do you really want to spend any more time talking about Brutus?" Trent asked, trailing one hand from her waist to her shoulder.

Erin gave him a quick kiss, then scooped up Brutus and headed toward the stairway. "Good point. But just so you know, I think it's adorable how much you care for this little guy. You can grumble and growl all you want, but I know you love Brutus."

Adorable? Dang. What guy wanted the woman he could hardly wait to sleep with to find him adorable? Irresistible, sure. Sexy-as-sin, absolutely. But not adorable. He was going to have to do his best over the next few hours to get Erin to rethink her image of him.

But first, they needed to deal with the furball. Erin had a doggy bed set up in the spare bedroom, and because it hadn't been that long since he'd slept in it, Brutus thankfully settled right down.

The second Erin closed the door, Trent wrapped his arms around her waist, lifted her off the ground until she was eye level with him, then said, "I'll show you who's adorable."

The kiss he gave her was deep and hot and sexy. He carried her like that with her feet off the ground down the hall and into the room he suspected was her bedroom.

Breaking the kiss, he gave her a self-satisfied male smile. "I bet you don't think I'm so adorable now."

Obviously breathless and aroused from the kiss, Erin stared at him for a couple of seconds. Then a smile slowly grew on her face.

"I wouldn't, except you just walked us into the linen closet. Now *that's* adorable."

Trent glanced around. Ah, hell, he had. He'd taken them straight into a walk-in linen closet. So much for his lady-killer instincts.

He did the only thing a guy could do in these circumstances, he laughed.

"Dang. I give up. I'm trying to get you all excited and turned on, and all I'm managing to do is make you think I'm adorable. Do you know what a word like that does to a man?"

Erin pressed her body against his and obviously felt how aroused he was. "In your case, it seems to get your engine revved." Taking his hand, she said, "This time, follow me."

"Yes, ma'am." He let her lead him out of the linen closet and down the hallway to the last room on the left.

"I should warn you, I haven't redecorated this room since I moved in. It's a little…odd."

"Does it have a bed?"

"Yes. But it's—"

"As long as it has a bed, it's great."

As soon as they entered the room, he leaned down to kiss Erin, but a flash of orange out of the corner of his eye made him stop and look around. "What the—"

The bedroom looked like a disco. The walls were painted vibrant orange and pink, with small, geometric-shaped mirrors placed all around. With a grin, Trent looked up and laughed when he saw that instead of a traditional overhead light, the room had its very own disco ball to flash splatters of light around the room.

"Now *this* is what I call a bedroom." He slowly studied the room. "Definitely makes you want to strut your stuff. Are you sure you didn't decorate this?"

"Hardly," she said dryly. "It looked exactly this way when I moved in. So far, all I've redone is the kitchen. I keep meaning to redo this room, but since I'm the only one who sees it—"

He grinned. "Until now."

She grinned back. "Until now. Anyway, I

haven't a clue who did this. I was told when I rented the building that it had been vacant for a long time.''

''Not that long.'' He studied the room again. ''The previous tenant was Tina Zeffner. She ran an arts and crafts shop downstairs.'' He walked over and turned on the disco ball. ''Tina was almost eighty. She closed her shop a couple of years ago to go live by her daughter in Des Moines. The lady was always a lot of fun.'' He watched the globe spin overhead. ''I guess I didn't realize just how much fun she was. Way to go, Tina.''

''Well, if you find the room too distracting, we can go to your house,'' Erin offered. ''Of course, we *will* be wasting time, but it's your call.''

And Trent wasn't in the mood to waste any more time. Seeing Erin standing in the middle of this wild room with the sparkling effect of the lights dancing off the mirrors was making him crazy.

''I'm through wasting time,'' he said, kissing her slowly. When he slipped his tongue into her mouth, she made a little mewing noise that fired up his blood. Man. This was good. Really good.

He broke the kiss and glanced around. The bed was about six paces away. ''Hang on.''

''What are you—'' She squeaked when he picked her a couple of inches off the floor and headed over to the bed.

''I do know how to walk,'' she said dryly.

"I know. But I'm in a hurry." When he reached the four-poster sitting in the middle of the room, he asked, "Is this a waterbed?"

She shook her head. "No. Sorry."

"I'm not. Considering what I have in mind, we might both end up seasick if it were," he teased.

"You have big plans, do you? I can hardly wait." She untucked his T-shirt.

"Very big plans." Figuring two could play at this game, Trent untucked her T-shirt.

She pressed against him for a moment, then smiled. "Yes, the plans are big. Very, *very* big."

Trent laughed. "Lady, you're bad."

"You have no idea." With a few tugs, she pulled his T-shirt over his head.

Bending slowly, Trent feathered a teasing kiss across her soft lips. Despite his casual attitude, he was wired. He'd never wanted a woman as badly as he wanted Erin. His kiss turned firm and hungry, coaxing her willing lips apart and thrusting his tongue inside to taste her sweetness. His chest rumbled with a satisfied growl as she met his ardor with her own.

Her fingers threaded through the hair on the back of his head, sculpting him to her. Rising on her toes, she burned her body against his, her mouth closing around his tongue and keeping it prisoner.

Yeow.

Finally, with a shudder, Trent tore his mouth free. "Erin, hon, I don't know how long I can last."

She kissed his neck, her mouth gliding over his skin, her tongue trailing moisture on his flesh. "I'm sure you can manage. Anticipation is part of the fun."

His fingers tightened on her waist. "Oh, yeah?"

She kissed his chin and his jaw. "Um." She dropped her hands to the top button of his jeans and popped it open. "Waiting for something makes you appreciate it all the more when you finally get it."

He chuckled and tugged her T-shirt over her head. "So in other words, if I do this…" He leaned down and kissed the creamy skin showing over the top of her bra. "Then you'll have fun anticipating what I'll do next?"

He could hear her struggling for breath as he continued his leisurely exploration, slowly learning her taste. "For instance, you don't know if I'll do this," he said as he slipped his tongue beneath the edge of her bra, causing Erin to sigh. "Or if I'll do this," he eventually said, capturing one taut nipple through the thin fabric and sucking hard.

Erin held him to her, obviously enjoying herself as much as he was. When he lifted his head and flashed her a grin, she smiled back.

"You think you're pretty smart, don't you?" she teased.

"Smart? No. Talented? Maybe."

She laughed and shoved him onto the bed. "Talented definitely." Reaching down, she carefully slid down the zipper on his jeans. With his help, she tugged them down his legs, leaving him in his boxers.

"Boxers. I knew it," she said, sitting next to him on the bed.

"Oh really? How?" He reached behind her and unhooked her bra. She made no comment as he slipped the flimsy garment off her, but when he cupped her naked breasts, a soft murmur of pleasure escaped her. He nudged her until she lay on the bed and closed her eyes. Then he used both his hands and his mouth to explore her full, pretty breasts.

For a few moments, he simply enjoyed the feel of her silky skin. Then he leaned over her and whispered, "Erin?"

"Hmmm." She ran her hands over his shoulders. "What?"

"You never told me. How did you know I wore boxers?"

She opened her eyes and her gaze locked with his. "Men like you always do."

Men like him? He wanted to pursue that remark, but at that moment, she slipped one hand inside said boxers, and he pretty much forgot everything. Man, he wasn't the only one with talent on this bed.

When he felt precariously close to losing it, he helped Erin out of the rest of her clothes. Then he slipped off his boxers and grabbed his wallet out of his jeans.

"Give me a second while I—"

Erin pulled open the drawer of the bedside table and took out a condom. "Here," she said, tossing it to him.

"You keep condoms in your nightstand?" he asked.

"You keep condoms in your wallet?" she countered.

Okay, good point. But despite what everyone in town thought, he didn't sleep with every woman he met. The condom in his wallet had been there for several months.

But as stupid as it sounded, the thought that Erin had stocked the nightstand surprised him, although he couldn't say why. Erin was a vibrant, pretty woman and just because no man had been in this bedroom in the couple of months since she'd moved here didn't mean she hadn't planned on one stopping by soon.

"Planning on using that condom or just admiring it?" she teased.

"I definitely plan on using it."

He opened the condom, but before he had it in place, she leaned forward and kissed his chin, then his neck, and then his chest, her tongue doing wild things to his blood pressure.

"You're distracting me," he said, although he didn't really want her to stop.

"Poor baby," she murmured and she skimmed her hands over his chest, her fingers kneading his muscles. "I can't believe how mean I am to you."

Trent turned his head and kissed her deeply, giving her talented lips something else to do for a minute. "If I don't get this condom on, neither of us is going to be too happy."

She laughed softly and scooted toward the headboard of the bed. "Fine. I'll leave you alone. But you really do need to practice your multitasking skills. It seems to me I should be able to do a little exploration while you're otherwise occupied."

The condom in place, Trent grinned at her. "Darlin', at the moment, I have a one-track mind."

"Good, because I can't take any more."

"What about that whole 'anticipation makes it better' thing you mentioned?"

"I think we've both anticipated enough for one day," she said.

He couldn't agree more. He quickly joined their bodies, savoring the feel of her against him. Man, this was heaven, and he wanted this experience to last for a long, long time.

Erin must have felt the same way, because as they loved each other, she kept encouraging him with her hands and her lips and her body. He couldn't remember ever being this close to a woman. It was way more than just physical. He felt like his mind and his soul and even his heart were also making love to Erin.

It felt wonderful.

When she finally gasped and went rigid, he released the tight control he'd held on himself and pushed them both over the threshold. As he crossed, he called out her name, clutching her to him.

Afterward, he buried his face into the soft, scented skin of her neck. Slowly his heart rate returned to normal. When he started to move off her, she protested, holding him close.

"Not yet," she murmured, kissing his cheek.

He looked at her. "Aren't I too heavy for you?"

"No. I like the feel of you, the sensation of being with you." She moved ever so slightly. "It feels amazing."

His heart constricted at her words. "Yeah. Amazing pretty much sums it up," he told her.

Surprised by the sensation, he studied her face, wondering if she'd felt more than merely physical pleasure, too. For a heartbeat, she stared back at him. Then she smiled.

"I'm pretty sure even my toes had an orgasm," she teased.

Okay, that wasn't exactly what he'd expected her to say, but like any other guy, he was thrilled he'd made her happy.

"Good for your toes," he murmured, kissing her lightly. "I told you I was talented."

"And you didn't lie. Any chance I can talk you into proving it again?"

The weirdest thing was happening to him. Here, this beautiful, passionate woman was complimenting his lovemaking skill, and all he could think about was how much he wanted her to say the experience had meant something more to her. More than just flesh meeting flesh. More than just hot sex on a cool night.

Talk about ridiculous. He wasn't interested in emotions and commitments and relationships. Hot sex was just fine with him.

Forcing himself to brush aside the sensation he'd been feeling, he instead focused on the woman beneath him. He refused to go all sappy and stupid about this. He and Erin were perfect together because neither of them wanted any strings.

"I'll be happy to prove anything you want anytime you want," he told her.

Then he did.

ERIN WOKE WITH A START. Something was different. She glanced down at the masculine arm wrapped around her waist.

Oh, yeah, something was most definitely different.

Hoping Trent was a sound sleeper, she tried to

slowly slip free of his arm. Gingerly she lifted a couple of his fingers in an attempt to loosen his grip. But the man proved as stubborn when asleep as he was when awake.

"Stop fussing with my hand. I like it exactly where it is," he murmured in her ear. "In fact, I can think of a few other places I'd like my hand to be as well. Let me see." He shifted his hand lower. "Here's good."

Erin let out a squeak when he indeed started exploring her body. "Cut it out."

"Okay. Not your favorite spot. How about here? You like this?"

This time, she giggled. "Trent. I'm serious."

He shifted closer to her. "Fine. I'll be serious, too."

This time when his wandering hand came to rest, a sigh of pleasure slipped from her lips. Trent Barrett might be stubborn as the day was long, but he also was one heck of a lover. So much so that for a long time, she forgot about trying to get away from him.

But eventually, reality returned when Brutus started yapping from down the hall.

Trent chuckled as he slowly kissed Erin. "I think the furball is getting the hang of this male bonding thing. This time, he waited until I was done before interrupting me."

He gave Erin another kiss but kept it short this

time. "Let me take him out for a bathroom break, then I'll be right back." He winked and added, "Don't go anywhere."

Erin laughed and assured him, "I'll wait right here."

"Thanks." As she watched Trent pull on his jeans and then head out the door to get Brutus, she leaned back in the bed, contentment filling her. She'd never been with a man just for fun before, but she had to admit, there were distinct advantages.

For starters, there were no awkward moments this morning. She and Trent had fooled around simply for pure enjoyment. And she'd had a terrific time. A really terrific time.

And now today, there were no awkward attempts at small talk. They weren't worried if the other person liked them or would fall in love with them. Instead they were two people enjoying each other's company for as long as it lasted. Simple as that.

Trent came back into the bedroom with Brutus hot on his heels. The puppy jumped up on the bed, but Trent scooped him up and sat him on the floor.

"No, stay there, furball."

Brutus wagged his tail, and after Trent sat down on the mattress next to Erin, the puppy immediately hopped up on the bed again.

"Dang, this dog is never going to learn." Trent put him on the floor again.

"Born to be wild?" Erin teased.

"Something like that." Trent leaned over and kissed Erin, but before the kiss could catch fire, Brutus jumped on the bed yet again.

"That's it," Trent said, standing and picking up the pup. "If monkeys can learn to read, you're going to learn to listen to me."

Erin couldn't help smiling because the whole time Trent was delivering his stern speech, he was scratching Brutus under the chin. The he-man chief of police was a real softy at heart.

And one heck of a nice guy.

"Brutus likes you and wants your attention," Erin said.

"Well, I like you and want *your* attention," Trent counted.

"I'm pretty sure if we give each other any more of our attention, neither of us will be able to walk straight."

Trent shrugged. "Walking straight is overrated in my opinion."

She laughed and tucked the sheet firmly beneath her arms when he made a move to join her once again on the bed. "Be that as it may, I have a business to run. I need to get up and dress. You and your puppy need to leave."

Trent sighed and grabbed his shirt off the floor where she'd tossed it last night. "Guess you're right, although I hate to admit it. But I need to run Brutus home and head into work myself.''

After he'd gotten dressed, he kissed her one last time. ''Can I see you tonight? Maybe even take you to dinner this time?''

Erin nodded. ''Absolutely.''

''And we're still going to the wedding together next week, right?''

The wedding. She'd completely forgotten she'd been invited to Trent's brother's wedding. When she'd agreed to go, she hadn't expected to go with him. What she had with Trent was so new, it felt odd to think about letting everyone know.

By the same token, she didn't want to keep what was happening with Trent as a secret forever. She had nothing to be ashamed of, so there was no reason the world couldn't know they were seeing each other. No reason to keep it hidden.

Besides, this was Paxton. Secrets lasted about as long as an ice cube in the Amazon. Sooner or later, everyone would know.

''Sure,'' she said.

''Great. See you tonight.'' With that, Trent headed out the door. She heard him talking to Brutus on the way down the stairs.

The man really was adorable.

And she could hardly wait until tonight to see him again.

8

"YOUR BROTHER IS HERE," Trent's secretary, Ann Seaver, announced. "Shall I send him in?"

Trent rubbed his neck. Man, he was exhausted, but for a spectacular reason. Like every other night this week, he and Erin had spent hours making love, only to fall asleep for a little while, then wake up, and make love again. The past few days with Erin had been unbelievable.

He was one happy camper today, and he didn't feel like putting up with either of his brothers or their nonsense. They'd take one look at his goofy, I-had-a-great-time-last-night face and razz him like crazy.

"Tell whichever one it is that I'm not here," Trent said.

After a pause, Ann asked, "What do I do if there's two of them?"

"*Both* of them are here now?" He needed this like a kick to the head this morning.

"Yep. The second one just walked in. Want me to tell them you aren't here? I don't think they'll believe me since they can tell I'm talking to you, but I'm willing to give it a try.''

Trent sighed, resigned to his fate. ''Very cute. Fine. Send them in.''

The door to his office flew open before he'd even finished speaking.

''Hey, there, baby brother,'' Chase said, crossing the room and dropping into one of the chairs facing Trent's desk. ''You look like hell this morning.''

''Good to see you, too,'' he said dryly, then looked at Nathan. ''Go ahead. Say it. Say I look like hell.''

Nathan sat in the other chair facing his desk. ''You don't look like hell.'' He studied Trent for a second, then added with a laugh, ''You look...stupidly happy. Doesn't he, Chase?''

Chase leaned back in his chair. ''Why, I do believe you're right, Nathan. He does look stupidly happy. I wonder if the fact that he had lunch with Erin Weber at Roy's Café yesterday has anything to do with his expression. Megan heard from Hailey that Trent and Erin looked cozier than a newlywed couple.''

Ah, hell. He should have known better than to meet Erin for lunch so soon after they'd become lovers. Now the whole blasted town knew they were involved.

''Is that a fact?'' Nathan smiled at Trent. ''You and Erin had lunch together?''

Trent ignored the questions since they obviously already knew the answer. "Why are you two bozos here? To see if I'll tell you anything?"

Chase glanced at Nathan, then back at Trent. "I don't believe we need any answers. I think most of Paxton has heard what's going on between you and Erin Weber. So much for your claim that you were never going to fall in love and get married."

Trent held up his left hand. "Do you see a ring here?"

Nathan held up his left hand. "I don't have my wedding ring on yet, either. The ceremony's not for three more days. But that doesn't mean I'm not in love and in a committed relationship."

Trent started to tell his brother that he wasn't in love and he wasn't in a committed relationship, but for some insane reason, the words refused to pass his lips. The truth was, he might not be in love yet, but he sure did feel like he and Erin had a lot going for them.

He stared at his brothers, uncertain for the first time in his life what to say.

"We seem to have left him speechless," Chase observed. He stood and said to Nathan, "Let's leave him alone to think things over. We'll see him at the wedding on Saturday."

"Bring Erin," Nathan said.

"I'm not in love," Trent finally managed. "We're just having fun."

"Megan and I were just having fun, and now we're happily married and still having fun," Chase pointed out.

"Hailey and I were just having fun and our wedding is on Saturday," Nathan stated.

"It's different with Erin and me," Trent said, but for the life of him, that's all he could think to say.

"You just never know," Chase said. Then he headed for the door. "Come on, Nathan. I think our work here is done. I want to head on over to the library and see if I can corner Megan in her office and make her blush."

Trent watched his brothers walk out. Despite what they thought, things really were different between him and Erin.

Weren't they?

"HECK OF A WEDDING, wasn't it?" Leigh nudged Erin. "Doesn't it make you long to walk down the aisle? To have flower girls drop rose petals at your feet? To have a handsome, wonderful man waiting to spend the rest of his life with you?"

"Not particularly," Erin said, taking a sip of her champagne. And boy did she mean it. Today's wedding had been lovely, but it had brought back more than a few memories of her own wedding day fiasco. At least Nathan Barrett had actually married Hailey Montgomery, not told her he'd changed his mind and then sprinted toward the exit with the maid of honor in tow.

"No weepy moments of envy? No mental images of china patterns flashing through your mind?" Leigh prodded.

"Not a one," Erin assured her. In fact, the only images that had drifted through her mind were of the amazing things Trent had done with and to her last night. The man was phenomenally talented.

"Not even a teensy, weensy thought about wedded bliss?" Leigh continued.

Erin sighed. "Leigh, I'm not marrying your brother, so stop pushing on me. Today's wedding was wonderful for Nathan and Hailey. But I don't want to get married." Deciding to turn the tables, she asked, "What about you? Any deep-seated marital desires bubble up inside you during the ceremony?"

Leigh rolled her eyes. "Puh-lease. I'd rather remove my own appendix than tie the knot."

Okay, so maybe Erin didn't feel quite as strongly about avoiding commitment as Leigh did. But she did like her life the way it was. No strings. No ties. No heartache. Just really great sex.

It definitely worked for her.

Thinking about Trent made her wonder where he was. She glanced around the crowded wedding reception. As far as she could tell, the entire population of Paxton had turned out for the wedding.

And Leigh was right—it had been a lovely ceremony. Very sweet, with the bride and groom writing their own vows and looking so very deeply in love.

Love suited some people. That was true. But it was also true that she didn't happen to be one of those people.

Erin was still searching the crowd for Trent when a pair of strong arms circled her waist from behind.

"Want to dance with the best-looking guy in the room?" Trent asked over her shoulder.

Erin leaned back against him and pretended to glance around. "Sure. Where is he?"

Leigh laughed and pointed at her brother. "You should see your expression—it's hysterical. You two are cute together. Despite what you said, Erin, I bet it won't be long before I'm at your wedding, too."

Trent's arms around her waist tightened the tiniest bit, but Erin hadn't a clue what that meant. Hopefully it meant he had as little interest in orange blossoms and wedding bands as she did. But something in his attitude the last couple of days made her wonder. He'd been acting...oddly. More interested in cuddling after lovemaking. More interested in talking about hopes and dreams and plans over dinner.

Not exactly the behavior of a man who was only

interested in sex. Of course she could be wrong about what he was thinking.

But when he said to his sister, "You never know what the future will bring," Erin realized maybe she wasn't wrong after all.

What kind of denial was that? Erin tipped her head and looked at him. The scary part was that he didn't seem to be kidding. But he had to be kidding. She insisted he be kidding.

"He's joking," she told Leigh firmly. Then more to Trent than to his sister, she added, "He feels the same way I do—why mess with something that's working. And what we have together is working beautifully."

From over her shoulder, Trent said, "I still believe that no one knows what the future will bring. Things change. People change. Agreements change."

Erin sighed. Oh, no. She and Trent needed to have a long, hard talk and soon. Glancing at Leigh, she asked, "Would you excuse us for a moment? I'd like to dance with your brother."

Leigh laughed. "Okeydokey. You two go dance. And let me know how your dance turns out. Keep in mind that my schedule for the fall is pretty much booked. At the moment, I only have a couple of weekends free in November and one in early December. See if any of those dates work for you."

Then before Erin could once again explain that

she had no interest in getting married, Leigh spotted an opening in the buffet line and bounded off.

Trent snagged Erin's hand. "Come on. I think you had a great idea. Let's dance."

Erin trailed after him, teasing as she went, "I guess I'll dance with you since that good-looking guy is nowhere to be found."

Trent flashed her a wicked grin. "Oh, you're going to pay for that later."

"I sure hope so," she said hoping his light-hearted comment meant he'd only been kidding earlier with Leigh. He had to be kidding. Trent Barrett wasn't the type to marry and settle down. She was absolutely positive about that.

Well, close to positive.

When he took her in his arms, he slowly swayed to the music.

"Um, Trent, you know they're playing a fast song, don't you? Why are you slow dancing?"

He ran one hand up from her hip to her shoulder. "Because this way, I get to slide my hands all over you and pretend I'm just dancing instead of taking advantage of you," he said, demonstrating once again as his hand made the return journey to her hip, lingering a few places on the way.

Erin laughed. "You're a rascal, that's for sure."

"I am, but only with you."

"For the moment," Erin said, figuring now was a good time to clarify her feelings. "That's what's so nice about our casual relationship. There aren't any long-term expectations.''

For a couple of seconds, Trent was quiet. Then he said, ''We could always think about making things between us a little less casual. Like I told Leigh, things change.''

Erin stopped dancing and leaned back in his arms so she could look him dead in the eyes. ''Trent, don't let this wedding make you get all gushy and sentimental. We agreed we'd keep things between us simple. No strings. No ties. No broken hearts.''

''First off, I'm never gushy. I'm the chief of police. I don't gush.''

She hoped his nonsense meant he really wasn't getting serious on her. ''Fine, you're not gushy. But there's no reason to change things between us. We're doing great. Having fun. It's perfect.''

Trent started dancing again. ''I can't believe I'm going to say this, but I'd kind of like things to move forward. If not completely forward, then a couple of steps in that direction.''

Stunned, Erin stared at him. ''Excuse me, but huh?''

''I'm talking about feelings,'' he said.

''You mean the kind of feeling your left hand is doing at this very moment,'' she couldn't resist saying, all the while hoping he'd say yes.

''No,'' he said. ''Not that kind at all.''

Drat. What were you supposed to do when a flirt

like Trent Barrett got serious on you? She'd really thought he'd be the last man on earth to pull this sort of thing.

He dipped his head and whispered, "I'll admit, I have a lot of fun feeling you. Just like you seem to be enjoying yourself."

Despite the seriousness of their discussion, Erin couldn't help laughing. "But Trent, that's the only kind of feeling I'm comfortable with us doing right now."

She expected him to argue with her, but he didn't. All he said was, "Just keep an open mind, okay?"

"Fine. But for the record, my mind may be open, but I absolutely never change my mind once it's made up."

"Never?"

Her nod was firm. "Never."

"Ever?"

"Never ever," she said slowly. It was incredibly important that Trent not think she was going to want anything serious to develop between them. It simply wasn't going to happen, and the sooner he accepted that, the better. "I'm serious. I won't change my mind about this. The only reason I ever agreed to getting involved was because you don't get serious."

"I never have before," he admitted. "But like I said, things change. People change their minds."

"I won't."

"Okay. If you say so."

Despite what he'd said, Erin knew he no more believed her than he thought horses could fly.

Well, she'd simply have to show him she was serious. What they had together was fine the way it was.

No sense messing it up by getting serious.

"I CAN'T BELIEVE THIS is happening again," Erin said as she walked into Trent's office. "Here."

She handed him an old straw hat with plastic grapes decorating the brim. "And this would be?"

"You tell me. Is it another gift? I found it hanging on the antenna of my car this morning."

He studied the hat. Man, it was beat-up. "And you think it was put there deliberately."

"I think the chances of the wind blowing it and making it land on my antenna are slim."

He set the hat on his desk. "I wish I'd been able to see it."

"Yeah, I know. I should have left it there and called you, but I was upset when I saw it and I didn't think." She came over to his side of the desk and looked at the hat. "Trent, I thought this non-sense had stopped."

So had he. Nothing had happened for almost a month. He'd figured it was over with. He studied the hat. It was really ugly and looked familiar, but he couldn't place where he'd seen it before. If he had to guess, though, history said it belonged to Delia.

"So this hat was on your car. As usual, there was no note, right?"

Erin sighed. "No. No note. This is driving me crazy. Whoever is leaving these things for me is acting like a jerk. Plus, everyone in this town has known for the last month that you and I are—" She waved one hand in the air. "You know."

Trent frowned at her. He didn't like what was happening between them dismissed like that, but now wasn't the time to get into this discussion again. They'd let it drop at the wedding reception, and he didn't want to open up that can of worms right now.

Instead he wanted to know who was leaving these things for Erin.

"Who would do this knowing I'm involved?" Erin shook her head. "It all seems too juvenile for words."

That's when it hit Trent. Juvenile. Erin was right. It did seem juvenile. Like something a person with a crush would do.

Like something a kid would do.

He grinned. "You're brilliant."

Erin gave him a dubious look. "Why? Because I'm tired of having stuff left for me by a stranger?"

"Because you've given me an idea." He kissed

her soundly. "I'll stop by your store later to talk. Right now, I've got to go see someone."

"Someone who might know something about these presents?"

He nodded. "Could be."

"Who?"

Trent was tempted to tell her his idea, but he couldn't. Not until he knew if he was right. But his gut told him he was, and his gut was never wrong.

"I'll tell you later. Just head on back to your store."

Erin didn't look a bit happy about doing as he said, but she headed toward the door anyway. "I hate it when you become secretive."

"I thought women loved men of mystery," he said with a chuckle.

"Not this woman," she said right before she walked out the door.

Trent sighed. Yeah. He knew. Erin didn't love a man of mystery. She didn't love any man.

What completely amazed him was how much that bothered him. He'd never wanted a woman to care about him before, to expect things from him. He'd always figured he'd go through life without falling for anyone.

But he'd been wrong. Because he no longer could pretend he hadn't fallen for Erin. He'd fallen all right, and fallen hard. Man, what a surprise.

He sighed and grabbed the hat off his desk.

Sooner or later, he was going to have to talk with Erin about how he felt. Of course, she hadn't exactly been thrilled when he'd tried to bring up the subject at the wedding reception. And he couldn't imagine she'd be happy to hear him say he'd fallen for her.

But he couldn't worry about that now. Right now, he had to go talk to someone about a hat.

ERIN BUMPED INTO LEIGH the second she stepped out of the police station.

"Hey," the younger woman said.

There was something about Leigh's expression that convinced Erin this meeting wasn't an accident. Leigh must have seen her enter the building and had planted herself outside.

"Hey to you, too." Erin turned and headed toward her shop. Not surprisingly, Leigh fell into step next to her.

After they'd taken only a couple of steps, Leigh said, "So enough small talk. How are things between you and Trent? Am I going to be in a wedding party again soon? 'Cause if I am, you should know that I come with a lot of experience. I've married off two of my brothers this year already."

Erin kept walking. "I told you, I'm not interested in getting married. Not to anyone."

Leigh bobbed her head. "Gotcha. Not interested

in marrying anyone. But Trent isn't just anyone. So are you interested in marrying him?''

"*Arrrgh.*" Erin stopped and looked at Leigh. "What does it take to make you leave me alone about this?"

Leigh shrugged. "Marrying my brother."

"You're impossible," Erin said flatly. Then she started walking again.

"Yeah, I know I'm impossible. But that's my style. Besides, I'm curious if things will work out between you two. I've never seen Trent act like this before."

Despite herself, Erin had to ask, "Act like what?"

"Like he's crazy about a woman. He's always been footloose, but suddenly, you're all he talks about. Erin this and Erin that. It would be annoying if I didn't really like you." She grabbed Erin's arm and added, "Plus you two have been dating for almost two months. That's forever in Trent romance years. I can't remember him ever dating anyone that long. It's like…" She shrugged. "Amazing."

Trent had never dated anyone for two months? Rather than being comforted by the thought, it unnerved her.

"I don't think it's amazing," she told Leigh. "I think it's sad that Trent's such a player he's never spent even two months with the same woman."

Leigh put her hands on her hips and snorted.

"Give me a break. He's not a player." At Erin's dubious look, she added, "Not in the sense you mean. Sure, he's always been a guy interested in fun, but do you know why?"

"He likes variety?" Erin offered, ignoring the little pang she felt when she said the words.

"No. Because when we were young, life was not a lot of fun. Dad left Mom for a waitress in town, then Mom got sick so Chase, Nathan, and Trent had to pretty much raise me. Trent got to the point where he figured life was short and damn hard. Might as well have a little fun along the way."

When all Erin did was shrug, Leigh tapped one foot on the ground. "You're looking at Trent all wrong. Okay, so he had some fun in his life. But now that he's found you, he's becoming more settled. That means something, Erin, even if you refuse to admit it."

But Erin wasn't sure she wanted it to mean anything. Sure, the more time she spent with Trent, the more she cared about him. And knowing about his background sure explained a lot about his attitude. She couldn't blame him for wanting to have a little fun when it sounded like his early years had been tough.

But she was convinced the reason she and Trent got along so well was that they kept things casual. Up until now, they'd had a great time. Not only in bed, although their sex life was wild and wonderful.

No, they'd also had fun going to the movies, having dinner together and taking Brutus for walks.

She had to admit, no matter what she and Trent were doing, they seemed to have fun. They spent a lot of time talking and laughing and truly enjoying each other's company.

Things were going well. Or they had been up until the wedding reception, when not only Leigh, but also Trent, had suggested they make their relationship something more.

Erin wasn't sure she was ready for something more. She wasn't sure she'd ever be ready.

The most frustrating part was she simply didn't know what to do. She cared for Trent, but she also was realistic about him. He was an outrageous flirt and she couldn't see him ever settling down. Maybe in time she'd change her mind about him, but she needed that time to figure out her feelings.

There was, however, one thing that Erin was absolutely positive about. Having Leigh meddling was not good and needed to stop right now.

"Leigh, whatever happens is between Trent and me. I appreciate that you love your brother and want the best for him, but you need to give us breathing room."

Leigh rolled her eyes. "Breathing room. For what?"

"To…" Erin groaned. "To breathe. To make up my own mind. To make my own decisions."

"Erin, this is Paxton. No one here has breathing room. That's what we all like about the town. We fit very nicely into each other's hip pocket."

"Well, I'd like everyone to get out of my pocket, thank you very much."

"You can say that all you want, but it won't happen. People in Paxton like each other. We're curious about what's happening in each other's lives. We want the best for our friends and neighbors. Hence the constant curiosity. You'll get used to it."

Erin sincerely doubted that. "I appreciate your interest, Leigh, I honestly don't know what's going to happen with Trent." And she didn't. These days, she wasn't even certain what she wanted to happen with him.

Wow, she was one confused woman.

"I need to get back to my shop," she said, wanting time alone to think.

"Fine. But remember what I said. Trent's never, ever acted this way about a woman in his whole life. It means something, Erin. Whether you want it to or not."

9

TRENT FOUND ZACH SITTING on the front porch of his grandmother's house all alone. Poor kid. He probably hadn't made any friends this summer since moving to town. So instead, he'd developed a crush on Erin. Not that Trent could blame the boy. Erin was one special lady.

"Hey, Zach," Trent said, coming up the walkway to stand next to the porch. In his left hand, he held the straw hat that he'd bet anything was Delia's. Zach's attention fixed on the hat, and he turned bright red. Yep, no doubt about it now. The boy was the culprit.

"Is your grandmother home?" Trent asked when Zach didn't say anything.

Zach slowly shook his head, his eyes wide, fear on his face. Trent knew if he didn't say something soon the boy was either going to run away or cry or both.

He dropped down on the porch step next to Zach. "You know what I like about summer?"

Zach made a sniffling noise. Oh, no. Here come tears. Trent decided to bypass them.

"I like the fact that in the summer, you can just laze around doing nothing. I think I may take today off. For instance, I'm supposed to be out finding the person who left this hat on Erin Weber's car. But maybe I'll just be lazy instead. I'm sure the person who's doing this knows it isn't right."

"Are you going to arrest..." Zach swallowed hard "...somebody?"

"No. I'm pretty sure *somebody* knows to cut it out." He nudged Zach with his arm. "Don't you think so?"

Zach nodded. "Erin's nice."

"Yes, she is. But finding stuff left outside her store bothers her."

For a second, Zach once again looked like he might cry, but then he said, "I'm sorry. I thought she'd like it."

Trent dropped his arm around the boy's shoulders and gave him a quick hug. "I know."

"What are you going to do to me?"

Trent sighed. "For starters, you need to tell your grandmother what you did. Then you should tell Erin you're sorry."

Zach bobbed his head. "Okay. Do I have to go to jail, too? My grandmother won't like that."

Trent imagined not. Glancing around the yard, he noticed Zach had a soccer ball. An idea came to him. "Hey, you know what? I coach one of the boys' soccer teams. Sign-ups for the fall are going

on now. If you own up to what you did by telling
your grandmother and paying a visit to Erin, then
I'll ask your grandmother if you can join my team.
Of course, you'll have to help me with the equipment.''

For the first time since Trent had arrived, Zach
smiled. ''I'm good at soccer. I used to play on a
team in Dallas. I didn't think Paxton had any
teams.''

''Sure we do. And we always need more players.''

Noticing the time, Trent stood, and handed the
hat to Zach. ''Tell your grandmother she can call
me if she likes.''

Zach took the hat. ''Okay. I really am sorry. It's
just that Erin's so nice and I really, really like her.''

Trent knew exactly how the boy felt. He really,
really liked Erin, too.

''Yeah, but you know, it would've never worked.
Erin's thirty. Kinda old for you.''

Zach looked surprised. ''Oh boy. Thirty. She is
old. Guess I should have realized she wouldn't fall
in love with me.'' Then, he added, ''But she's still
nice. Even if she is old.''

Trent laughed. Yeah, she was nice. Unfortunately
she wasn't any more likely to fall in love with him
than she was with Zach.

ERIN LOOKED UP AS SOON as Trent entered her
store. He no longer had the hat with him.

"Where did you run off to? And what did you do with the hat?" She came around the counter and walked over to stand next to him.

"The hat belongs to Delia. I returned it to her grandson. Then I had a talk with the boy."

Why would he talk to Zach about the...oh. Understanding dawned on Erin. "Is he the one who's been doing all these things?"

Trent nodded. "Yep."

She never would have guessed. Zach was always so polite when he came into the store with Delia. He hardly seemed the type to leave presents on her doorstep. And now that she knew the gifts were coming from a sweet little kid, Erin wasn't upset. Obviously Zach had been trying to be nice.

"I hope you weren't mean to him. He only moved to town a few months ago when his mom came back to live with Delia. I don't think he has many friends."

Trent slipped his arms around her waist. "That's part of his punishment."

She frowned. "What?"

"He's going to join my soccer team, and he has to help me lug the team equipment to all the games. He also has to tell Delia what he did. And he has to apologize to you." He brushed a quick kiss across her lips. "That seemed like the best way to handle this. The kid didn't mean any harm, but he also needs to know he shouldn't do something like that again.''

Erin stared at Trent, surprised at how thoughtful he'd been. ''You're so sweet.''

The grin he flashed was pure devil. ''I am, aren't I? I'm a real sweetheart. Any chance I can talk you into closing your store early? I mean, after all, I did solve the crime. I ought to get a reward.''

She laughed and slipped out of his arms. ''I officially take back my comment. You're not sweet at all. You're incorrigible.''

''No. I'm *encouragable*. One smile from you, and I am definitely encouraged.'' He grabbed her hand and slipped his fingers between hers. ''If you can't close the store early, how about having dinner with me?''

''Um, I don't know.''

''I'll cook. Heck, I'll even buy the food to cook. Now how can you possibly pass up that invitation?''

She couldn't, although she knew she should. Things with Trent were supposed to be light, casual. But they weren't turning out that way at all. They were becoming complicated. And complicated wasn't something she wanted in her life right now.

Still, how could she turn him down? He really had been terrific in the way he'd handled Zach. And she loved spending time with him. Maybe a couple more nights wouldn't hurt.

"Okay. I'll come to dinner since you're cooking and buying."

He grinned again. "Great. And I'll help you run the store until it's closing time."

"I'm not going to change my mind, so you don't have to stay and guard me," she pointed out.

Trent seemed surprised by her statement. "I'm not guarding you. I happen to want to be around you." His expression turned lecherous. "If I'm around you, then I can steal a few kisses."

He leaned down and demonstrated, and Erin didn't complain one bit. In fact, she was having so much fun kissing Trent that it took her a second to realize the bell over the front door had rung.

"Oops, you've got a customer," he said.

Erin sucked a deep breath into her lungs. Yikes, but that man could kiss. She only hoped she didn't look as wobbly as she felt. Heading toward the front of the store, she found Zach standing by the counter. Delia stood outside, peering through the glass in the front door.

"Hi," she said to Zach, who seemed to find his sneakers fascinating since he was staring at them.

"Hi," he said so quietly that Erin had to strain to hear him. Then he blurted, "I'm the one who left you all that stuff. I'm really sorry, and I'll never do it again."

Erin knew confessing was hard for Zach, but she appreciated him doing it.

"Thank you for telling me, Zach. And I know you're sorry."

She glanced over her shoulder and watched Trent walk out of the back room. Zach looked up and saw him as well. For a second, Erin was afraid seeing Trent would make Zach nervous, but instead, the boy smiled.

"I did what I promised. I told my grandma and I apologized to Erin. So can I be on the team now?"

"You bet. I'm very proud of how you handled yourself, Zach. You showed a lot of responsibility," Trent said.

The boy beamed at the compliment, and Erin had to admit, Trent had handled this situation well. Not only had Zach learned his lesson, but he'd also learned how to take responsibility for his actions. Trent had managed all of that without making the boy feel badly about himself.

Oh, yeah, there were no two ways around it— Trent Barrett was one heck of a guy.

TRENT POPPED OPEN THE TOP to the paint can and frowned. The paint was blue. A nice, ordinary, everyday blue. Dang.

"You don't want to use this paint," he told Erin. "It will make your bedroom look—"

"Normal," she said, before he could finish his sentence.

"Boring, not normal. I like the room the way it is. Why are you so gung ho on changing it?" He winked at her and walked over to slip his arms around her waist. "Seems to me we've had a lot of fun in this room. I like the mirrors and the disco ball and the bright orange paint. They put me in the mood."

To prove his point, he kissed her. But before he could woo her into a little hanky-panky, she gently removed his hands from her oh-so-soft body.

"As far as I can tell, anything puts you in the mood," she said with a laugh. "Last week, you pounced on me when we were discussing the best way to cook shrimp."

"Hey, cooking makes me hot."

She laughed. "You're insane."

"Probably, but knowing my family, does that come as a surprise?"

Ha. He had her there and he knew it.

"No," she admitted. "Not at all. Now stop pouting and help me paint the room." With a sexy little smile that got his blood pounding through his veins, she said, "The sooner we're done, the sooner I'll reward you for all your manly effort."

"Incentive. I like that. What did you have in mind?"

She pretended to think. Finally she said, "I know, I'll make dinner for you."

"Dinner? Not exactly what I had in mind. Try again. I'm going to need a serious bribe to get me to agree to paint these pretty orange walls a dull blue."

With great exaggeration, she fluttered her eyelashes at him. "Why, Mr. Barrett, what could I possibly have that would be of interest to you?"

He chuckled. "I'm going to enjoy showing you later."

"Fine. But first you have to help." She poured paint into both of their trays. "You want to do the baseboards or start on the walls?"

"I'll do the walls. If I'm not allowed to touch you until this room is done, then I want to get it finished in a hurry," he said, meaning it. Although he liked just spending time with Erin, he also was burning with need for her. He'd been stuck at work late last night and hadn't been able to see her. After only two days, he'd missed her so much it hurt.

He started rolling the paint onto the walls, figuring if he had to keep his hands to himself for the next hour or so, then he could at least use the time to talk to her about how he felt. Now all he had to think of was a subtle way to start a conversation about their relationship. Subtle wasn't exactly his strong point, but there had to be a way to do it.

After forty-five frustrating minutes during which

no brainstorms rained on him, he blurted, "So, Erin, what's new with you?"

She was carefully painting the baseboard by the closet. Now she turned her head and looked at him. "What?"

Yeah, he deserved the strange look she was giving him. Dang, he was handling this all wrong.

He admitted the truth. "I'm trying to find a nonchalant way to bring up our relationship."

"Ah."

That was it. That was all she said. Then she turned back to painting the baseboard.

Trent went back to painting the walls. But frustration churned inside him, until with a groan, he turned to face her. "So do you?"

"Do I what?"

"Want to discuss what's happening between us." Granted, he'd never before had a relationship like the one he had with Erin, but he'd always heard women liked to talk about their relationships. But, man, if the expression on Erin's face was anything to go by, she'd rather be dunked in mud and hosed down with grease than talk about the two of them.

"Why can't we just leave everything the way it is? Why does it have to change?" she asked softly.

"Because I've changed," he admitted.

She tipped her head and studied him. "How?"

For a second, he almost decided not to tell her. After all, he knew she didn't want to hear what he had to say. But he'd never backed down from anything in his entire life, and he sure wasn't going to start now.

"I'm in love with you," he said.

She blinked. A couple of times. Then she asked slowly, "You're in love with *me? Are you sure?"

Was he sure? Hell, yes, he was sure. "Well, I'm in love with someone, and it sure isn't Brutus."

This wasn't going at all the way he'd wanted it to go. He hadn't expected her to say she loved him in return, but then again, he hadn't expected her to look horrified by the idea, either.

"Erin, why are you so surprised? We've been dating for the last couple of months. We spend all our free time together. We spend almost every night together. Is it really so unbelievable that I'd fall in love with you?"

She nodded her head. "Yes. It is. I mean that was the whole point of us. We knew we wouldn't fall in love. We agreed we'd keep it simple. No strings. Your being in love with me is a really big string, Trent."

"Tell me about it. I didn't do this on purpose. I've never even thought I was in love before let alone actually been in it. It's…weird. I know I should feel panicky and nervous, but I'm not. Actually the opposite. I feel good. Incredibly good. Like I've found a missing piece of a puzzle."

Erin's expression softened a little at his description, but she still didn't seem too thrilled by the whole love thing.

Figuring he was in for some serious pain, Trent asked, "Don't you feel anything for me?"

She set the brush carefully on the side of the paint tray and said, "Of course I do."

Okay. That wasn't much, but at least it was something. "What do you feel?"

"I like you, and admire you, and think you're a great guy," she said with a soft smile.

Although he appreciated the sentiment, those sure weren't the words he'd wanted to hear.

"Erin, I've never told a woman I love her before. I've never even come close to love. My entire life, I've avoided it like a big old tar pit. But this much I know—we're great together. And we're great for each other. I can't help thinking we're meant to be together. You honestly don't feel the connection between us? There's a lot more going on between us than just killer sex, and you've got to know that."

A light blush colored her cheeks. "Of course I know we're great together. But I also thought Don and I were great together. That we were meant to be together. That is, until he sprinted from the church."

"Hey, I'm not Don."

"I know that. But I'm still me," she said.

She'd lost him there. "What does that mean?"

"It means, I need more time. Sure, things between us seem to be going great. But things between Don and me seemed great, too. I completely misjudged our relationship. Heck, I completely misjudged him, too. Do you know he's divorcing the woman he left me for? I used to be so certain that Don was a steady, dependable guy. Shows you how bad of a character judge I am.''

"Thanks for the compliment,'' Trent said dryly.

"You know what I mean.''

"I don't think I do.'' He wasn't the type to get upset about things usually. In fact, that was one of the main reasons he found being chief of police enjoyable. He rarely got upset. But he sure was upset now.

"Trent, I just need time,'' she said, coming over to stand next to him. "Is that so much to ask?''

"It is because you want this time so you can figure out that I'm not the same kind of jerk as your ex-fiancé. Well, you should know that by now. I shouldn't have to prove it to you.''

"I don't mean it like that,'' she said.

But he knew she did. She needed time because she wasn't sure. But he couldn't help thinking she should be sure by now.

"Let's forget about it and finish painting this room,'' he said.

She didn't say anything, so he turned his attention back to the walls, quickly finishing the painting. Then he set the roller down, and headed toward the door.

"You know where to find me if you ever decide I'm not a jerk," he said.

"Trent, wait."

He stopped, turning slightly to look at her.

"I just need more time," she said. "Maybe then I'll change my mind and want a relationship."

He sighed, feeling incredibly defeated. "You know, Erin, I never believed in love before I met you. Never believed there was one perfect person for everyone. But I've changed my mind. I now think that when something's meant to be, it's meant to be. And when you find something this great, you need to be brave enough to grab hold of it and not let go."

He willed himself not to weaken when a couple of tears slipped free and rolled down her face.

"I'm not letting go," she said. "You are."

"That's just because you're not willing to hold on," he told her.

Then he left.

"MIND IF I JOIN YOU?"

Erin glanced up from the menu she'd been studying. Megan Barrett, Chase Barrett's wife, stood next to the table. The last thing Erin wanted to do at the moment was talk about Trent. She'd spent the better part of a week thinking about him. And even after all that thinking, she still wasn't certain how she felt.

But good manners forced her to say to Megan, "Not at all. Please sit."

Megan took the chair across from Erin, and opened her own menu. "I never know why I look at the menu each time I come to Roy's Café. I mean, it's not like I haven't eaten here a million times before. And since nothing on the menu ever changes, it's not like I don't already know what my choices are." She smiled over the menu at Erin. "Guess I keep hoping something better than my current choice will appear."

Erin frowned. Was that a veiled message of some sort or just a vocalized wish for more variety on the menu? She started to ask Megan, but the one waitress in the café stopped by and took their order. Megan ordered what she'd obviously ordered the million other times when she'd been here before.

After the waitress walked away, Megan leaned back in her chair. "Are you enjoying Paxton?"

That didn't seem like a loaded question, so Erin said, "Yes. It's a nice town."

"It is, isn't it? Very friendly. Filled with wonderful people."

Erin frowned again. Was Megan once more saying something without actually saying something?

It seemed difficult to believe considering that every time she'd ever talked to Megan before, the woman had been very open and friendly. Surely she wasn't trying to nudge Erin in Trent's direction.

Was she?

"When I first moved here, I was eight years old," Megan said. "I didn't know a soul, and I had quite a bit of trouble with a town bully. But then one day, Chase showed up and scared off the bully for me. I fell in love with him in that split second, and I've never fallen out of love with him."

Okay, this time there was no doubt. The woman was here on a mission.

"Megan, no offense, but I don't really want to talk about Trent."

"I wasn't talking about Trent," the other woman said. "Just talking about when I first moved to Paxton."

"And when you fell in love with your husband," Erin added.

"Oh, yes. But I only mentioned that because I wanted you to know what a great guy Chase is."

Erin sighed. "And naturally you think Trent is a great guy, too."

"Yes, he is," Megan said. They sat quietly while the waitress placed their lunches in front of them. As soon as they were alone again, she said, "He really is a great guy, Erin."

"I take it he told you what happened?"

Megan nodded. "Sort of. Actually his brothers dragged the information out of him, which is pretty much the way that family works. But yes, I know he's in love with you but you don't love him back.''

Erin opened her mouth to respond, then suddenly realized the entire café had gone silent. Pin-drop silent. She glanced around. Everyone was obviously listening to her conversation with Megan.

What was with this town?

As softly as possible, she said to Megan, ''I told him it's possible I'll eventually come to love him. All I asked was for a little more time.''

Apparently she hadn't been quite quiet enough, because a low buzz of gossip erupted when she finished speaking.

''What'd she say?'' someone in a far corner asked.

Erin felt like banging her head against the table when someone answered, ''She said she doesn't love Trent.''

She looked at Megan. ''You'd think if they were going to eavesdrop, they'd get it right.'' Turning, she said to the crowd, ''I said it's *possible* I may come to love him. Eventually.''

The patrons of the restaurant pretended they were interested in their own meals and hadn't been listening to her, but as soon as she turned back around to face Megan, she heard the person in the corner ask, ''What'd she mean by eventually?''

''Don't let them upset you,'' Megan said gently. ''They just really like Trent and want him to be happy.''

"Leigh already shared the hip-pocket philosophy of this town with me," Erin said.

"It's a mixed blessing," Megan admitted. "So you were saying that you may eventually come to love Trent before we got distracted. What exactly does that mean?"

"It means I need time."

Megan nodded, and for a second, Erin thought the other woman might understand. At least she did until Megan asked, "Time for what?"

"To figure out my feelings for him."

"Okay. So you need time. Mind if I ask you a question?"

Truthfully Erin minded this entire conversation, but at this juncture, she didn't see much point in protesting. "Sure. Ask away."

"What is Trent supposed to do while you're figuring out whether you love him or not?"

Erin stared at the other woman, dumbfounded. She'd never considered that before. What did she expect Trent to do while she had more time to think about their relationship? Did she expect him to wait for her? To keep seeing her on the chance that she might one day love him, too? Or did she expect him to start dating someone else, someone who could quickly decide whether she was in love or not.

She honestly had no idea.

"I don't know," she admitted. Then listened

while her answer was relayed to the person in the corner who was obviously hard of hearing. What a town.

Megan patted her hand. "Why don't you figure that out. I think once you know what you expect Trent to do, then you'll also know how you feel about him."

With a nod, Erin turned back to her salad. She wasn't hungry anymore because Megan had given her a lot to think about. But for the sake of appearances, she pretended to eat her salad.

But her mind wasn't on food. It wasn't even on the fact that the entire café was now openly discussing what she'd said. Most of the room seemed to be of the opinion that she should marry Trent. A few ladies, though, firmly maintained that Trent wasn't the type to settle down.

But Erin couldn't listen to them chatter at the moment. Her mind was on Trent. What in the world was she going to do about him?

She really had no idea. None at all. But she knew Megan was right. Once she knew what she expected Trent to do while she made up her mind, then she'd know what her feelings were for him. Right now, she had no answers. But hopefully she would soon.

For her sake. For Trent's sake.

She sighed. And based on the heated discussions going on in the café, for the sake of the town as well.

10

TRENT RUBBED BRUTUS'S BELLY, glad the puppy had finally stopped throwing up. Man, but that dog had been sick. A couple of times during the last few hours, he'd been really worried about the furball. He'd ended up taking him to the vet around midnight just to make certain Brutus was going to be all right.

Who'd have ever thought he'd come to care this much about the puppy?

He knew the answer—Erin had. All along she'd told him he'd come to love Brutus, and he did. Brutus seemed to love him right back. All it had taken was being nice to the puppy, and Brutus had come right around.

Too bad he couldn't figure out a way to make Erin love him as well.

"Maybe if I sit with her when she's sick she'll decide she loves me," he said to the dog.

Brutus flopped his tail once, a sure sign he still wasn't one hundred percent better. Poor little guy. This was all Leigh's fault. She should have been watching him closely. Then she would have seen

Brutus eat the dead crickets that had been covered in bug spray.

"Women," Trent said, still rubbing the puppy's stomach. "They'll let you eat poisoned crickets and break your heart all without batting an eye."

Brutus sighed a big puppy sigh, obviously agreeing with Trent.

"I mean, come on. I told her I loved her. I've never told another woman that ever." Warming to his topic, Trent added, "I went out on a limb, put my feelings out there for her to see, and she said she needed time.

"Time. Time for what? To see if I'm a jerk?" He scratched the puppy behind the ears. "See if I'm the same sort as her ex-fiancé? What about faith? What about trust? Don't those count for anything? Haven't I convinced her that I'm nothing like that Don guy? Haven't I shown her I really love her?"

He looked at Brutus. "You know, I'm going to go have another talk with her. I thought I'd let this sleeping dog lie, but I can't. I'm not giving up. Not yet. Not by a long shot. I'm the right guy for her, and if she doesn't see that, then I'll have to help her see that. I've never been in love before, and I know in my bones, I'll never be again."

He glanced again at Brutus and saw that the puppy had finally fallen asleep. Since the furball was asleep on the guest bedroom floor, Trent decided to sleep in here as well. He wanted to be nearby just in case the pup had more trouble during the next few hours.

And then tomorrow, once he had taken Brutus to the vet's again to make certain the pup really was all right, he was going to go see Erin.

Things between them weren't over. Not nearly over. In fact, even with everything that had happened over the last couple of weeks, he couldn't help believing that things between him and Erin were just beginning, not ending.

They were meant to be together. He was absolutely positive of that.

ERIN WAS FEEDING THE hamsters when the bell over the door jangled. Leigh Barrett walked inside, her expression determined. Uh-oh. That couldn't be good. Leigh at the best of times was like a human tornado. A determined Leigh could only be big trouble.

"Hi," Erin said, hoping against hope that she'd misread Leigh's expression. Maybe the younger woman wasn't here on a mission.

"Sick puppy," Leigh said. "One sick puppy."

Okay, now that seemed way too harsh. "Excuse me?"

"Do you know what Trent's been doing all night?" Leigh asked in return.

"I don't know, Leigh, but whatever it is, it won't

change my mind. I've told every member of your family and most of the town of Paxton that I really care about Trent but I don't think it's a good idea for us to get too serious. We had agreed when we first started—''

''Messing around?'' Leigh supplied.

''Not exactly the way I would have put it, but yes. We both agreed we weren't interested in getting serious.'' Trying one more time to get the other woman to see her viewpoint, Erin explained, ''It wasn't all that long ago that I thought I'd found the perfect man for me. It turned out to be a disaster. I was completely wrong about him and only saw what I wanted to see. I'm not looking for more heartache.''

Leigh nodded thoughtfully, then said slowly, ''Sick puppy.''

Okay, that was it. ''I'm not a sick puppy just because I don't want to have my heart smushed by your brother.''

''Of course you're not a sick puppy. Brutus is. That's what Trent's been doing the entire night— tending to the sick puppy.''

The puppy was sick? The little guy had been the picture of health and mischief the last time Erin had seen him.

''What's wrong with Brutus?''

''He ate some dead crickets and has been grossly sick all night.''

"How was he able to eat the dead crickets? Trent always watches Brutus carefully."

Leigh's gaze darted around the shop. "Someone had taken him for a walk and her...I mean, that person's cell phone rang. That person was talking about a real cool job offer and for one split second didn't watch the dog."

Erin sighed. "Leigh, you have to watch Brutus all the time. He's like a goat. He'll eat anything."

"Hey, goats do not eat just any old thing."

"But Brutus does," Erin pointed out.

Leigh drummed her fingers on the counter beside her. "We're getting off the main point here. It doesn't matter how Brutus got sick, just that he was. And my brother drove him to the vet in the middle of the night, then sat up with him until morning."

She leaned toward Erin and added, "Plus, he even rearranged his schedule so he could stay home from work today and make certain the little guy is better."

Trent had done all that for the puppy? Heck, adopting Brutus hadn't even been his idea.

"Does he know you're here?" Erin asked.

With a snort, Leigh said, "As if. He'd bust a vein if he knew. But when I went over there this morning and saw what he'd been up to, well, I had to come and tell you. You're all wrong about Trent. Sure, he can be a little wild. Maybe a lot wild. But he's a good guy. He's nothing like that jerk you were engaged to marry.''

"I appreciate what you're doing. It's very sweet of you to come defend your brother. I agree that Trent is a great guy. He's smart and funny and can be unbelievably sweet. But I'm not looking for a serious relationship right now. I've just moved to this town and opened my business. Love can wait.''

"No, it can't. And it won't. Love doesn't stick around where it's not wanted. If you don't grab hold of the love Trent's offering you, it will disappear. And you'll be left alone and sorry.''

With that pronouncement, Leigh spun on one heel and headed toward the door.

"Leigh—''

The younger woman stopped and turned. ''Do you realize you're walking away from a man who's willing to clean up after a sick puppy? A really sick puppy filled with dead cricket parts. Come on, how many guys do you know would clean up that kind of mess, especially when they didn't really want the dog in the first place?'' She shook her head. ''You're never going to find anyone else even half as great as Trent is and you know it. He's loyal to his job. He's loyal to his family. For crying out loud, he's loyal to Brutus. He'd be loyal to you, too.''

Then Leigh yanked open the door and walked out.

"Guess I've been told," Erin muttered to the hamsters after the door slammed shut behind Leigh. One of the small, furry pets seemed to stare directly at her, almost as if he were listening.

"But I'm right," she said.

The hamster tipped his head and looked as doubtful as a hamster can look. Great. Even small rodents thought she was being a fool.

"Fine, maybe I *am* a fool, but just because someone loves you doesn't mean you have to love him back." The hamster continued to watch her with his small, black eyes. "Oh, all right, even if I do love him, that doesn't mean we have to get married and have a couple of kids and buy a minivan and go to soccer games. We're not required to live happily ever after."

She said the last sentence with enough force that the hamster wiggled his nose and ran off. Apparently he was unconvinced by her argument.

Well, too bad. It was a good argument. A sound argument. So maybe Trent wasn't like Don. Maybe he wouldn't run off with another woman. Maybe once he settled down, he really would be settled for life.

Did that mean she had to be the woman he settled down with?

Of course not.

Feeling unbelievably dejected but refusing to give in to the mood, she finished feeding the hamsters, then moved on to the fish. Thankfully none of them looked at her with accusatory eyes. They blithely went about their fish lives, ignoring her.

"You don't care a bit that my heart's broken," she said, shaking more food into the goldfishes's tank. When what she'd just said hit her, she froze.

Her heart was broken? Really? When had that happened? Why hadn't she noticed when the first tiny fracture lines had appeared?

This was exactly what she'd been trying to avoid—a broken heart. She'd gone to great lengths to prevent this very circumstance. She'd moved to a new town. Started all over again. Gotten involved with the one man who absolutely would not break her heart.

And yet she'd still ended up hurt because what she hadn't counted on was how crazy in love she'd be with Trent. He was so wonderful, how could she not love him? The man had sat up all night with a sick puppy. Who could resist a guy that terrific?

Not her. The only reason her heart was broken was that she refused to accept the love he was freely offering.

"I really am a fool," she told all the animals in general, realizing she'd been avoiding facing the truth for a long, long time. So her ex-fiancé had been a jerk. Trent was a different man. A man she knew in her heart she could trust.

She didn't need any more time to know that. She didn't need any more proof of his love.

She just needed him.

"Well, that's a problem I can fix." And she could. All she had to do was say yes. Yes to loving him. Yes to spending her life with him.

She could do that. In fact, she could hardly wait to do that.

Glancing at the clock, she saw she had three hours before it would be time to close the store. She could only hope those hours went quickly because she could hardly wait to see Trent.

TRENT HEADED DOWN the sidewalk at a clip. He'd spent a long night thinking about this whole thing with Erin, and dang it all, he was going to say his peace. She was making one huge mistake keeping them apart, and he was going to let her know that.

Feeling stoked, he shoved open the door to Precious Pets and headed inside. Erin was with Delia and Zach, apparently helping them pick out some more bird food, but he didn't care. For once in his life, he was going to ignore his mama's teachings and be downright rude.

"Excuse me, Delia and Zach, but can I have a few minutes alone with Erin? We need to talk." He planted his feet firmly and knew she could tell he meant business.

Rather than looking upset, Erin seemed pleased.

Well, she probably wouldn't be once he was done, but at least she'd know how he felt.

"I'm so glad you stopped by," she said. "I want to talk to you, too."

Now that was a change in her tune. But before he could get his hopes up, he reminded himself that she'd probably just thought of another reason why the two of them had no future. Well, whatever she'd come up with, he'd find a counterargument. He might not be the brightest searchlight in the sky, but he knew he and Erin should be together and he wasn't giving up or backing down.

He glanced at Delia, who flashed him a wide grin. She obviously knew he was a man on a mission.

"I'll stop by tomorrow for the seed, Erin." She nudged her grandson, who was looking from Trent to Erin then back to Trent. "Come on, Zach. Let's go look for soccer shin guards for you."

"Great." Zach must have figured out what was going on, too, because on his way by Trent, he said, "Good luck."

Trent patted the boy's shoulder. Yeah. Good luck. He could use some of that.

Delia winked. "Remember, you have handcuffs if you need to get her to stand still and listen to you."

Then, with a laugh, Delia and her grandson headed out the door. Once they were alone, Trent faced Erin. She still looked very happy and for a split second, he worried that the speech he'd worked up would make her unhappy. But he pushed that thought aside. She definitely needed to hear what he had to say.

"Isn't this how we met? You standing there with your handcuffs all set to arrest me?" Erin asked, a twinkle in her eyes.

"I wasn't going to arrest you. I just had some questions."

She smiled. "And today? Do you have questions?"

Yeah, he had one. One very important question. But first, they needed to get some things straight. Trent squared his shoulders and took two deliberate steps forward until he stood toe-to-toe with Erin. "We need to talk."

She arched one brow and didn't look the least bit intimidated. "Oh, really?"

"Yes, really. I've had a long night, and I've done a lot of thinking. I've come to a few important conclusions."

"Okay. Such as?"

At least she was being reasonable about this. "For starters, just because we originally thought we'd keep things casual doesn't mean they always have to stay that way. Life is about change, Erin. And when something wonderful happens, you don't push it away because you didn't expect it. You grab on to it with both hands even if it wasn't part of your original plan.''

She nodded. "I know.''

She did? Well…good. But he wasn't nearly done. "And you're dead wrong about me. I'm not the kind of guy who would tell a woman he loved her if he didn't mean he'd love her forever.''

Erin gave him a soft smile. "I know.''

Momentarily disconcerted, he gathered his thoughts, running through the other points he'd come up with during the long night. Oh, there was another really important one.

"You also don't give yourself enough credit. It wasn't your fault that your ex-fiancé was a moron. You're a trusting person, and you thought you'd found someone who was equally trustworthy. That doesn't mean your judgment in men is off. It just means you had the bad luck to choose the wrong guy.''

Her smile grew. "I know.''

She did? He ran one hand through his hair. "But that guy wasn't the right guy. I'm the right guy. I've never told a woman I loved her. I've never even come close. This is the real deal, Erin, and you can't let it pass us by.''

She leaned closer to him. "I know.''

For crying out loud, what was going on here? Was this some sort of game? She'd made it clear time and again that she didn't agree with him, so why wasn't she putting up a fight now?

He blew out an exasperated breath. "Why are you agreeing with everything I'm saying?"

"Because I think you're right."

He frowned. "Since when?"

She laughed. "You simply can't believe that I agree with you, can you?"

"No. Not really. You never have before," he pointed out.

She placed one hand on his arm. "I do now. Earlier, I reacted without thinking. But when I really stopped to consider everything, I realized you aren't my ex-fiancé. And I truly believe you're the right man for me."

Dang. Now he knew something was up. "Not that I'm not thrilled with what you're saying, 'cause I am. But I have to ask—what changed your mind?"

"Leigh did."

Ah, hell. If Leigh was involved this couldn't be good. He stared at Erin, hoping he'd heard her wrong. Although he loved Leigh, he couldn't exactly say she'd been a big help in his life. In fact, he could readily think of about a hundred times when she'd caused him trouble. The woman was a walking disaster zone.

"Are we talking about my sister Leigh?" he asked, just to make certain.

Erin laughed. "Don't be so cynical. Of course I mean your sister."

"I'm not cynical. I'm just trying to figure out what Leigh could have possibly done to make you agree with me."

With one small step, Erin moved close enough to lean against him. "Leigh told me how you took care of Brutus last night."

What did the sick pup have to do with all of this? "Of course I took care of the furball. He was sick and needed me."

"Exactly. You were there for Brutus. Just like you're always there for everyone who needs you. At first, I thought you were a hopeless flirt and a wild man. But over the past few months, I've come to realize that you're actually a great guy. Leigh told me about how you took care of Brutus through the night. It reminded me just how great you are."

He liked the sound of that. Things were definitely moving in the right direction. "So since you think I'm great, where does that leave us?"

"First, I have to ask how Brutus is."

Trent laughed. "Figures. I'm standing here more nervous than I've ever been in my life and you're talking about the furball."

She placed one hand on the side of his face. "You love Brutus and you know it."

"Yeah. I do," he admitted. "He's grown on me. And to answer your question, he's fine. Under the weather last night, but perky as all get out today. I took him to the vet this morning and was assured he's out of the woods.''

''Good. I'm so glad to hear that,'' she said.

''So now that you know Brutus has recovered, I'd like to return to the conversation about us. I believe you were saying how great you think I am.''

She looked downright adorable when she gave him a flirty, sexy look. Man, he loved this woman.

''I do think you're great.''

''That's it?''

''No. I love you, too.''

At her words, his heart raced in his chest. She loved him. Just to make certain, he asked, ''Sure?''

She nodded. ''Positive.''

Life did not get any sweeter than this. He leaned down and kissed her. For several long minutes, he simply held her in his arms and enjoyed kissing the woman he loved. Finally he broke the kiss, but still held her firmly within the circle of his arms.

''So what happens now? You said you needed more time.''

She shook her head. ''Not anymore.''

He took a deep breath and plunged ahead. ''So if I ask you to marry me, is there any chance you'll say yes?''

''Um, are you asking me or just asking me if it's okay to ask me?''

"Whatever's the best way to get a yes," he admitted.

"Just ask," she said softly.

He readily complied. "Will you marry me?"

"Yes."

He grinned. *All right!* He was about to kiss her again when he felt obligated to admit, "You know Brutus is part of this deal, and I can't promise he's completely housetrained yet. I've tried, but that dang furball has a mind of his own."

She laughed. "I think I can help with that problem."

"Oh. Good. Then we can tell everyone we're getting married for the sake of the dog," Trent teased.

"That and because I'm crazy about you."

Trent couldn't remember ever feeling this fantastic. "I'm crazy about you, too. And you'll see. We really will live happily ever after because you're the right woman for me, Erin. I've never felt this way before, and I know I never will again."

"I know. You're meant for me." She wrapped her arms around his neck. "And I'm meant for Trent."

He chuckled. "I like the sound of that. It's corny, sure, but effective."

"And oh so very true," she said right before she kissed him.

Leigh's for Me
Liz Jarrett

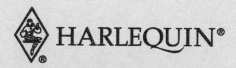

TORONTO • NEW YORK • LONDON
AMSTERDAM • PARIS • SYDNEY • HAMBURG
STOCKHOLM • ATHENS • TOKYO • MILAN • MADRID
PRAGUE • WARSAW • BUDAPEST • AUCKLAND

HOMETOWN
HEARTTHROBS

ERIN
+
TRENT

LEIGH
+
JARED

1

SHE WAS GOING TO KILL HER brothers. All three of
them. Slowly. In front of the entire town of Paxton,
Texas.

How dare they invite Jared Kendrick to Trent's
wedding? No, not only invite him, but also have
him in the wedding party. Were they insane? Was
this some kind of lame joke?

Whatever the cause, they were dead men for sure.

"The wedding was beautiful," said Amanda
Newman, wife of the minister who'd performed the
ceremony. "Trent and Erin seem so happy. Now
all of your brothers are blissfully married. Guess it
won't be long until you follow their example."

Leigh barely resisted the urge to gag. As if. She'd
rather go swimming with piranha. Here she'd finally married off her last meddlesome brother and
from this point on, she'd be an independent woman.

No way was she giving up her freedom anytime
in this century.

"I'm too young to get married," she told
Amanda. Standing on her tiptoes, she scanned the
wedding reception crowd, looking for her brothers.

How hard was it to spot three tall men in tuxes? Apparently impossible, since she didn't see them.

Maybe the weasels were hiding from her. Yeah. That was a distinct possibility. At least it was if they had the slightest inkling as to what she was thinking at the moment.

"Oh, now I'm sure this wedding is giving you ideas." Amanda patted Leigh's arm and smiled. "I can see you're studying the decorations, maybe coming up with plans for your own reception."

Leigh stared at her, stunned. Amanda was a sweet older woman, but boy, she didn't have a clue what Leigh was thinking. Not that she could exactly enlighten her. After all, how did you tell the minister's wife that you were looking for your brothers so you could kill them? Hmmm. Emily Post probably didn't have any etiquette advice for this particular circumstance.

Deciding not to go into it, Leigh said, "I'm not interested in getting married. Thanks."

Figuring that was settled, she returned to scanning the crowd. Where were those bozos? She finally spotted two of her sisters-in-law, Megan and Hailey, over by the buffet table. Wherever they were, their husbands and her brothers, Chase and Nathan, wouldn't be far behind.

Bingo. She'd found them.

She started to head in that direction when Amanda once again put her hand on Leigh's arm.

"Getting married and starting your own family

is one of life's precious gifts," Amanda said. "As I know your brothers have discovered."

Leigh bit back a groan. Would this woman never stop? She didn't want to get married. She didn't want to fall in love.

She only wanted to talk to her ratfink brothers and then maybe kick Jared Kendrick out of here.

Was that too much to ask for?

"No offense, Amanda, 'cause I know you're happily married," Leigh said. "But I have no desire to live in a house with a white-picket fence."

"Do tell. Because I could have sworn that the house you're renting from Megan has a white-picket fence out front," a deep voice said from behind her.

Oh, just great. While she'd been looking for her brothers, Jared Kendrick had walked up and was apparently standing directly behind her. Man-o-man, this day just kept getting worse.

"Hello, Jared," Amanda said. "I heard you moved back to Paxton. You're turning your parents ranch into a rodeo school, right?" Without waiting for an answer, Amanda continued. "Mary Monroe said she saw you riding that motorcycle of yours around town. And she said you were going quite fast. I told her you probably weren't, but I don't think she believed me."

Leigh rolled her eyes. Of course the man had been driving fast. This was Jared Kendrick. If there was a rule in Paxton, he broke it.

"I might have been going a couple of miles over the speed limit," Jared admitted. "Tell her I'll slow down from now on."

Unable to stop herself, Leigh snorted. "That will be the day."

"Hello to you, too," Jared said.

Turning slowly, Leigh braced herself for the wallop she knew she'd feel when she made eye contact with this man. Despite no longer liking him, she was still female. And females of all ages found it difficult to resist Jared. He was tall, over six feet, and had amazingly thick dark brown hair and equally dark eyes. The man was serious eye candy.

Darn his hide.

Predictably, as soon as Leigh looked at him, her DNA betrayed her. Her stupid heart raced. Her equally stupid breathing seemed to have grown rapid and shallow.

This world was one screwy place when the man you disliked more than any other turned you on like crazy.

Sheesh.

Taking a deep breath to calm her raging libido, she flashed him a completely insincere smile. "Why, hello, Kendrick. I thought you'd be in jail by now. Did the Parole Board take a liking to you?"

Jared laughed, the sound deep and rich and way too appealing. "Glad to see you haven't changed since last summer, Leigh."

Amanda frowned and made a *tsking* sound. "Oh, Jared, were you really in jail? My, my. I thought you were riding with those rodeo people. Of course, you were a trifle wild while growing up here, but I had no idea you'd run into serious trouble."

Leigh waited patiently for Jared to correct the older woman, but he simply shrugged. Oh, for the love of Pete. Was he really going to let this go? The Paxton rumor mill would have a field day. Leigh knew that before the night was over, all the good folks of Paxton would swear up and down that Jared had been in jail for murder.

"Maybe my husband could counsel you," Amanda offered. "He's very good with things like this."

Leigh groaned. "Amanda, Jared wasn't in jail. I was kidding."

Amanda laughed softly, and Leigh rolled her eyes.

"Oh, good. You two are joking," Amanda said. "I'm happy to hear that. Although I will admit I was surprised to see you in the wedding party today. I didn't know you were friends with Trent."

"Everyone seemed surprised to see me," he said. "Leigh more so than most. I especially liked the way she screamed when she noticed me standing next to her brothers by the altar. You'll have to check with your husband, Amanda, but I bet she's the first bridesmaid to scream like that during a ceremony."

"Oh, pulleese. I'm sure a lot of women scream around you," Leigh said, and then she felt like whacking herself on the side of the head when she realized the interpretation that could be put on her words. From the grin on Jared's face, he'd taken it as a compliment to his lovemaking prowess.

Leigh shook her head. "Hey! Don't go there. I only meant—"

Jared held up one hand and drawled, "I know exactly what you meant, Leigh, and thanks. Maybe one day you can find out for yourself if it's true."

Keenly aware that Amanda was watching them, Leigh said in her sweetest voice, "Kendrick, I'd rather polka with a rattlesnake. No, wait, it wouldn't be much different, would it?"

Amanda frowned and looked from Leigh to Jared then back at Leigh. "What are you talking about, dear? Are you teasing Jared again?"

A sexy grin slowly crossed Jared's handsome face. "Yeah, Leigh, are you teasing me again?"

"I'm completely, absolutely sincere," she said firmly, which only made Jared grin more.

Typical.

"Oh." Amanda looked confused. "I see. Well, I guess we'd better find our seats now. It looks like the toasts are about to start," Amanda pointed out.

Leigh glanced around. People were quickly finding their places at the small round tables. With a quick goodbye to Amanda, Leigh headed over to the table near the front where she was supposed to sit. Now she'd have to wait until later to talk to her brothers, but at least she'd be away from Jared.

Boy, he really got to her. Big time. Why in the world had her doofus brothers invited him to be in the wedding party? Had love turned their brains to mush? They hated Jared, and ever since their dating fiasco a few months back, he was the last man she ever wanted to see again.

So what in the world was he doing here?

And why in the blazes did he still get to her so much?

JARED CHUCKLED AS HE watched Leigh weave her way through the tables. She was mad at him. Really mad at him.

Good. Mad meant he still got to her. Mad meant she hadn't forgotten what had happened last summer.

Mad meant he had a good chance of making his plan work.

"It was lovely to see you again," Amanda told him.

Before the older woman could wander away, Jared jumped at the chance to secure another ally in this town.

"I really enjoyed seeing you, too," he told her. "Now that I'm going to settle down in Paxton, I'm hoping the townsfolk will rethink their opinion of me." With a deliberately self-effacing smile, he added, "You know, maybe forget a couple of those wild things I did when I was a kid."

With a nod, Amanda told him, "I understand. You'd like a second chance."

"Exactly."

"Changing people's minds may take a little doing," she warned him. "I've heard quite a few stories about you. And there was that time shortly after my husband and I first moved here when someone covered all the trees in front of the church in pink toilet paper."

Okay. He deserved that. "Actually, Amanda, I covered all the trees on Main Street in toilet paper, not just those in front of the church. It was nothing personal."

She seemed surprised that he'd owned up to the prank. "Oh. Yes. I guess I knew that. Still, it was a mess."

He moved forward and told her, "I'm very sorry about the mess. And to make up for it in some small way, I hear you're collecting money to do some landscaping next spring."

She blinked. "We're hoping to raise enough to plant some shrubs and maybe more flowers."

"I'd like to help. Tomorrow when I come to church, I'll give you a check to help cover those expenses."

She blinked even more. "You're coming to church? Really?"

Jared bit back a sigh. Changing everyone's opinion of him wasn't going to be easy. "Yes."

She rewarded him for his answer by giving him a sweet smile. "We'll be happy to have you. But, Jared, I hope you aren't trying to buy my goodwill."

"Of course not," he said, even though in a way he was. He had to start somewhere. If he didn't get the people in this town on his side, he'd never make a go of Kendrick Rodeo School. Deciding to be honest with Amanda, he said, "I want to be a part of this town, and from now on, you and your husband will find me sitting in church every Sunday."

"It's good to have you back. And I'm sure, with time, everyone will welcome you home." She leaned a little closer, "But you might want to try being nicer to Leigh. I don't think you did much to win her over tonight. She seemed very perturbed with you."

Oh, yeah, she was perturbed all right. But that was just fine with him. He'd already decided his approach with Leigh had to be different from the one he used with everyone else in town. With the rest of the people, he could win them over with kindness.

But kindness wouldn't work with Leigh. Especially after what had happened last summer. No, to win Leigh over, he'd need to be a lot like her—downright sneaky.

Not that he'd share that with Amanda. He doubted she'd approve of his plan.

After saying goodbye to the older woman, he wandered over to the table near the back of the room where he'd put both his and Leigh's place cards. It wouldn't take her long to discover he'd moved them from the table near the front to this table by the back door. And once she figured it out, she'd have a fit.

Should be fun.

He leaned against his chair and waited, smiling as he watched her approach the tables near the front and search for her place card. She searched one table. Then another. Then another.

"Five, four, three, two, one..." he counted down slowly to himself. Suddenly Leigh spun around and glared at him across the width of the room.

"Ignition." He chuckled. She looked ready to explode.

Although her slinky pink bridesmaid dress made her look like a princess, at the moment, Leigh more closely resembled a fire-breathing dragon. She literally stomped across the room until she stood directly in front of him.

"You are the lowest man on the face of the earth," she told him. "You're so low, you're whatever pond scum considers low."

He leaned close and said softly, "Flattery will get you nowhere."

Leigh made a growling noise, and he bit back another chuckle.

"Let me get this chair for you." He pulled her chair out with a flourish. "Have a seat, darlin'."

She narrowed her eyes and shot him a look that could melt the skin off a lesser man. Yeow. That was one mad woman.

Good thing he wasn't a lesser man.

"Don't call me darlin', Kendrick," she said slowly. "Your charm doesn't work on me." She pulled her chair away from him and sat.

Sitting in his own chair, he turned to face her. "Seems to me that just a few months ago you liked it when I called you darlin'. Or was that only because you thought dating me would rile your brothers? Now that your brothers and I are getting along, I guess you don't like it anymore."

Leigh rolled her eyes. "As if. I went out with you because I was delusional at the time. Must have been some sort of forty-eight-hour virus where your judgment disappears faster than a rodeo rider. And you did disappear, didn't you? Seems to me the last time we talked, you were going to take me to dinner. But you never showed."

Now this was fun. He'd missed these twelve-round verbal bouts with Leigh since he'd left Paxton.

"I'm here now," he said.

She glanced at her watch. "You're about... mmm, four months too late."

Leaning toward her so that no one would over-hear, he said, "You're not really mad that I cut out. You didn't care a thing about me."

"Hey, that's not true. Why else would I have gone out with you?"

Jared studied her pretty face. He loved looking at Leigh. Not only was she beautiful, with silky black hair and sexy blue eyes, but she was also full of life and fire and passion. Lots and lots of passion.

But she'd never seen him as a person. She'd only seen him as a way to upset her brothers.

"You're not mad *at* me," he told her. "You're just mad that I wouldn't have sex with you."

She blew out a huffy sigh. "That only proves that you're totally devoid of good judgment."

He laughed. "Do tell."

"Yes. And for your information, you had the per-fect opportunity, and you blew it. Your loss."

"Don't I know it," he said, laughing again when she stuck her tongue out at him. Leigh was never shy about expressing her feelings. It was one of the things he liked about her.

And there were lots of things he liked about Leigh. He'd always found her fascinating, even when they'd been kids. Leigh had a way of looking life in the eye and daring it to mess with her plans. You couldn't help but admire her spirit.

The fact that she was also gorgeous only made the whole package that much more appealing. But he didn't appreciate being used. And Leigh had used him. She'd gone out with him because he was the bad boy of Paxton. She loved to rock the boat, and being with him would have not only rocked the boat, but it would have capsized it.

So he hadn't played along. He'd never cared for being used and still didn't. If Leigh felt the need to ruffle feathers in Paxton, she'd have to do it without him. His feather-ruffling days were over.

He'd moved back to town a couple of weeks ago, figuring the family ranch would be a great place to open his rodeo school. Knowing that for his school to succeed he'd need to woo the goodwill of the people of Paxton, he'd started with the Barrett brothers. Each of them had proven tough to thaw, but he'd managed it.

He glanced at Leigh, and she shot him another icy stare. Looked like thawing her was going to take some doing, too.

"So how have you been?" he asked, figuring that was a safe enough topic.

She sighed. "I'm ignoring you, so don't talk to me."·

"But I'm not ignoring you, so why can't I talk? I know, you ignore me and I'll handle the conversation for both of us."

When she made no response, he asked, "So, Leigh, how have you been?"

Then in his best female voice, which he made deliberately sultry, he said, "Oh, Jared, this town hasn't been the same since you've been away. Like all the other ladies in Paxton, I've missed you so much I couldn't think about anything else."

Next to him, Leigh snorted. "As if."

He ignored her response and kept on. "Well, Leigh, I'm glad to hear you missed me. I missed you, too."

Again, she snorted, and this time shifted so her back was to him.

He used the female voice again. "Oh, Jared, did you really miss little ol' me? I'm all aflutter."

That got to her. Leigh spun around. "*Aflutter?* You're out of your mind. And for the record, I didn't miss you."

Again, he ignored her response and continued on. "Well, darlin', I'm glad to hear you're no longer mad about that misunderstanding we had. You know, I was tempted to take you up on your offer of hot sex, but I didn't like being used like that."

Leigh looked like a pressure cooker about to explode.

"I completely understand, Jared," he said softly in the female voice. "I should have realized it was unfair of me to ask you out for the sole purpose of making my brothers mad. I'll have to think of a way to make it up to you. Maybe I could make you dinner one night. Or help you decorate your house. Or, I know, I could make that hot-sex offer again, but this time because I want you, not because I want to shake up the good folks of Paxton."

Leigh jumped out of her chair, knocking it over in her haste. "In your dreams, hayseed."

Then she walked away. Actually she stomped away. And every person in the room turned to stare at him.

Yeah, he was back in Paxton all right. And it looked like his feather-ruffling days weren't completely behind him after all.

THE TOASTS WERE OVER, so people were wandering around again. Leigh finally found her brothers Chase and Nathan standing by the bar. Their wives, Megan and Hailey, were across the room talking to a group of ladies, so for the moment, Leigh had the boys to herself. Good, because the three of them needed to have a little family chat.

"Hey, kiddo, great wedding wasn't it?" Chase asked.

She wasted no time. "Why is Jared here?"

Nathan shrugged. "Who else could Trent ask when Joe got sick? We had to find someone who was the right size for the tux. I asked Jared, and he said he didn't mind helping out. He's a nice guy."

Nice? Nice?

"You're kidding, right? You don't like Jared. None of you have ever liked him," she pointed out.

Chase patted her on the shoulder. "Calm down. That's in the past. When he first moved back to town, he stopped by and talked to each of us. I don't think we made it easy on him, but he showed a lot of gumption and toughed it out. The man wants to settle here in Paxton and help the town. I think we all need to give him a second chance. Nathan, Trent and I have agreed we'd do what we could to help him.''

Openmouthed, Leigh stared at her oldest brother, unable to believe what he was saying. For the first time in memory, she was at a complete loss for words. Something was definitely wrong. These couldn't be her brothers. They had to be alien clones. Her brothers wouldn't act this way.

When she finally recovered from the shock of hearing Chase call Jared nice, she sputtered, ''So just like that—'' she snapped her fingers ''—you now like Jared where for years and years you couldn't stand him.''

Chase glanced at Nathan, then they both nodded.

''Pretty much,'' Chase admitted. ''But you have to realize, we took to disliking Jared when we all were in high school. We're adults now. Might as well bury old hatchets.''

This was unbelievable. She looked at Nathan, the most logical one of the whole Barrett family. ''A few months ago you went out of your way to warn me against Jared. You said he was all wrong for me.''

''He was. He was a rodeo rider, and we knew he'd pack up and leave town at the drop of a hat, which he did. But now he's back and trying to start a business. Got to admire a man who helps his parents out by paying top dollar to buy their failing ranch so they can retire to Florida. And he's set out to build a profitable business here, which will definitely be good for Paxton.'' Nathan took a couple of glasses of champagne from the bartender, then said, ''You should try to be nice to him, Leigh. Jared's actually a good guy. Everyone deserves a second chance.''

Before she could answer, Hailey and Megan walked up, and Leigh watched both of her brothers kiss their wives.

''Hi, Leigh,'' Megan said, giving her a smile. ''Wasn't the ceremony wonderful? Erin and Trent seem so much in love.'' She beamed at Chase. ''Looks like all the Barrett men have found love.''

''You should give it a try,'' Chase told Leigh. ''It might help with your disposition.''

''Har-de-har-har,'' Leigh said. ''My disposition is just fine, thank you very much. And I have no intention of falling in love, not when I finally have some breathing room now that you boys have your own lives to worry about.''

''Suit yourself,'' Chase said, slipping one arm around Megan's waist. ''But you don't know what you're missing.''

Yeah, she did. She'd be missing out on having another person keeping tabs on her day and night. Her brothers had done enough spying to last her a lifetime. Freedom stretched out before her, and she wasn't about to give it up.

Deciding she'd gotten nowhere with her brothers, she said goodbye and wandered the room, looking for someone to take her mind off of Jared Kendrick. The dancing had started, which would *definitely* take her mind off the man. She loved to dance, and since practically everyone in town had come to the wedding, it shouldn't be too difficult to find a willing partner.

She didn't have to look for long. Within minutes, she spotted Billy Joe Tate, a guy she'd dated a couple of times over the years. Billy didn't get her heart racing the way Jar—er, some men did, but he was a nice guy.

She tapped him on the shoulder. "Hey, Billy. Feel like dancing? They're playing our song."

At that particular moment, the band was playing a rather poor version of "Proud Mary."

Billy turned and smiled at her. "Hey, Leigh. This is our song? I didn't know we had a song. Well, except maybe the high school's anthem. You know, 'Go Mighty Panthers, pride and joy of our town. We're always there for you, even when…um, something is something something.'" He scratched his head. "Guess I don't remember all the words."

Leigh snagged his hand. Yep, Billy Joe Tate was exactly what she needed to get her mind off what's-his-name. When they reached the dance floor, she threw herself into the dance heart and soul, feeling free and alive and too happy for words. Gone were the pressures of the day. Gone were any worries. It was just the music, running through her body, feeding her soul.

When the band finished, they immediately started a slow song. Leigh reluctantly came to a halt and turned toward Billy. But his arms weren't the ones that circled her waist, and it certainly wasn't Billy's body she brushed against on the crowded dance floor.

"Where's Billy?" she asked Jared, none too happy to find herself dancing with him but deciding not to make another scene at her brother's wedding.

"His cell phone rang while you were dancing. I think he tried to tell you, but you were kinda lost in your own world. A few minutes ago, he wandered off to talk on the phone." His brown eyes twinkled with mischief. "I figured since you were out on the floor all by yourself, I'd come to your rescue."

"My *rescue?* What exactly do you think you're rescuing me from? Do you see any danger here?"

"You know what I mean."

"No, I'm afraid I don't." Annoyed by his attitude, a devious idea popped into her head. She placed her hands on his chest and waited until they got bumped again by other couples. Then she softly undid a few buttons on his vest. He was in for a surprise when this dance ended. A big surprise.

"From now on, Kendrick, don't do me any favors. I'm all grown up. I can take care of myself."

"For starters, I figured this was the only way

you'd ever dance with me. Plus, I didn't want you to be embarrassed when you realized your dance partner had left,'' he said, swaying them to the soft, seductive music. ''I thought I could do something nice for you.''

Leigh didn't know what to make of his answer. Frankly it surprised her. Was he serious? Was he really trying to be nice?

She didn't know what to think anymore.

But the one thing she was sure of was that he was dead wrong about her. She wouldn't have been embarrassed.

Of course, she couldn't say the same thing for him. She bit back a smile, thinking about Jared redoing his vest in front of the crowd once the song ended.

''I don't get embarrassed,'' she assured him. ''I'm not ashamed of the way I am. I know you think I only went out with you to upset my brothers, but that's not true.''

At his doubtful look, she relented a tad. ''Okay, getting my brothers riled up was a side benefit, but I went out with you because I'd always wanted to go out with you.''

''So you could have sex with me,'' he said.

''Yeah, well, is that such a crime? You've always been wild. So what's the big deal? I didn't think guys got all huffy about stuff like this.''

''So I wasn't the first guy you went out with solely for the purpose of having sex?''

She sighed. "Okay, yes, you were. But, Jared, it's not like you care. I know what you're like."

"How is that possible, Leigh? Up until our first date, we hadn't said ten words to each other in all the years we've lived in the same town. Did you consult a crystal ball with questions about me?"

Jeez, she hated this. He was making some really good points. She hadn't considered it from his side. Maybe she shouldn't have assumed just because he was majorly cute that all he was interested in was getting lucky.

"Fine. I apologize," she said, but she didn't really like doing it. "I shouldn't have thought that just because you chase women all the time that you'd be interested in no-strings sex. How foolish of me."

"Was that an apology or an accusation?"

She laughed. "Kendrick, just settle for it, okay? And we'll agree to *try* to get along."

"Not much of a truce, but I guess I can live with it. Who knows? Maybe we can be friends," he said, his body warm against hers as they kept time with the music.

She'd give him this—he was a great dancer. And he smelled like heaven. So much so that it took a couple of seconds for his words to penetrate her lust-filled brain.

Friends? He wanted them to be friends?

"I'm not sure that's possible," she admitted.

"Sure it is. Just give it a try." He twirled them

a little, causing Leigh to hold him tighter. "I apologize for messing up your plans last summer."

Plans. Right. That reminded her. Maybe she needed to rethink the whole undone vest thing now that they'd come to a hazy agreement. She might not be ready to be friends with this man, but maybe she shouldn't leave him on the dance floor with his clothes undone.

Too bad that thinking of any sort was proving difficult at this particular moment. Her hormones were having a field day being held this close to Jared. Being in his arms felt amazingly good.

When they got bumped yet again, he pulled her even closer. Leaning down so she could hear him, he said, "I'm glad we had this chance to talk. I'm back now, and for lots of reasons, things didn't work out between us. But that doesn't mean we can't get along. I really am settling here for good. I'd like to know you're on my side. I'd like to know you're my friend."

Leigh looked up into his devastatingly handsome face. There was the word again—friends. He wanted them to be friends. She was the type who generally got along with everyone, so surely she could find a way to get along with Jared. Everyone else in her family seemed to be getting along with him just fine these days.

So maybe a truce was the only logical thing to do. He skimmed the fingers of one hand slowly down her back to her waist, and she barely managed not to sigh. Friends. Was it possible to be friends with a man like Jared Kendrick? More importantly, was it possible to be friends with a man who'd repeatedly said "no" when you'd thrown yourself at him?

Um, she had to think about that one.

"I guess I can stop being mad at you," she relented. "Or at least I can *try* to stop being mad at you. I can't promise miracles."

"Ah, Leigh, but I'd like more. I'd like us to be people who help each other out in times of need."

Something in the way he said that made her frown. "When would we ever need to help each other?"

He leaned down until his lips were next to her left ear, then he whispered, "How about now? I'll rezip your dress if you refasten my vest."

2

SHE WAS GOING TO END UP blind, Leigh decided as
she squinted against the brilliant sun flooding in
through the window in the office of Gavin Monroe,
principal of Paxton High School. Why on earth did
Gavin insist on having his desk situated so his back
was to the window? She couldn't see a blasted
thing.

"Leigh, I asked you to stop by today for a couple
of reasons. First, I think you're doing a great job
with your student-teaching assignment. The kids
love you, and your fellow teachers have nothing but
wonderful things to say about you."

Mentally Leigh did a little happy dance. Yippee.
About time she got some good news. Ever since the
wedding reception a little over a week ago, she'd
been feeling out of sorts. Could have something to
do with Jared besting her on the dance floor, but
she doubted it. She was enough of a good sport to
give him credit for that one.

No, the reason she'd felt mopey was that she'd
been undeniably turned on during their dance—the
one where he'd talked about being friends. It was

happening all over again. She wanted Jared, but he didn't want her.

Talk about pathetic. She needed to find some sort of anti-Jared potion before she saw him again. Something that would make it so she could stand next to him without wanting to strip him naked and throw him on the floor.

Maybe the local drugstore had something. Hmm, probably not. Probably the only thing that would help was to avoid him completely.

That shouldn't be too hard. He lived out of town. She worked long hours. There was no reason for them to see each other again.

And now, judging from all the compliments Gavin was tossing her way, she was about to have a major pick-me-up. She could practically guess what Gavin's next words were going to be—he was going to ask her to join the staff full-time starting next year. After all those years of college, she'd finally get to be a teacher at Paxton High School.

"Thank you so much for the compliments, Principal Monroe," she said in her best teacher voice. Since Gavin was only thirty-five, the same age as her oldest brother, Chase, and they'd grown up together, it felt weird being so formal with him. She still clearly remembered him helping out at his family's drugstore and blushing like mad every time a good-looking girl walked in.

But hey, if Gavin wanted everyone to call him Principal Monroe, then that's what she'd call him.

Heck, she was willing to call him Santa Claus, if that was what he wanted. Anything to get the job.

Gavin smiled, obviously enjoying delivering the good news. "Since you've done such a good job, and you really fit in here at Paxton High, I'd like…" His words trailed off and his attention focused on something behind her.

Leigh leaned forward. Yes? Yes? Hello. She looked over her shoulder. What was he staring at? The picture of his wife? The clock? What?

Turning back to face him, she tried to verbally nudge him forward. "Yes, Principal Monroe?"

He blinked. "Sorry. I didn't realize it was so late."

This was getting annoying. Leigh slapped a smile on her face and said, "I'm sure our meeting is almost over. You were saying, you'd like…?"

Gavin nodded and thankfully directed his attention back to her. "Leigh, I'd like to offer you a job as—"

"Yes," she blurted.

He smiled. "So you knew what I was going to ask? I guess the school grapevine is working overtime. Well, I'm glad you know, and I'm glad you said yes."

"Frankly I'm thrilled. This is something I've wanted for a long time." Boy was it ever. A full-time teaching job at Paxton High. Life didn't get much sweeter than this.

Before she could say anything else, the door to

Gavin's office opened behind her and Leigh heard someone walk in.

"Sorry I'm late."

The deep male voice drifted over Leigh's shoulders. Oh, no. No, no, no. What was Jared doing here? He had no business being here. How was she supposed to avoid him if he kept appearing places he shouldn't be?

She tipped her head and looked at him. He gave her a quick wink, then walked around and sat in the chair next to her. Darn his hide, he looked gorgeous as usual. He had on jeans and a black T-shirt and looked less like a rodeo rider than a midnight fantasy.

Just great. This could not be happening. Not again. Stunned, she stared at him, but he looked at Gavin instead. Before she could say anything, Jared held one hand up and shielded his eyes.

"Whoa, that sun sure is bright. I think I may lose my eyesight," Jared said. "Gav, mind lowering the blinds so Leigh and I can see?"

Gav? He called the principal Gav?

Apparently so, since Gavin immediately apologized and quickly closed the blinds. "Sorry about that, Jared."

"No problem." Jared grinned at Leigh. "So, what do you think? Did Gav explain the plan? Are you on board with everything?"

What did she think? Was she on board? If they

were swapping questions, she had a good one—what was he doing here?

"So what do you think?" Jared prompted again. She stared at him. "About what?"

"The job." Jared looked at Gavin and raised one brow. As much as she hated to notice, Leigh didn't miss how the sunlight still seeping in around the blind slats made his dark brown hair shine. Jared had great hair. Soft and just long enough to give him a wild look.

Blinking, she brought her attention back to the conversation. She had to stop thinking about him that way. "Yes, I accepted the job," she said.

"Really?" Jared grinned at her. "Good. It should be fun."

Gavin leaned back in his chair. "Leigh's a great asset to the school. She already knew about the job when she got here, and she didn't hesitate a bit in accepting."

Why would she hesitate? Gavin had to know she wanted a full-time job at the school. Of course she'd said yes. Why did they find that so unbelievable?

Uh-oh. Suspicion slowly crept through her. Something wasn't right. There was no reason for them to be surprised. Was there?

She studied them. Their smiling faces. Their happy looks. Oh, yeah, something wasn't right. Quickly running through the conversation with Gavin in her mind, she bit back a groan when she realized she'd interrupted him. He hadn't completely finished speaking when she'd said yes.

But what other job could he mean? Naturally he was talking about a full-time teaching job.

Wasn't he?

But if it was, then why was Jared here?

Shoving aside the feeling of impending doom, she said to the principal, "I'd like to know a little bit more about this job."

"Certainly." Gavin folded his hands on his desk. "Homecoming this year is being called Wild Westival. Don't you think that's cute? The student council has arranged for the half-time show, the student dance and the alumni dance, but that still leaves the parade. No one has time to take it on. Then Jared stepped up, solving our problem."

Leigh felt her stomach drop to the floor. Rats. This wasn't about a full-time job. Not at all. It was about a homecoming parade.

How could she have been so stupid?

Acutely aware of Jared sitting next to her, she refused to let her disappointment show. Sure, she wasn't getting the teaching job. At least, not yet. But if she helped on this Westival thingee, then she'd be a shoe-in. Gavin always rewarded employees who pitched in on extra-curriculum activities.

"Why Wild Westival?" she asked Jared.

He was looking at her oddly, almost as if he'd figured out that she'd been thinking along different lines when Gavin had offered the job. Well, that was her own business, and she wasn't telling him about it.

"What did you have in mind?" she prompted when he didn't answer.

He leaned toward her. "Are you okay?"

"Why wouldn't I be okay?" she countered, hating the fact that he'd sensed she was upset while her boss was sitting there completely oblivious to the fact that he'd rained on her happiness by asking her to work on the homecoming parade.

Jared refused to let the subject drop. "Did you mean to agree to help with homecoming parade or did you think Gav was talking about something else when you said yes?"

There was no way she was going to tell Jared what she'd thought. Turning the tables, she asked, "What I want to know is why *you* agreed to help with the parade? You don't work for the high school, so why get involved?"

"Why are both of you asking questions and neither of you is answering?" Gavin interjected.

Jared chuckled. "Sorry about that. Okay, I'll answer first. I was talking to Gav, and he mentioned there might not be a parade this year because they were short on resources. I figured I might as well help. I know how much homecoming weekend means to this town." He grinned that famous sexy grin of his and Leigh felt her heart rate pick up. Talk about being seriously pathetic.

He leaned toward her. "Rumor has it that there are a couple of folks who have less than stellar memories of me."

Leigh laughed. "Ya think? Maybe it has something to do with you painting the water tower an ugly shade of lime-green with shock-pink stripes?"

"I had to paint over it," Jared reminded her. "Took me most of the summer. That pink was hard to cover up. I had to paint that water tower three times before you couldn't see it anymore."

Leigh remembered those days well. Jared, painting on the water tower. Often without a shirt. On any given day, you could find most of the female population of Paxton hanging out at that end of town, enjoying the magnificent view.

Of course, she hadn't joined the groupies at the bottom of the water tower stairs. Nope. Not her. Instead she'd been busy that summer acting as the receptionist for Danny Hoover, the local lawyer. She'd greeted his clients, answered his phones.

The fact that his office afforded whoever was seated at the receptionist's desk a stellar view of the water tower had just been a coincidence.

"See, Jared made up for his little prank," Gavin said. "He had to pay the price, and he did. That's all a person can do. We all make mistakes."

Gavin had to be kidding. Jared hadn't made mistakes; he'd run around like a wild man.

Unable to let this go so easily, Leigh asked, "And didn't you also switch the hubcaps on all the teachers's cars during a pep rally? It seems to me it took almost two weeks for everyone to sort out that little *mistake*.''

Jared shrugged. ''Maybe I switched a few hubcaps.''

Leigh snorted, and Jared laughed.

''Hey, it's true. I couldn't get all the hubcaps off. Some of them were locked on.''

Leigh knew she should drop the subject, but the truth was, she didn't want to work with Jared on a committee. She didn't want to be anywhere near him. Too much could go wrong, and she might end up making a fool of herself again. That was more than she could take.

Hoping to change Gavin's mind, she threw down her trump card. ''And let's not forget you ruined the homecoming parade your senior year when you freed all the dogs from the pound and let them loose on the town.''

''I guess next time I pick a friend, I'll find one with a shorter memory,'' Jared said, his brown eyes twinkling with humor.

Leigh knew he wasn't thrilled she was bringing up all of his past indiscretions, and realistically, she couldn't blame him. Even though she hadn't signed on board with that whole friend thing, she had agreed to try to get along with him. So far, she was doing a crummy job.

''But I guess you've reformed,'' she relented.

''When a man gets older, he starts to realize

what's important in life,'' Gavin said in his most pompous voice. ''Young people make mistakes, Leigh. If memory serves, your brothers made more than a few when they were young. And you may have made a couple yourself along the way. You should congratulate Jared for turning over a new leaf.''

Personally she wasn't completely convinced there weren't all sorts of creepy things under that leaf, but she kept her opinion to herself.

''How long do we have to organize the parade?'' she asked, hoping she could find a way to do this without actually having to see Jared.

''Not quite four weeks. The plans are already underway for the dances and the homecoming show, so you may find it a challenge getting student volunteers. Maybe a few of the freshmen and sophomores will be willing to help. The juniors and seniors are already running the other committees.''

That's right. They'd have student volunteers. Bodies that could help Leigh maintain her distance from Jared.

Whew. That was a relief.

Gavin leaned back in his chair. ''The school really appreciates this. The parade always sets the tone for homecoming weekend and helps draw in a lot of out-of-town visitors. I know all the local merchants were disappointed when we told them there might not be a parade this year. In fact, my parents were thrilled when I told them Jared had stepped up to the plate and would make sure it happened after all. You two should have a lot of fun.''

Oh, yeah, she'd bet they'd have a spiffy-doodle time. She gave Gavin a wan smile. ''Should be swell.''

Jared chuckled. ''See, Leigh's already so excited about this she's about to burst. Gavin, why don't Leigh and I go do some planning and stop back by in a few days to tell you what we've figured out?''

''Sounds good,'' Gavin said, then he stood and showed them to the door. Right before they walked out, he shook their hands. ''Thanks again, Jared. Leigh. I really appreciate this, and I know everyone in Paxton does, too. Homecoming wouldn't be the same without the parade.''

Leigh barely managed to keep her mouth shut until they were out of earshot of Gavin's office. Then she stopped and looked at Jared.

''Why?''

''Why what?''

''Why are you doing this?''

He tipped his head, pretending to be confused, but Leigh didn't buy it for a second.

''I told you. I want to help the town,'' he eventually said.

''Why with me? You can't tell me Gavin chose me to do this. You must have suggested I help. Why me?''

''I thought we'd agreed we were friends. Who else would I ask to help me?''

That blasted friend thing again. "For the record, all I agreed to was to *try* to get along. That's completely different from being friends."

Jared nodded. "Okay. Good enough. We'll be people who are *trying* to get along working together on the parade. I'll get some good publicity out of it, and you'll convince Gav to give you a full-time teaching position. Sounds like a win-win to me."

"How do you know that's what I want?"

"You are one suspicious woman." Taking a couple of steps toward her, he explained, "Chase mentioned it at the wedding."

For a second, Leigh studied him, trying to judge his sincerity. He seemed to be telling the truth as far as she could tell. Then, without meaning to, she blurted, "I hate it when you're nice."

He looked surprised at first. Then he laughed. "Damn annoying, isn't it?"

This time, she laughed as well. "Yes. It is. I don't want to like you."

"And here I go, being so incredibly likable." He pretended to think, then said, "I know. From now on, whenever we see each other, I'll be mean and surly. How about that? Will that make it easier on you?"

"I'd take it as a personal favor," she said. She knew he thought she was teasing, but she really would appreciate it if he at least tried not to be so darn appealing.

But how did you ask a man not to turn you on?

His gaze locked with hers, and Leigh felt her pulse rate pick up. Oh, no. Not again.

Maybe she'd given up on that potion idea too soon.

Turning, she headed toward the exit. She needed to get away from him, away from his sexy smile and seductive laugh. When she reached the door, good manners and a strong sense of fair play forced her to say to him, "This is a good thing you're doing for the town. It's nice of you to help."

"Homecoming seemed like the best way to get everyone in town to realize I've changed. After all, I don't think our mutual striptease at the wedding reception swayed anyone over to my side, do you?"

He had a point. Although only the couples closest to them on the dance floor actually noticed that she and Jared had to redress themselves once the music ended, this was Paxton. Gossip that juicy spread quicker than a lame joke on the Internet.

Frankly Leigh was surprised Gavin hadn't mentioned it today, since that seemed to be all anyone talked about these days. But no doubt the principal had kept his mouth shut because he didn't want to run the risk of chasing off two volunteers.

"No, I guess it didn't help your reputation," she said. "Didn't help mine, either." She shoved open the door but before she walked out, Jared stopped her.

"Do you think what happened on the dance floor might hurt your chance of getting a full-time job here?'' he asked as they headed down the steps outside the school.

''I don't know.''

''Want me to talk to Gav? I don't know if it would help, but I can try.''

She glanced at him as they walked across the parking lot. ''There you go, being nice again.''

''Oops. Sorry,'' he said. ''So do you want me to talk to Gav?''

Why did he care? Why was he so willing to help? And most importantly, since when did Gavin listen to Jared Kendrick?

''Is this the same *Gav* whose locker you filled with French fries?'' she asked sweetly. ''Oh, yes, and then you thoughtfully added ketchup, didn't you?''

He laughed. ''There you go again with that terrible long-term memory thing. You know, most people in this town don't remember every little infraction I did. Like the water tower thing. I'd be surprised if very many people in town still remembered that.''

Well, maybe the men had forgotten about it, but she'd bet most of the women remembered. Jared Kendrick without a shirt was not a sight a lady forgot.

But she wasn't going to admit that to him. All she said was, ''I guess.''

They'd reached her car, so she unlocked the

driver's side door. Jared stopped her before she got in.

"I think we can really help each other. If we do a good job with the homecoming parade, we'll both have a better shot at getting what we want."

She studied him, her gaze slowly drifting down to his full lips. When she thought about things she wanted, one of them was to kiss Jared. She'd always wanted to kiss him, but despite her many attempts, she'd had no luck.

But she knew that wasn't what he meant, so she answered, "I guess you're right. It could show them that I'm mature and responsible, that is if I actually manage to *act* mature and responsible."

He bumped her with his arm. "Is it really that difficult?"

"Seems to be when I'm around you," she admitted. "You don't bring out the mature side in me."

"I'll work on that, too." He patted the pockets of his jeans. "You got a piece of paper I can use? This list is getting long. Maybe I should write it down. Let's see, I need to stop being nice. And I have to stop bringing out the immature side of you. Anything else you'd like me to do?"

Oh, now there was a loaded question. Leigh yanked open her car door and climbed inside. "I'll let you know if I think of anything," she said dryly.

He grinned, and she knew *he* knew what she'd been thinking. "You do that."

Yeah, right. She'd rather eat worms than hit on Jared Kendrick again.

"YOU HAVE SUCH MASCULINE handwriting," Janet Defries cooed as Jared finished signing her up for his rodeo school. "It's so strong and forceful."

He looked at his handwriting on the registration form. It looked like chicken scratch. The woman was crazy.

"It's awful, but thanks anyway." He looked at Janet and her two friends, Tammy Holbrook and Caitlin Estes. The three of them had come racing up the driveway first thing this morning in Janet's red convertible claiming they were dying to learn about roping and riding and "horse stuff like that."

He didn't buy it for a second. Sure, these ladies were looking to rope something, but it sure as hell wasn't a calf. They were after what Leigh'd been after—a good time with a bad boy.

But a student was a student, and money was money, so he'd signed them up and taken their checks. He'd teach the basics of roping and riding. But that was all. Just as Leigh had discovered, he wasn't looking to be a belt buckle prize in anyone's personal rodeo.

"So, Jared, when do you want us to start?" Janet said, putting her hands on her hips and calling attention to the fact that there was about three inches between the bottom of her top and the top of her bottom. Her belly button and belly button earring were on full display, but rather than finding it erotic, all Jared could think about was how it must have hurt like the devil when she'd had it pierced like that. The little hoop she wore near her navel made him think of tagged cows.

He pulled his attention back to her face. "The first class starts next Saturday morning. Be sure to wear old clothes." He glanced again at her naked belly. "And, Janet, you have to be *completely* covered. I mean wear jeans that come to your waist, boots and long-sleeve shirts. We're going to be busy."

Janet pouted, but Tammy and Caitlin, who weren't dressed any more appropriately than Janet, laughed.

"Guess we'll all have to buy some boring clothes," Tammy said. "Or maybe Leigh has something we can borrow. She has a closet full of them."

Jared froze. "What do you mean by that?"

His tone must have conveyed that he wasn't too thrilled with the conversation because Tammy had the good sense to look embarrassed. "You know. Since she's been teaching, she's wearing old-lady stuff. I can't imagine why Billy Joe Tate asked her out."

That bit of information distracted Jared from the comment about Leigh's clothes. "Leigh's going out with Billy Tate?"

Janet must have noticed the undercurrent in his

voice, because she came over to stand next to him. "Billy told me he was taking her to dinner tonight at Roy's Café. And then after that, he's going to let nature take its course."

"Why in the blazes would he say that?" Jared asked, then felt like kicking himself for saying anything. Janet arched one well-plucked eyebrow.

"Jared, honey, you sound almost like you care," she practically purred. She placed one hand on his right arm and squeezed, "But that can't be true since you dumped Leigh last summer. I heard she undid your vest at the wedding 'cause she was mad at you for breaking up with her, and you unzipped her dress to get her back."

Yeah, that was pretty much what had happened. When he'd first felt her undoing the buttons on his vest, he'd thought her motive was desire. Then he'd quickly realized that her actions had nothing to do with desire and everything to do with revenge.

Typical sneaky Leigh. Oddly enough, that was one of the things he liked about her. The woman was never without a plan.

"I don't care who she goes out with. I just think Billy Joe's a jerk for saying something like that," he maintained.

Caitlin Estes, the owner of the local ice-cream shop and a notorious flirt, said, "The heck with Leigh and Billy Joe. I want it on the record that you can feel free to unzip my dress whenever you want."

All three of the ladies giggled at that one, but Jared was too preoccupied to care. Leigh was going to dinner with Billy Joe Tate? Was she crazy? Billy was a nice enough guy, but not exactly the sharpest spur in the county.

Janet leaned toward him, her stance deliberately provocative. "You want to go to dinner with me tonight to take your mind off Leigh?"

"I'm not interested in Leigh," he told her, knowing if he said anything different Janet would go out of her way to sabotage his plans.

"I see," Janet said, but he knew she didn't believe him. Tough. He wasn't about to tell Janet that he was interested in Leigh. But the truth was, he'd always been interested in her.

He glanced at Janet, Tammy and Caitlin. He sure didn't have any allies in this group. They were looking at him like he was prime rib on sale.

No, if he wanted allies, he'd have to see if Leigh's brothers might be willing to help him out. After all, his intentions toward their sister were honorable.

Unfortunately that was the part that made Leigh so mad at him.

"So you want to go to dinner," Janet asked again. "I'll buy." When Caitlin and Tammy protested she added, "They can come along, too."

"I don't think so," Jason said.

All three women crowded around him, and he felt as trapped as a trussed-up calf.

"You sure you won't change your mind?" Janet ran one red-painted nail down his chest. "We'll have a great time."

Jared shook his head and gently pushed his way out of the group. "No. Sorry, ladies."

All three women tried to change his mind, but he didn't waver. He had plans tonight. Plans he wasn't about to change.

He intended on hanging out at the café, no matter how long it took. Sooner or later, Leigh and Billy Joe Tate would show up. Then he'd see what he could do about putting the kibosh on this whole nature-taking-its-course idea.

He hadn't moved back to town and started this rodeo school just to watch the woman he wanted fool around with some other guy.

He hadn't been thrown from that many horses.

3

"SO NOW I'M FIGURING there's a problem with the fuel injection system on my car instead of the radiator," Billy Joe Tate said, drawing yet another picture of who-knew-what on his napkin.

They were at Roy's Café, waiting to order. This date with Billy was Leigh's first crack at enjoying her newfound freedom. Of course, it might have been a little easier to enjoy if he stopped rattling on about his car, but still, freedom was freedom, even if it did come with a few boring stories. And with any luck, tonight would take her mind off Jared.

She glanced at Billy, who at the moment was tucking his napkin into his collar. Okay, maybe he wouldn't completely take her mind off Jared, but being here beat the heck out of sitting at home.

Desperate to change the subject, Leigh asked, "So have you decided what you'd like to eat?"

Billy nodded. "Chicken fried steak, same as every time I come here. It's good for the soul."

Ick. But bad for the arteries. Fortunately Billy's coronary health was none of her business. "I think I'll have a salad."

"Chick food," Billy said with a laugh.

"Intelligent food," Leigh corrected. "Some of us want to live to see fifty."

Billy frowned. "Fifty what?"

Grrr. "Forget it."

"Wish I could forget about my car," Billy said, circling right back into the same old conversation. "Like I said, this time, I think I've finally figured out what's wrong. And once I take the system apart, maybe I'll also see where that spare part I have should go."

Oh, pulleese. Billy was a menace. Maybe she should talk to her brother Trent, the chief of police, and see if they could issue a restraining order keeping Billy at least 150 yards away from anything mechanical.

Loyalty to her fellow human beings forced her to say, "Give it up, Billy. You don't know what you're doing, so you may create even more problems than you're trying to fix. You may even make your car unsafe, which could end up hurting some innocent person. You need to get a mechanic involved."

Billy squinched up his face and looked like he planned on arguing the point, so Leigh added, "Do it for me. Please?"

That worked. He grinned. "Sure, Leigh. I'd hate for you to worry about me. I'll take my car to a mechanic and get it done right." Brightening, he added, "And this way, I'll have plenty of time to work on my phone. There's something wrong with it. A little tweak or two should fix it right up.''

Leigh made a mental note not to take any phone calls from Billy in the near future. Who knew what damage he could do when he tore apart his phone. On the brighter side, at least he wouldn't be driving it around town.

She opened her mouth to once again tell Billy to be careful but before she could say anything, someone else jumped in.

''Be careful when you take apart that phone. Especially the base. You can hurt yourself.''

Leigh spun around. Sure enough, Jared Kendrick sat at the table directly behind them. He was pretty much hidden by the huge potted fern between the two tables, but still, why hadn't she seen him sooner?

This couldn't be happening yet again. ''What are *you* doing here? Can't I go anywhere without you showing up?''

''I'm having dinner and for the record, I was here first.'' He leaned a little to the right and waved. ''Hey, Billy.''

''Hey, Jared,'' Billy said. ''You all by yourself?''

Oh, no. No, no, no. Billy couldn't be planning on doing what he sounded like he was planning on doing.

''Billy, it doesn't matter if Jared is by himself,''

Leigh said sweetly. "We're on a date. We should be alone."

When Billy gave her a doofy smile, she thought he'd understood her not-at-all-subtle message that she didn't want Jared to join them. They might have reached a truce, but that didn't mean she wanted to spend any more time with Jared than the homecoming parade forced on her.

But apparently Billy didn't get her hint, because not two seconds later, he said to Jared, "Leigh and I don't mind. You should join us. I can tell you about my car."

Jared stood and walked over to their table. "Leigh, is this okay with you?"

He expected her to say no. She could see it on his face. Well, if he was going to be mature and adult and reasonable about their relationship, then darn it, she was, too.

Still, all she could manage was, "It's fine. Sit."

Of course, Jared decided to sit in the chair next to her. Now the two of them were sitting together and Billy was across the table. To the casual observer—not that there were any casual ones in Paxton—it looked like she and Jared were together, and that Billy had joined them.

Sheesh.

Billy, however, seemed as happy as a dog with a steak. He launched back into his fuel injector story and continued along that vein on and off throughout dinner. Once or twice either she or Jared tried to negotiate the conversation away from Billy's car, but he stuck to that topic and refused to budge.

Finally, in what seemed to be desperation, Jared said, "So, Billy, enough about your car. Did you ask Leigh how her day was?"

Billy blinked. "Why? She taught school, like she always does during the week."

"But I'm sure she'd like to talk about her day, too," Jared said.

Wearing a stunned expression, Billy asked, "*You* did something interesting today, Leigh? But you were at school. School's boring."

Okay, there was only so much a woman could take. Here she needed Billy to rise to the occasion and be the perfect date in front of Jared, and instead he was doing a terrific impersonation of a dweeb.

Biting back a groan, she said, "School went very well today. The class I'm in is wonderful. In fact quite a few of the kids are accelerated."

Billy scratched his head. "I think you should tell Gavin about that. They don't like the kids takin' stuff."

"No, no. I don't mean accelerated in that sense," Leigh said. "I just meant they're ahead of the rest of the class."

Billy bobbed his head. "Gotcha. So you should tell them to slow down and wait for everyone else. Man, I hate it when people run ahead and leave you in the dust. The kids on the track team used to do that to us all the time. It stunk.''

Leigh stared at Billy, wondering why on earth she'd asked him out in the first place. A snicker from Jared quickly reminded her. Oh, yeah, she'd been hoping Billy could distract her.

Billy chose that moment to burp.

Sheesh.

''Speaking of going fast, how do you like your new car, Leigh? It's sweet. What kind of mileage do you get?''

She could tell Jared found all this oh-so amusing. Heck, she'd find it funny, too, if it wasn't all playing out in front of Jared. Life was against her. There were no two ways about it.

''Billy, why don't you ask Leigh about the work she's doing on the homecoming parade?'' Jared asked.

A wide grin grew on Billy's face. ''You're helping with homecoming? Cool.'' He turned to Jared. ''Remember that time you snuck into the other team's locker room and curled the fur on their costume? The mascot came out at half-time and looked like a kitty cat rather than a ferocious lion.''

Billy made a loud guffawing noise. ''Man, that was sweet. None of the moms wanted us kids to go around you after that. You were trouble, they all said. Even my mom said I needed to stay away, and *she* let me eat cake for dinner.''

"I was young," Jared said. "But people change, Billy."

"Dang, I hope not. I thought since you'd come back to town, you'd liven things up. Like that time you put orange food coloring in the school fountain. That was a hoot."

Leigh glanced at Jared. Although he was smiling, she knew he wasn't happy that Billy was trotting out his escapades.

Of course, she'd done the same thing during the meeting with Gavin, but this was different. Billy was acting like Jared couldn't have possibly outgrown his wild days, while she'd mentioned some of Jared's past antics because she'd wanted to…ah, darn it, there was no difference. She was as bad as Billy.

He burped again. Okay, maybe she wasn't quite as bad, but she was close.

Ignoring the headache she was rapidly getting, she decided to steer Billy in a new direction. "Why don't we talk about the homecoming parade? Hey, I have an idea. You should enter a float. A lot of local businesses are."

Billy frowned. "I own a dairy. What could I enter?"

Leigh thought for a minute, and then decided he could enter a decorative banner. "What about a—"

"Big, fat cow," Billy said, as if he really believed that's what Leigh had been about to say. "I could use my car, if it's fixed by then. I could ride around inside it." He snickered. "Kinda like I'd been eaten by a cow."

"Um, okay, that sounds good," Leigh said, shooting a perplexed look at Jared, who was obviously trying not to laugh.

Billy nodded. "Yep, it should be sweet. I can tie a few tarps to my car and paint them to make the cow body." He tipped his head. "I wonder what I should use for the udders?"

Jared laughed. Really loud. Leigh tried not to, but it was impossible. Even Billy laughed.

"I have no suggestions," Jared finally managed to say, wiping his eyes. "None at all."

"Yeah, me neither," Billy said. Apparently deciding to give that one some thought, he added, "Homecoming is such a blast. Remember that game our senior year when Jeff threw you that sweet pass, but that bozo from Greenville tried to snag it away from you? Man, I slammed into that kid so hard his grandparents felt it."

"Billy, I don't think Leigh wants to talk about football," Jared said.

Oh, now he was wrong there. "Pulleese. This is Texas. I always want to talk about football. But for the record, Jared barely caught that pass because he was too busy checking out the other team's cheerleaders."

When Billy chortled, Leigh added, "And you didn't slam into that kid from Greenville on purpose. Your helmet slipped so you couldn't see well, and you hit him by mistake.''

Both men stared at her. Jared recovered first. "You were at that game?''

"Of course. I have three brothers, all of whom played ball for Paxton. I never miss a Paxton Panthers home game.''

Jared arched one brow. "Why does your liking football not surprise me?''

"You'd make a great tackle,'' Billy assured her. "You'd be the kind who hunted down the person with the ball and didn't let them get away. You'd smush them into a big ol' pile of...'' He blinked, obviously thinking. Finally he said, "A pile of smushed person.''

Now wasn't that a wonderfully flattering compliment from a man she was dating.

"Nice to know I'm the type of woman who would hunt someone down and smush them,'' she said dryly. "Gee, thanks.''

Her sarcasm was lost on Billy. He just smiled. "You're welcome.''

Next to her, she heard Jared stifle another laugh.

"Don't you have someplace you need to be?'' she asked him. Her exasperation meter was pretty much off the scale tonight. Much more of this and she'd go running out into the street screaming.

For his part, though, Jared looked perfectly content. "I'm in no hurry to leave. In fact, I can visit with you two all night. Thanks for your concern, though.''

Leigh shot him a frown, but he only winked in return. He knew good and well what he was doing, but she couldn't figure out *why* he was doing it. Jared had made it clear he had no interest in her, so why the me-and-my-shadow routine? Here she'd finally gotten her freedom from her brothers, and now she had to put up with Jared tailing her?

As if.

Inspiration struck her. "Come on, Billy, let's head on to my place. I'm renting Megan's old house now that she and Chase are married. Want to see how I've decorated the inside?''

Billy shrugged. "Not really. I'm not much on decorating. So, Jared, why didn't you ever go pro? You had magic hands.''

That was it? She offered to show Billy her "decorating,'' and he'd rather discuss football with Jared? The man didn't deserve his Y chromosome.

She could feel Jared looking at her, waiting for her response. No doubt he found this funny. After all, he'd also turned her down when she'd offered to show him her "decorating.''

What was it with the men in this town?

Okay, to be honest, Billy probably hadn't understood what she'd meant by *decorating*. Subtle hints tended to zoom right over his head.

But Jared had completely understood her when she'd made her desires clear to him. He'd known he'd been invited to do a lot more than comment on the color of her drapes, but he'd said no.

Pffft.

Well, she didn't care anymore. About any of it. She'd wasted enough time with these two men tonight. She could have stayed home and defrosted her nonfrost refrigerator and had a better time.

"Billy, I'm going to walk home now," she said, standing. "You can stay here and shoot the breeze with Jared."

"Um, okay," Billy said. "Can I have your dessert then? Apple pie is my favorite."

He sure sounded crushed that she was leaving. That whole running-through-the-street screaming thing was starting to look like a real possibility.

"Sure," she told him, beyond caring anymore. "Eat the rest of my dessert. Talk to Jared about football. Figure out how to turn your car into a giant cow. Whatever."

Billy grinned. "Okay."

That was the last time she wasted any time on Billy Joe Tate. He was officially off her list of men with whom she could enjoy her freedom.

With as much dignity as she could muster, she headed out the door and started toward her house. It was only a little after eight, so a lot of people were still wandering around downtown. Thankfully none of them stopped to talk to her. She wasn't in the mood tonight.

She'd only made it half a block when she heard Jared holler from behind her, "Leigh, wait up."

He had to be kidding. Well, she wasn't stopping. No way. Deliberately she picked up her pace.

Within a couple of seconds, though, he was even with her. "Are we power walking?" he asked when she made no move to slow down. "Because if we are, shouldn't we swing our arms?"

He demonstrated and looked so downright silly when he did it that Leigh had to slam her mouth closed to keep from laughing. How could he be so annoying and yet so amusing at the same time?

It wasn't fair.

"You're not going to make me forgive you," she told him once she had herself under control again. "You ruined my date on purpose."

"You didn't say good-night to me." He had a wide grin on his face. "Guess we're even."

That got her. She stopped and turned to face him. "You're kidding, right?" When he shook his head, she said, "Why should I say good night to you? You weren't my date. I didn't ask you to join us. Go have Billy say good night to you."

Jared chuckled. "He's too busy not only eating your dessert, but also mine. And when I left he was polling people in the café for suggestions about the cow thing. Steve Myerson said he should use plastic trash bags but Kenny Herbert said they'd drag on the ground."

Leigh sighed. Why did these things keep happening to her? More importantly, why did they keep happening in front of Jared? Tonight was supposed to be fun. Instead it had become a fiasco. No, wait, a debacle. Yes, definitely a debacle.

She glanced at Jared, who was smiling at her.

Leigh groaned. "Good night. There, I've told you good-night, so you can go away." She started walking again. Not surprisingly, Jared fell into step next to her.

"So did you enjoy your evening with Billy?" Jared asked after they'd walked a while. "I had a good time, but I thought he burped too much."

"I would have had fun, but this incredibly rude guy butted into our date and spoiled the whole evening."

"What nerve." He lightly bumped his arm against hers. "You weren't really going to take Billy back to your place and show him your *decorating,* were you? I mean, the guy single-handedly disproves Darwin's Survival of the Fittest theory."

Leigh laughed, then abruptly sobered. "Stop it. Stop it right now. Don't be nice now that you ruined my date."

Once again, he bumped her arm. "Come on. I didn't really ruin your date, did I? I thought I was helping. You didn't seem to be having a very good time with Billy."

No, she hadn't been. But that still didn't give Jared the right to butt in.

"Why are you following me?" she asked.

He glanced around. "I'm not following. I'm walking *next* to you. It's entirely different. If I were following you, I'd wear a trench coat, maybe some dark glasses, and definitely a hat."

Grrr. "You *know* what I mean, so don't play dumb. You keep showing up wherever I am. The wedding. The homecoming thing. Now dinner." She narrowed her eyes. "What are you up to?"

His expression was completely sincere as he said, "Not one thing. Guess it's fate or something."

Leigh snorted. "As if. You're up to something as sure as a pig likes to roll in mud."

Jared grinned. "Interesting analogy."

"Appropriate. And just so you know, sooner or later, I'll figure out what you're up to."

He bumped her arm yet again. "Leigh, no offense, but we live in a town the size of a postage stamp. How can we avoid seeing each other?"

His explanation sounded reasonable enough, but she couldn't shake the feeling there was more going on here. But what? And more importantly, why? What possible motivation could Jared have?

"Besides, we're friends now," he said. "We should be happy to see each other. And since we're friends, if you want me to go talk to Billy, I will. I'm sure he'd love to go out with you again."

"That's okay. I don't think Billy's what I'm looking for after all." She kept walking, wishing he'd leave her alone.

"You didn't answer my question," he said after they'd walked for a few minutes in silence.

She glanced at him. "Which one? You ask so many it's hard to keep track."

He stopped walking. "You weren't really going to ask Billy home, were you?"

"Just because you weren't interested in me doesn't mean no man is interested. For your information, there were many, *many* times back in high school when I had to pry Billy off me. He may be more interested in dessert than in wild sex these days, but he's not the only fish in the sea. Nor is he the only guy in Paxton."

"Hey, I know you'll have no trouble finding a whole string of guys to show your decorating to," he said. "Heck, I know quite a few from my rodeo days who'd jump at the chance."

"Kendrick, you're being deliberately obtuse."

Jared scratched his jaw. "Is that anything like being oblique, 'cause I'm sure I've been that a couple of times as well."

Leigh snorted. "You're confusing *oblique* with *elongated.*"

Jared hooted a laugh. "Damn, Leigh, I can't believe you said that."

Well, she couldn't, either. And the more he laughed, the harder she had to try not to laugh, too. But he wasn't going to do this to her. He wasn't going to make her forgive him for butting into her life.

Once she'd finally gotten herself under control, she said, "I'm not looking for a bunch of meaningless affairs. But I would like to enjoy my freedom. For my entire life, I've had one brother or the other breathing down my neck. Now that they're all happily settled, I'd like to enjoy myself. Go out, have some fun."

In the fading evening light, she couldn't quite see him clearly. It made it difficult to tell what he was thinking, since Jared didn't always say exactly what was on his mind.

"But wasn't that why you hit on me? Just to have sex?" he asked.

She shrugged and gave the only explanation she had, "You got my brothers in a lather, and besides, you're cute."

"Ah. Nice to know I'm cute." He started walking again.

She groaned loud and long. "Don't pretend to be insulted. You are cute, and you know it."

"So does that mean you're going to ask me out again, now that you have your freedom?"

She shook her head. "Nope. I'm still not interested in something serious, which is what I gather you want."

"What makes you think that?" he asked.

"You told me."

"When?"

"When I tried to kiss you on our last date. You said you weren't going to have sex with me just so

I could make my brothers mad. You also said you were at a different point in your life than I'm at, and that you weren't looking for a fling."

He nodded. "I meant that. I still do."

"Fine, I understand." Her headache now felt like there were football players holding a scrimmage in her brain. She rubbed her left temple. "Good luck finding what you're looking for."

"Thanks. Hey, maybe you can help. Know any women in town looking for a serious relationship who might go out with me?"

Leigh stared at him. Hello? What universe was she in? Jared wanted her to fix him up with other women?

When she finally recovered enough to speak, she asked, "You're kidding, right? Ha, ha. Very funny."

Jared shook his head. "Of course I'm not kidding. Your brothers told me what a great job you did finding the perfect women for them. I thought that since we're friends, you might be willing to help me out, too."

Leigh continued to stare at him, trying to figure out how she hadn't noticed until now that the man was flat-out crazy.

"You're kidding, right?" she repeated when she realized he was waiting for her answer.

Jared laughed and assured her, "Don't be so surprised. Since we're friends, naturally I'd ask for your help. And hey, like I said, if you want me to hook you up with some of the rowdier boys from the rodeo circuit, just say the word.''

''No,'' she told him firmly.

''No to which part? No, you don't want to help me or no, you don't want me to hook you up with some of the guys?''

How aggravating could one man be? Scratch that. She knew how aggravating a man could be because she had the world's most aggravating one standing right in front of her.

''No to both ideas,'' she said.

Jared sighed. ''I'm sure sorry to hear that. I was hoping you'd help me.'' He leaned closer and said softly, ''I'm not exactly the most popular person in town. A lot of women may be reluctant to go out with me, considering the kinds of things I got up to as a kid.''

Leigh was trying to follow what he was saying, but it was darn near impossible with him standing this close. The man smelled like heaven, like sandalwood and the outdoors. And when he spoke softly, like he was now, a woman couldn't help thinking about satin sheets and warm nights and wild sex.

For a nanosecond, she allowed herself the luxury of simply enjoying the experience. Then she gave herself a good, hard mental whack upside her head.

''I'm positive you won't have any trouble getting the ladies in this town to go out with you,'' she said, cringing when her voice came out sounding breathless and squeaky.

"Yeah, but they'll be like you. Only wanting to find out if all the stories of my sexual escapades are true. I want to go out with nice women interested in a relationship," he said. "So will you help me?"

Leigh held up one hand. She needed a minute to get her brain to let go of that whole sexual escapades idea he'd brought up.

She wasn't having much luck, what with him using his soft voice and all, and Jared was obviously getting impatient.

"Leigh, stop staring at me like you're picturing me swinging naked from a chandelier. I'm asking you for help."

Now why'd he go and say that part about the chandelier? More importantly, why'd he go and say that part about being naked? She was only human.

"You're not going to help me," he said finally. "I can tell."

Leigh snapped. "Fine. Fine. Don't pout. I'll help you. But I still think you're being silly. No one is going to hold what you did in high school against you."

"You did. You brought up all that stuff during the meeting with Gavin."

Oops. Okay, he had her there. But still, he was wrong. "But other people won't."

"Billy did."

"Yeah, well he also ate both our desserts. No one who's not crazy will."

Jared chuckled. "I'll let it slide that you just put yourself in that crazy category."

Based on everything that had happened during the last couple of days, that seemed to be where she belonged. They'd reached her house, so she headed up the walkway. "Have a nice night."

He put one hand on her arm. "Hey, wait a minute. So you will help me, right? Any ideas who I should ask out first?"

Leigh blew out a breath of disgust. When she'd agreed earlier, she'd only said yes to close the subject. She hadn't actually *intended* on finding him dates, maybe just make it appear that she was finding him dates.

But now she realized he actually expected her to find real dates for him. What to do, what to do.

She always tried to be a good friend and help out other people. And it really wasn't Jared's fault that the two of them didn't want the same things out of life. Both of those were great reasons for her to agree to help.

Of course, on the other hand, she'd rather slow dance with a grizzly bear than set Jared up with other women. She wanted him to want her. Naked, with or without the chandelier.

Jared waved one hand in front of her face. "Hello, Leigh, are you still with me?"

Leigh gave him a narrow-eyed look. "Give me a sec. I'm thinking."

Jared started whistling. "Let me know when you're done thinking."

"Cute."

He winked. "You already told me that, but thanks again."

When he started whistling again, Leigh opened her mouth to tell him to cut it out, when suddenly, a blast of inspiration hit her. If she got to pick the women he dated, she could make certain they were completely wrong for him.

Ooooh. Now this was a plan with possibility.

"Sure. I have an idea," she said. "Ask out Maureen Sturnham. She moved to town a couple of months ago. She's single and very nice."

To her complete amazement, Jared hugged her. Really hugged her, not one of those quick friend hugs. Nope, this was a full-body contact hug with lots of *oomph.*

Never one to miss a chance, Leigh hugged him back. Yep, this friend thing could definitely work to her advantage.

"Thanks," Jared told her when he moved to release her. "I appreciate it."

Then, even more amazingly, he kissed her left cheek, and slowly, carefully, slid his mouth across her lips, lingering there a long, long time, before he finally dropped another kiss on her right cheek.

When he finally moved away from her, Leigh gaped at him.

"Excuse me, but what *was* that?" Leigh could feel her lips tingling, her heart racing in her chest. She wasn't complaining, not by a long shot, just confused. "You. Kissed. Me."

Jared shrugged. "On the cheeks. Nothing wrong with that. We're friends."

"Oh, no. That wasn't a kiss between friends. You kissed my lips, too," she pointed out, not sure whether she was accusing him or congratulating him, but baffled all the same.

He shrugged. "By accident. I was only trying to get from one cheek to the other. Seemed like the best way to go about it."

With a wave, he headed back up her walkway. "Anyway, I'll see you Wednesday night at the parade-planning meeting. And thanks again for your help. I'll give Maureen a call."

"I must be crazy," Leigh muttered under her breath as she watched him leave.

When he reached the sidewalk in front of her house, he turned briefly and said, "Oh, and for the record, I don't think you're crazy."

Then he walked away.

For the longest time, Leigh just looked after him. Then she snorted and said to herself, "I'm going to help the man I want to have an affair with find the woman of his dreams. If that's not crazy, I don't know what is."

4

JARED ENTERED THE HIGH school gym exactly eight minutes late for the parade-committee meeting. That should give Leigh enough time to get aggravated, and nothing was more fun than an aggravated Leigh. Plus, it guaranteed he was in the forefront of her mind.

That fit perfectly in his plan. So far, he'd gotten Leigh to agree to be his friend. Now, he was going to make certain he was the only man she thought about.

And based on her choice of date for him, she wasn't exactly trying to fix him up, either.

Sooner or later, he was certain she'd come to realize they were perfect for each other. He knew she was the right one for him. And she'd soon figure out she needed someone in her life who could go toe-to-toe with her.

The town might not like him signing himself up for the job, but he was determined to be the man Leigh needed and deserved. No matter what it took.

As soon as he walked into the gym, he spotted Leigh. She stood in the middle of a group of people who were all talking at the same time. When she noticed him, she put a couple of fingers in her mouth and let out an ear-deafening whistle.

"Okay, now listen up. I need all those people who are interested in walking in the parade, regardless of what they want to be dressed like, to go to the left side of the gym."

A couple of people started to argue, but she quelled them with a stern look. "I know, I know, the Mime Society wants to go before the clowns but the people dressed like panthers think they should go before everyone. I got it."

She turned her back and looked at the rest of the group. "Those of you wanting to create floats go to the right side of the gym and for goodness' sake, do a reality check. You can't drive a float down the street if you can't see out of the windows. Period. No negotiations. I'm not having you run over the crowd just so you can fulfill your artistic vision."

Once again a few people started to argue, but Leigh made a kind of growling noise, and everyone wandered off in the direction she'd indicated.

Then she turned her attention to him. She crossed the room and when she was a couple of feet from him, said, "You're late."

"Sorry. I was on the phone with Maureen. She wanted to talk about our date last night."

Leigh's expression made it clear she was surprised he'd moved so quickly. "I gave you her name on Monday, and you went out with her on Tuesday. You don't waste any time."

"Neither does Maureen." He took a step closer to her. "And I guess it comes as a total surprise to you that Maureen is sixty-two. She's a delightful woman with two sons who are both older than I am."

Leigh bit her bottom lip, and he knew she was trying not to laugh. "She's sixty-two? I had no idea. Well, don't worry. Women reach their sexual peak later than men. I'm sure you two will hit it off."

"Afraid we won't. She called me right before I came over here to tell me that her sons disapprove of her dating me, so we'd better not go out again."

Leigh made a sputtering sound. "Really? You poor thing."

"Mmm. Yes, well I agreed it was for the best." He took another step closer to her. "I thought you were going to help me find someone right for me."

Tears were forming in Leigh's eyes, obviously from trying not to laugh. "I am."

He made the snorting noise she liked so much and said, "As if."

Like a dam giving way, laughter burst out of Leigh. Long, loud laughter. Jared stood patiently while she laughed. And laughed. Wheezed a little. Then laughed some more.

Although he'd do his best to pretend to be mad, he was thrilled she'd set him up with a bogus date. That meant Leigh didn't want him to find Ms. Right any more than he wanted her to enjoy her freedom with any other guy.

His plan was percolating along nicely.

After a couple of minutes, he sighed. "Okay, okay. Enjoy laughing. And from now on, I expect you to fix me up with women my age."

Leigh bobbed her head. "Sure. Okay. Sorry."

"Sorry my—" He glanced around the gym. Everyone was watching them, and no doubt listening to every word they said. "Appaloosa."

Leigh must have also noticed they were the center of attention, because she took a deep breath and said, "Let's get started with this meeting. Go find Tommy and Kate."

He nodded toward the crowd. "First, tell me, why are most of the store owners here? Usually only a few enter the parade."

"Not this year. This year, seems like almost everyone wants to either walk in the parade or enter floats. Apparently Billy has been going around town bragging that he's going to drive a cow, and so now they want to do the same thing."

Jared studied the group, many of whom were shooting dirty looks his way. Man. Memories died hard in this town. "They want to decorate their cars like something you milk?"

"At this point, truthfully, I'd settle for more cows," she said. "Based on a couple of the ideas I've already heard, Billy's cow may be the tamest one in the whole parade. Did you know Pete Tunney wants to enter a giant toilet to represent his plumbing company? And Lilah Pearson wants to enter a coffin to represent the funeral home.''

"Yuck."

"Exactly." She sighed. "Billy's cow is looking better and better. Now will you go find Tommy and Kate so we can start this meeting?''

Jared stood quietly waiting for Leigh to remember that he still had no idea who Tommy and Kate were, let alone where to look for them. Leigh was scanning items scribbled on a piece of paper, and it took a while for her to realize he was still standing in front of her. When she finally looked up, he smiled.

"What's a Tommy-and-Kate?'' he asked sweetly.

She sighed. "The student volunteers on this committee. I sent them to get a flip chart, but so far, they're about as much help as…''

"Udders on Billy's car?'' Jared suggested.

Leigh groaned. "Yes. About as helpful as that. Can you go find them? They should be the only teenagers wandering around this time of night.''

Before he could say anything else, a disagreement broke out on the left-hand side of the gym. Two of the store owners had the same idea of dressing all their employees up as panthers and apparently they were willing to fight for the right.

"My ladies will make wonderful panthers,''

maintained Patty Stanley of Patty's Powder and Primp.

"You'll make sissy panthers," bellowed Bud Knuke of Bud's Boats and Bait. "My boys will be so ferocious, they'll scare off real panthers."

Jared leaned over and murmured to Leigh, "His boys can do that without even being in costume."

Leigh sighed. "It's going to be a long night. Go find Tommy and Kate so we can get this over with."

Seemed like a simple enough task. "Sure. I know all the nooks and crannies of this school."

"Yeah, and you've gotten lucky in quite a few of them, haven't you?"

"Oh, now, I thought we'd agreed to play nice," he pointed out.

Leigh rolled her eyes. "Fine. Fine. I'll no longer fix you up with women twice your age, and I'll no longer bring up the fact that in high school, you scored more than the football team. Just go find them."

Jared chuckled. Yep, he was getting to her all right. He was about to head off when she said, "Please."

Turning, he raised one eyebrow and gave her a slight smile. Then he tapped his ear and said, "I must be hearing things. I thought for a second you said please, but I know that can't be true. You'd never say please to me." He paused, then deliberately added, "Unless, of course, we were naked in bed."

As he predicted, that got to her. She snorted and said, "Like I keep telling you, in your dreams, Romeo."

"You bet. Every night." Then before she could throw something at him, and he was pretty sure she would, he walked out of the gym and went to find the teenagers.

Even though Leigh didn't hint that Tommy and Kate were anything other than student helpers, he couldn't shake the feeling that these two weren't wandering the halls looking for supplies. Every kid in school knew where the second-floor supply closet was. It didn't take but a couple of minutes to get a flip chart.

But if you intended on doing something more creative in that closet, like maybe getting a little romantic, well, that could take some time.

Whistling softly, he took the stairs two at a time. When he reached the second floor, he silently made his way down to the supply room door.

Then he banged on it as loudly as he could.

"Cut it out in there," he hollered, smiling at the scream he got in return.

Oh, yeah. These two weren't out looking for supplies.

Figuring he'd give them a couple of minutes to compose themselves, he wandered back toward the stairwell. Then, he waited.

And waited.

And waited.

Finally the door to the supply room opened a fraction of an inch. They must not have been able to see him, because with a lot of whispers, a slim blond girl and a bulky brown-haired boy snuck out of the closet.

They turned toward the stairs, then skittered to a stop when they saw him.

"Well, hello there," Jared said. "Let me guess, you're Tommy and Kate. Ms. Barrett told me you were getting her a flip chart." He glanced at their empty hands. "But it looks like you've forgotten it."

Both kids blushed. Tommy sprinted back to the closet, presumably to get the missing flip chart. Kate stayed behind, her attention fixed on her sneakers.

Jared left her alone until Tommy got back with the chart. Then he said, "I'm Jared Kendrick. I'm going to be working on the committee with Ms. Barrett and you. That is if you remember to actually come to the meetings from now on."

Tommy took a protective step in front of Kate. "I'm Tommy Tate and this is Kate Monroe. We were just…I mean we just…"

Jared held up one hand. He didn't want to hear whatever excuse the boy was going to give him. Truthfully he was having trouble getting over who these kids were.

He studied Kate. "You're principal Gavin Monroe's daughter? Little Katie?"

She nodded. "Yes."

Oh, this was too precious for words. Jared barely caught himself from laughing. Gavin had always been the straitlaced kind. The kind who never broke a single rule.

And who, Jared would guess, had no idea his daughter was hanging out in supply closets with Tommy Tate.

The urge to laugh was getting stronger, so instead, he nodded toward the girls' room. "I think you should go clean up, Kate, before we go downstairs. Your grandmother and grandfather are at the meeting. If you go in there looking the way you do, they'll know what you've been doing. No offense, but you look like you put your lipstick on while trying to bust a bronc."

With a screech, Kate hurried off to the rest room. Based on the mess she had to clean up, Jared figured he and Tommy would have time for a nice visit.

After Kate disappeared, Jared shifted his attention to Tommy. "Are you Billy Joe Tate's brother?"

Tommy had been looking at the door to the girls' room, but now he glanced at Jared. "Yeah. He's one of my brothers. What are you going to do to Kate? You can't tell her dad. He'll ground her for like a million years. Maybe more."

This was priceless. Billy Joe Tate's brother defending Gavin Monroe's daughter. Growing up, Billy Joe had spent the better part of his high school years tormenting Gavin.

Yep, this was too ironic for words.

"What do you think I should do about you and Kate?"

Tommy asked hopefully, "Is letting us off the hook one of my choices?"

Jared could no longer stop himself from laughing. Tommy was priceless. "You're kidding, right?"

"But nothing happened. We were just kissing, you know? That's all."

At this moment, Jared felt older than dirt. Not too long ago teachers were finding him in that very same closet kissing girls.

"I'll have to think about it," he finally told Tommy. "But while I'm thinking, you and Kate cool it. Deal?"

Tommy shifted his weight from one battered sneaker to the other. "I guess, but that's going to be hard. Kate is such a great kisser and I—"

"Whoa, whoa." Jared held up one hand. "Too much information. A simple 'Yes, Jared' is enough."

"Enough what?"

At the sound of Leigh's voice, Jared slowly turned. She stood at the top of the stairs and looked none too happy.

"Enough for what?" She arched one eyebrow and tapped one foot. Yep, she was one unhappy camper, or in this case, one unhappy homecoming coordinator.

Jared asked, "Enough what what?"

She groaned. "Don't play dumb."

"Want me to play smart instead?" he teased.

Leigh rolled her eyes and snorted. "That'll be the day."

Jared chuckled. "I'm so glad we're friends. You're so kind to my ego."

He could practically feel frustration oozing off Leigh, but he didn't want to tell her about Tommy and Kate. Not right away. After giving it some thought, he'd decided to give the kids a break.

"From what I can see, your ego is in great shape." She looked at the flip chart in Tommy's hands. "Anyone want to explain to me why it's so difficult to bring that downstairs? Half the town is in the gym, waiting for that chart so we can start planning the parade." She gave both Tommy and Jared a narrow-eyed look. "Do you know what it takes to entertain that many residents of Paxton?"

Jared nodded toward the chart. "We're all set."

Leigh looked thoroughly exasperated. "Good. I was starting to think this hallway was the Bermuda Triangle. People keep coming up here and then never come back downstairs. Now let's go."

She took a couple of steps, then stopped. "Wait a minute. Where's Kate?"

Tommy blushed and looked at Jared. In turn, Jared looked at Leigh, who repeated, "Where's Kate?"

At that moment, Kate came out of the girls' room. She looked slightly better, but not enough that Leigh didn't immediately know what had happened.

"You've got to be kidding me." She stared at Tommy. "You two were making out up here?"

"Ms. Barrett, it's not like we planned it or anything," Tommy said. "We were in the closet, getting the stuff you asked for, and Kate said she thought I'd rocked in last week's game." He shrugged. "Next thing I knew, we were kissing."

Kate bobbed her head. "That's right. Tommy and I have never even talked to each other before you sent us to that closet."

Oh, now this was too good to let slide. Jared couldn't resist saying, "So, Leigh, when you think about it, if you hadn't sent them to that closet, they wouldn't have started talking. And if they hadn't started talking, well, then they certainly wouldn't have started kissing." Leigh glared at him, but he couldn't help adding, "So when you think about it, this is really your fault."

With a groan, Leigh turned and headed down the stairs. "This is so unbelievable," she said as they all made their way back to the gym. "As if I don't have enough aggravation in my life what with my family and this homecoming thing and Jared, you two end up making out in the closet. Jeez. What's next? A tornado? Or how about a swarm of locusts? We've never had one of those in Paxton, but hey, the way my life is going, I'm sure there's one just around the corner waiting to pay us a visit.''

They'd reached the bottom of the stairs. Leigh stopped and faced them. ''I don't want anything like this happening ever again.''

As Jared watched, quite a few of the parade committee members wandered out of the gym and stood directly behind Leigh. Apparently they were wondering what the ruckus was, but Leigh was too wound up to hear them. Instead she was busy glaring at him, Tommy and Kate.

Figuring he'd better warn her that she had an audience, Jared said, ''Um, Leigh, there's a crowd—''

But Leigh cut him off. ''I'm trying to land a job here, and you people aren't helping. So from now on, I want everybody to keep their body parts to themselves. Got it?''

A gasp ran through the crowd, and Jared laughed. Well, Leigh was right about one thing. It sure was going to be a long night.

LEIGH TURNED SLOWLY, hoping she'd been wrong. She had to be wrong. No one was standing behind her. They couldn't be.

But true to the way her life was going these days,

not only were there people behind her, but there were lots and *lots* of people behind her.

Great. Just great.

She forced a smile on her face. "Hi. I guess we're ready to start."

Mary Monroe, Gavin's mother and Kate's grandmother, stepped forward. "What were you talking about a second ago?"

Silently Leigh sighed. Okeydokey. Here went her career, up in flames. "You see, there was—"

Jared stepped forward. "Leigh's upset because rather than hurrying with the flip chart, Tommy and I got talking about football. I was showing him a play we made during the homecoming game in '88, and I almost ended up shoving them all down the stairs."

Leigh stared at him. Didn't he realize he was giving this town one more reason to think badly of him? She looked at him, and shook her head slightly. He didn't need to throw himself on this grenade.

But he only grinned and winked. Then he walked over to Mary Monroe, and said, "I'm sorry. I'll have to be more careful next time. But at least Kate wasn't hurt."

The older woman frowned. "You're still as wild as you were growing up."

With a huff, she headed back toward the gym with Kate in tow. The rest of the town eventually followed, and Jared would have, too, but Leigh stopped him.

No matter how long she tried, she would never be able to figure out Jared Kendrick. Here he was trying so hard to get the town to forget his past, and then he'd just voluntarily given these people yet another reason to say bad things about him.

"I don't get you," she admitted.

Jared chuckled. "Is this where I'm supposed to say you could get me if you tried?"

"Har-de-har-har." Moving closer, she poked him with one finger. "You know what I mean. Why did you tell Mary you'd almost knocked her precious Kate down the stairs? You know she's going to tell every single person who comes into the drugstore how irresponsible you are. That can really hurt your rodeo school."

Apparently he wasn't too thrilled with her poking him in the chest, because he wrapped one hand around hers. "For starters, ouch."

"Oh, pulleese. You're a big, bad rodeo rider. I'm not hurting you."

His grin was sexy as all get out, and as usual, it made Leigh's heart race.

"Maybe I'm more sensitive than you think," he told her with a twinkle in his amazing brown eyes. "Maybe I'm easily hurt."

"Ha. That will be the day. You've had horses toss you a bunch of times. You're big, and strong, and tough."

He lightly stroked her hand, which he still held against his chest. "Oops. Watch yourself there, Leigh. You came awfully close to complimenting me."

Maybe she had. She hadn't really intended on doing anything but chewing him out for not backing her up when she'd been lecturing Kate and Tommy.

But now that she thought about it, maybe his approach was the right one. He'd gone out of his way to make sure those kids weren't humiliated in front of the citizens of Paxton.

"Maybe you deserve the compliment. This time. That was a good thing you did for Tommy and Kate tonight," she admitted.

His grin grew wider. "Mary Monroe hasn't liked me since I bought a box of condoms in her store the day I turned eighteen. Unlike Kate and Tommy, I had nothing to lose."

She playfully shoved at his shoulder. "How am I supposed to stay mad at you if you do nice things?"

He grinned that slow, sexy grin of his that made her tingle all over with awareness. She loved it when he grinned like that.

"Maybe you'll just have to stop being mad at me," he said. "We're friends, now. We should work harder at getting along."

Friends. That was right. They were friends.

She took a step backward, away from all the temptation she felt whenever she was near Jared.

"Thank you for being nice to Tommy and Kate," she finally managed to say.

"Do you realize you gave me both a please and a thank-you tonight? I'm on a roll."

"Let's hope so. Let's hope your noble deed doesn't end up hurting your new business," Leigh said.

With one last slow caress, he released her hand and opened the door to the gym for her. "The funny thing is I seem to be attracting customers *because* of my wild reputation."

Leigh stared at him. "Let me guess. These customers are all female."

"Seems like you're not the only lady in town who'd like to find out what sort of talents I have," he said dryly. "Like I told you on Monday, that's exactly why I need your help figuring out which women in this town are interested in a serious relationship not just a quick roll in the hay."

Leigh frowned. Women were signing up at his school in the hopes of seducing him? Boy, that stunk. She taught school during the week and was busy on the weekends. She couldn't sign up for classes.

She was getting another of those headaches she only got when she was around him. "Let's get this meeting over with."

Jared nodded. "Good idea. And who knows? Maybe you'll notice someone at the meeting tonight who's perfect for me. What do you think?"

His comment felt like ice dropped down her shirt. "I know someone who might like to go out with you," she said, biting back a smile. "In fact, she's here tonight. In Mr. Buckingham's classroom."

Jared looked confused. "In the classroom? I thought all the teachers had left for the night."

Although she knew it wasn't fair, Leigh was enjoying this little game. "They have. But Connie Pearl Reardon always stays here. She's very loyal."

"Is she on the cleaning crew?" he asked.

Leigh shook her head. "No."

With a sigh, Jared said, "I'm lost, then. Why is this woman here? For the meeting?"

With effort, Leigh held in a laugh. "No. She's not coming to the meeting. But now that you mention it, she might be interested in joining the parade."

"Leigh, dang it, what are you talking about? Who is this woman?"

She couldn't help herself anymore. She laughed. "Connie Pearl Reardon happens to be a dummy."

"Seems to me you had some trouble with algebra in the ninth grade," Jared pointed out.

Leigh laughed again, her good mood rapidly returning. "No, you don't understand. She's a real dummy. You know, the kind they use to teach CPR."

With a groan, Jared said, "I get it. Connie Pearl Reardon—CPR. So the only female in the whole place you think will go out with me is a rubber dummy in health class? Man, I must be losing my touch.''

No, that wasn't the only female she thought would go out with him…as he well knew. ''I think you're missing out on a golden opportunity with Connie Pearl. She's quiet, and polite, and definitely wants to settle down. In fact, she's the type of woman who stays where you put her.''

''No offense to Connie Pearl,'' he said slowly, ''but I prefer my women a lot more animated.''

The sexy way he said the word *animated* made the air in Leigh's lungs sort of whoosh out. She stared at him for a second, and then with effort, slammed her brain back in gear.

''I'll make a mental note,'' she said dryly. ''And store it someplace safe in my brain.''

Jared chuckled and fell into step next to her as they crossed the gym. ''You know, sometimes I get the feeling you're not really intending on helping me find my soul mate.''

Gee, now how'd he figure that one out?

''I think you're capable of trolling for your own dates,'' she told him. ''But if you really want me to keep trying, I will.''

Thankfully they'd reached the center of the gym. Anxious to get the meeting going, Leigh sat in the first empty chair she found and said, ''Who has the list of parade entrants?''

Tommy brought it over and gave it to her. She didn't miss that he no longer looked her in the eye.

Too bad. The kid had a bright future. This was his senior year, and because of his football skill and good grades, it looked like he was going to get offered a lot of scholarships to some very impressive colleges. But if he got involved with the daughter of the principal, there was no telling what might happen to those scholarships.

"Thanks, Tommy." Leigh studied the list and immediately saw some serious problems. When someone dragged out the chair next to her and sat, she didn't even bother to see who it was. She knew it was Jared.

Refusing to let him distract her yet again, she looked at the crowd and shook her head. "Nope. This order for the parade isn't going to work."

"But we like it," said Patty. "We took a vote while you people were off doing whatever it was you did."

Leigh resisted the temptation to roll her eyes. Instead she forced herself to say calmly, "No offense, but you've got the horses leading the parade."

Bud stepped forward. "That's right. We figure since it's Wild Westival, we should start the parade off with a Western theme."

She could hear the muted sound of Jared's chuckle.

"No offense, Leigh," Mary said, "but if you're going to wander off during the meeting, you really shouldn't criticize the plans we develop."

Hey, she had *not* wandered off. She'd gone to

find out what had happened to Tommy and Kate and Jared. If anything, she'd been on a rescue mission.

"I don't think she's criticizing," Jared said. "Just pointing out an obvious fact."

Leigh appreciated his support. "That's right. If the horses go first, the rest of the parade will have a lot of dodging to do."

Steve Myerson leaned forward. According to the list, he planned on walking in the parade, towing his lazy dog Rufus in a wagon.

Sheesh.

"Isn't there some way we can teach the horses not to do that?" Steve asked. "Then there wouldn't be a problem."

This time, Leigh was the one who bit back a laugh. "Yeah, Kendrick. Just tell your horses to wait until they get home."

Jared looked at Steve and said, "Sorry. These horses aren't housebroken."

The committee members did a lot of moaning and groaning, but eventually, once the band teacher, Annie Croft, said there was no way she and the marching band were following horses, the rest of the group went along with the change in plans.

Over the next hour, they negotiated then counternegotiated, then counter-counternegotiated the order in which everyone would be in the parade. Finally most people seemed happy until Annie Croft said, "I still think the band should go near the end rather than right at the beginning of the parade.''

"The music might startle the horses," Jared pointed out.

"Couldn't we work with them to get them used to it? I'd like the band to be the grand finale," she persisted.

Leigh shook her head. "Annie, it's too risky."

"But think how exciting the finale would be if we could teach the horses to do tricks." Annie waved one hand. "It would be a triumph."

Jared looked confused as he said, "These horses have been trained to do barrel racing and I have some cutting horses that can—"

Annie shook her head. "No, no. What I want to know is, can they dance?"

Jared made a choking sound. "You want my horses to *dance?*"

Annie nodded. "A little. If they can. You know, maybe sway side-to-side. See, the band is considering playing the 'Hokey Pokey,' and I thought it would be cute if the horses followed us and danced to the song."

Leigh was unable to stop her mouth from dropping open, but at least no one noticed her, because Jared burst out laughing. Really long. And hard.

At first, Leigh figured Annie was kidding. But the expression on the woman's face made it clear she was perfectly serious.

She truly wanted Jared's horses to dance the "Hokey Pokey."

Looked like they still had a lot of negotiating left to do tonight.

5

"THANKS A LOT FOR CHANGING your mind," Steve said, pumping Jared's hand. "I know my brother's family is going to have a great time here."

Jared scuffed the ground with one boot heel. Glad to know someone was going to enjoy themselves, because he sure as shooting wasn't going to. He'd just agreed to host Steve's brother and his family for a week. No, host was the wrong word. He was going to *entertain* them, like some kind of six-foot-tall amusement park.

Now, not only did his students mostly consist of women who were more interested in coming on to him than in learning how to barrel race. They also consisted of dude ranchers, people who wanted to spend a week on a ranch so they could play cowboy.

Looking downright gleeful, Steve climbed back into his purple minivan. "I really appreciate this, Jared. My brother is tickled pink." Then, with a wide grin, he added, "And I don't care what anyone says about you, you're one heck of a guy."

With that as his final comment, Steve honked his horn, waved frantically out of the window and drove away like a big grape rolling down the driveway.

"Damn," Jared muttered. "You're one sorry excuse for a businessman." After Steve had disappeared, Jared headed up the porch steps to his house. This rodeo school was turning out to be just about everything else but a rodeo school. So far, his school was a combination dude ranch and ladies' club.

He dropped into one of the rocking chairs on his porch. But what choice did he have? Setting up a rodeo school took money. Lots of money. Money he didn't have.

He'd hoped students would sign up, and he could reinvest their tuitions into upgrading the school. Unfortunately he'd discovered there were two types of rodeo school customers: the ones with money, who immediately signed up with the established schools, and the ones without two dimes, who immediately gravitated to him.

He already had two guys, Stan and Dwayne, who were helping out in exchange for lessons. He didn't need any more down-and-out students.

He needed students with money. So at least for now, he'd work with the local ladies, even if they had about as much interest in learning to rope and ride as they did in splitting the atom. And he'd let Steve's brother and his brood stay at the ranch, because at this point, money was money.

Leaning back in his chair, he watched a truck

pull in his driveway. The way his luck was going, this was probably some local dad wanting to know if Jared did pony rides for children's birthday parties.

But thankfully, once the truck got closer, he saw it was Chase Barrett. Good. Chase might not be a prospective student, but he also wasn't about to ask Jared to teach him to "ride the pretty horsies."

No, if he had to guess, Jared would wager Chase was here on an official big brother mission. The Barrett brothers were probably hearing all sorts of things about him and Leigh. Knowing those three, they'd want some strong reassurance that his intentions toward their baby sister were honorable.

No problem there. *His* intentions were honorable. Leigh's, however, weren't.

"Hey," Chase said, getting out of his truck and heading up the porch steps. "How's it going?"

"Good. What brings you here?"

Chase sat in the chair next to Jared. "This and that."

Jared nodded. "Which you want to talk about first, this or that?"

With a chuckle, Chase pulled off his Stetson. "Let's start with *this* first."

"This being Leigh, right?"

"You're one smart fellow," Chase said.

Yeah, well, it didn't exactly take a rocket scientist to figure out the direction of this conversation. "What do you want to know about Leigh?"

"For starters, mind running me through what happened at the reception? I know that dance floor was mighty crowded and people got kinda squashed, but you and Leigh were the only ones who had trouble with their clothing."

"Noticed that, did you?"

"Most of the town did since when the song ended, you two had to get dressed again. Then I understand things got kinda chummy with you and Leigh at the café a few nights ago."

When Chase took a breath, Jared added, "Plus things got a little dicey at the parade-planning meeting last night."

Chase nodded. "That's what folks are saying."

"So what do all those 'folks' think is going on? Do they think I'm trying to seduce Leigh and lead her astray?"

"I believe that's the popular theory."

Man, this was amazing, but unfortunately, not very surprising. "Have any of these people actually met your sister? Do they honestly believe anyone could lead Leigh anywhere?"

Chase laughed. "Yeah, I see what you mean. She's always been a tough one."

"If you know Leigh's not about to let anyone do anything she doesn't want, why are you here, Chase?"

He shrugged. "I'm her brother, and I love her. I'd be falling down on my brotherly duties if I didn't at least ask why you unzipped her dress at the wedding reception.''

''I unzipped her dress because she unbuttoned my vest.'' Before Chase could say anything, he went on. ''You should know that Leigh unbuttoned my vest first. And not because she was overcome with lust. She was mad at me.''

''And why is that?''

Jared debated for a second just how honest to be with Chase. Finally he decided he might as well put his cards on the table. ''Last summer when Leigh went out with me, she only did it because she wanted to drive you and your brothers crazy,'' he confessed.

Chase didn't seem surprised. ''Yep, that's my sister. Born to drive her kin insane.'' He tipped his head and looked at Jared. ''But see, what I can't understand is why she's mad at you. Seems natural to me you'd be irked at her, but she's got nothing to be upset about.''

With a shrug, Jared explained, ''I didn't go along with her plan.''

Chase chuckled. ''Okay. Now I get it. She had you pegged as some easy fun, right? But you refused to cooperate. That sure would fry Leigh's bacon. When she makes a plan, she doesn't like it foiled.''

''So she's explained to me in her own special way,'' Jared said dryly.

''What happens now?''

"Nothing. Leigh and I have decided to be friends." Even saying the word made him crazy, but he knew he had to take things slowly. But before he was through, he was going to move heaven and earth to make sure they became a lot more than friends to each other.

For the moment, though, he'd bide his time. If he rushed her, Leigh would figure out what he was up to and never speak to him again.

"You know, Megan and I started out as friends," Chase pointed out. "Now we're happily married with a ba—" He abruptly stopped talking.

Jared turned to look at Chase. He knew why the other man had stopped talking, but he couldn't help teasing. "You and Megan have a ba? What kind of ba? Where'd you get it? In Dallas? I hear they have the best bas around."

Chase chuckled. "Shut up. You didn't hear a blasted thing from me."

Understanding that Chase and Megan weren't ready for the news of their impending parenthood to be spread all over Paxton, Jared nodded. "Gotcha. I'll keep your ba a secret until such time as everyone knows about it." He couldn't help adding, "And congratulations."

Chase grinned. "Thanks. But my point was that sometimes you start out as friends, but then you fall in love and end up being—"

"The parents of a ba."

With a chuckle, Chase agreed. "Something like that."

Jared liked to think that was a possibility, but a lot had to change before he could even think about having a family with Leigh. For starters, he had to get her to see him as more than stud material.

From what he could tell, that alone was going to take some doing.

"So if you and Leigh did become more than friends, do you think something might come of it?" Although Chase pretended to be casual, Jared knew he wasn't at all.

"I want to settle here and put down roots," Jared confessed. "Unfortunately, at the moment, Leigh wants to enjoy her newly found freedom. She wants to be independent and have some long-awaited fun."

"If you ask me, you're being too nice, Jared," Chase told him. "I love my sister and I'd do anything for her, but the way she's feeling now, she may not even give you a chance if you're looking for something more long-term. Guess the boys and I kept her on too tight a rope. She's a wild one, and we never wanted to see her get hurt. Bad mistake, because now she's going to run since she's finally got some room."

"Seems that way."

Chase leaned back in his chair. "I guess we all have to let her make her own choices."

There was nothing Jared could say to that, and for a few moments, they sat in silence.

Then Chase said, "Yep. She'll make her own choices. Like tonight, for instance. She's going to that new multiplex in Tyler with some guy who works for Nathan. The guy told Hailey they're going to go see that tear-jerker movie. Guess that's what Leigh wants out of life. To go to see sad movies with some guy who just moved into town a week ago and who no one knows a blasted thing about. But hey, it's her choice."

Jared frowned. Leigh was going all the way to Tyler with some guy she didn't know? Some guy no one in Paxton knew?

Didn't seem too wise. But all he said to Chase was, "I'm sure this guy is nice. Otherwise, Nathan wouldn't have hired him."

Chase snorted. "A person can seem real nice at work and be completely different on a date." He stood. "Another person can have the whole town convinced he's no good just because he was a little wild when he was a kid. But that man actually would be the good guy. The one a woman might not realize is the right guy for her. Not if she was too busy going out with the wrong guy. Who might act like who knows what on a date."

Jared laughed. "That's the most convoluted explanation I've ever heard. You could have hurt yourself just saying it."

Chase put his Stetson on. "Yeah, well, just for the record, you didn't hear any of it from me."

With that, Chase climbed into his truck and headed down the driveway. Jared watched him go. Man, that had been one bizarre visit. But then again, most of his encounters with the good people of Paxton were strange. This town had to be too close to a toxic waste dump or something because the inhabitants were peculiar.

"Strange, strange, strange," he muttered to himself as he headed inside his house. It was almost time for dinner. He could go out to eat or maybe cook something he'd picked up at the grocery store this morning.

When he reached the kitchen, he opened the refrigerator. Nothing inside looked good. And the thought of going to Roy's Café in Paxton didn't sound appetizing, either.

What he really felt like eating was…popcorn. A big barrel of movie popcorn.

Was he really going to drive all the way into Tyler to bust up Leigh's date with this guy? He grinned. Hell, yes. Sure, some might think he was a conniving jerk, but Leigh was the woman for him. He had to fight for her, didn't he?

Besides, going to a movie sure did sound like fun. And no one said he had to go to the one Leigh was going to see. Maybe he'd go to a completely different theater and see a completely different movie.

He walked over and grabbed his keys off the hook by the back door. "Guess I'm getting as peculiar as the rest of this town because now I'm lying to myself."

Still, that didn't stop him. He headed out the back door and off to Tyler, figuring the worse that could happen was Leigh would hate him for the rest of his life.

But hey, at this point, he'd try anything.

"YOU'RE REALLY QUIET. You okay?"

"I'm fine." Leigh glanced over at her date, Travis Armstrong. They were on their way to the movies. She should be having a great time. A terrific time. Travis was a nice guy, and she was certain their date would be nothing like her last one with Billy Joe Tate.

But ever since Travis had picked her up, she hadn't been able to pay a bit of attention to anything he'd been saying. Instead she'd been thinking about what she was always thinking about—Jared. She hadn't seen him since the parade-committee meeting two days ago, and already she felt antsy. Restless.

Talk about being stupider than a rock. Why would she waste perfectly good time thinking about Jared? There were so many other interesting and important things she could think about. Like...well, if she thought long enough she was sure she could come up with a few.

Focusing her attention on Travis, she asked, "What movie do you want to see?"

Travis parked his car in the crowded movie parking lot. He'd driven them all the way to Tyler since Paxton didn't have a movie theater. But Tyler had several multiplexes, and Travis had picked the biggest of the bunch.

"I figured you'd like to see *Buckets of Tears*," he said. "So that's what we're going to see."

He had to be kidding? She wasn't the three-hanky kind at all. Resisting the impulse to make a gagging noise, she said subtly, "That's sweet of you, Travis, but why don't we see *Spies and Lies* or maybe that campus comedy, *Idiot U* instead? They both look good."

Travis shook his head. "Ah, Leigh, that's nice of you, but Carla always said...I mean, I know ladies like sad movies."

"Who's Carla?"

Leigh watched with fascination as a bright red blush colored Travis's round face.

"She and I used to date," he finally said with a shrug.

Since Leigh knew practically everyone in Paxton and she didn't know Carla, this woman had to be someone Travis knew from before. "How long did you date her?"

"A while."

Uh-oh. That didn't sound good. "What's a while?"

Travis sighed long and loud. "We met when we first started school."

"When you were freshmen?"

When he shook his head, suspicion crept up Leigh's spine.

"Before that. Let's just forget Carla and enjoy this movie."

Leigh put one hand on his arm. "No way. Tell me when you first met Carla."

It took a lot of moaning and groaning, but finally Travis blurted, "In kindergarten. We met in kindergarten."

Leigh's mouth dropped open. "You're kidding? But you didn't start liking each other until much later, right? Maybe until you met again in college."

This time when Travis sighed, Leigh was the one who groaned. "You're seriously telling me you were together with Carla from kindergarten on? When did you break up?"

"Recently," was all Travis said, but the way he said it in such a gloomy voice pretty much spoke volumes.

Uh-oh. That didn't sound good. "Until *how* recently?"

"Um, you know when I moved to town last week to go to work for your brother, Nathan?"

Ah, jeez, she could see where this was going. "Travis, are you telling me you just broke up with your girlfriend of twenty years *last* week?"

He hung his head. "She broke up with me. She

didn't want to move to Paxton, but I wanted this job.''

This was much, much worse than her date with Billy Joe Tate. At least Billy had only been hung up on his car.

''You're still in love with Carla, aren't you?'' Leigh asked, knowing full well that this date was going to be a dud before it even started.

''I thought if I went out on a date, I might feel better. I know it's very important to get on with my life.'' Travis sighed again. ''I'll admit, dating someone else actually feels kind of...bizarre. But I'm sure I'll get over that feeling.''

Bizarre? Going out with her felt *bizarre?* Now wasn't that romantic? What was wrong with the men in this town? What did it take for a reasonably attractive woman to have a little fun?

She looked at Travis, who had a sad, puppy-dog expression on his face. Drat, drat, drat. She could tell he wanted to pour his heart out about his ex-girlfriend. Somehow she'd become a shoulder to cry on rather than an object of lust.

Ah, for crying out loud. She wanted some fun. Some wildness. She'd gotten her blasted brothers married off. This was supposed to be the time of her life.

But she couldn't just ignore Travis, so she said, ''Tell you what, let's go see something funny. Maybe that will cheer you up.''

''You're so nice,'' he said. ''But really, I want

to see what you want to see.'' He pushed open his door. ''Let's hurry. We don't want to be late to *Buckets of Tears.*''

As far as she was concerned, *late* was the only way to arrive at that movie. She'd rather tie her own arms into a pretzel knot than spend almost three hours watching that film.

But Travis seemed adamant, so rather than upset him, Leigh decided she could use the time to nap. ''Fine. Let's see the sad movie.''

Secretly she hoped the film might be sold out when they got to the ticket booth, but no such luck. It was a Friday night and most everything was sold out. Not only were there no seats left for the two movies she'd suggested, there were also no seats left in the next showing of the kid's movie with a talking alligator, the ninja movie, the good cop/bad cop movie and the two foreign films. The choice became either wait around for over an hour for one of the other movies to start…or go to *Buckets of Tears.*

''Come on. It won't be so bad,'' Travis said, buying the tickets.

Yeah right, and waxing your legs didn't hurt. She just knew this movie was going to be right up there with having a root canal on the enjoyment scale.

But she didn't want to hurt Travis's feelings. He was already so upset that she felt the least she could do was pretend to have a good time. Plus, she wasn't about to let another of her dates end before it really started. A woman could only take so much.

After getting a big tub of popcorn, they entered the theater. Surprisingly, a lot of people were there, although Leigh didn't miss that most of the patrons were women.

"Where would you like to sit?" she asked, still hoping he'd suggest they sit in the next theater.

"Anyplace is good." Travis glanced around. "Hey, look over there. A crowd has formed. Someone sure is popular."

Leigh leaned around Travis a little and studied the group. Five or six women stood clumped around one seat, all of them chattering loudly and laughing.

"Must be one of their friends," she said, glancing toward the back of the theater. Napping would be easier if she was away from a crowd. "Why don't we sit near the top?"

With a shrug, Travis started up the stairs. They'd only taken a couple of steps when a loud giggle made Leigh turn toward the group of women again. The one giggling moved a fraction of an inch, and Leigh caught a glimpse of the person sitting in the seat.

Jared. Jared was sitting in the middle of the theater being fawned and fussed over by all those women.

"That rat," she muttered. "That absolute rat."

"Who's a rat?" Travis followed her gaze. "Look, there's Jared. Let's go sit by him."

"You *know* Jared?"

"Not personally. But I read about his rodeo school in the *Paxton Times*. I know a lot of the people in town talk about him, but he seems like a great guy."

Oh, no, Jared was most certainly not a great guy. A great guy wouldn't follow you around and drive you crazy. A great guy wouldn't ask you to be friends and find him dates. Most importantly, a great guy would have sex with a lady when she asked him to.

Whatever else Jared was, he wasn't a great guy.

"I'd rather sit higher up," Leigh said, hoping against hope they could find seats before Jared noticed them. Unfortunately good luck had deserted her long ago, because just as she tugged on Travis's arm, Jared turned his head and caught sight of them.

Darn it all.

A slow, sexy smile crossed his face, and then he said something to the women because they eventually wandered off.

"Hey, Leigh. I didn't know you were coming to this movie," Jared said.

Before she could do a thing to stop him, Travis headed over to introduce himself to Jared, and then plopped down in the seat next to him. Oh, wasn't this just peachy. First Jared had ruined her date with Billy Joe, and now he was butting into her date with Travis.

Reluctantly she came over to where the men

were sitting. "What are you doing here?" she asked Jared.

He grinned, but she didn't miss for a second the sparkle in his eyes. "I was planning on watching a movie. Isn't that what most of the people are doing here?"

"This can't possibly be a coincidence. Not this time. Stop following me," she said.

Travis looked at her, obviously confused. "How can he be following you if he was here first?"

Leigh opened her mouth to respond, and then realized she didn't have an answer to that. She might have conceded the point, but Jared looked way too pleased with himself for her to believe this wasn't planned.

"Trust me, I'm not following you," Jared said, although he looked like he was going to laugh at any second. "Why would I do something like that?"

She didn't know why he was doing it, she just knew he was. She was prepared to keep discussing this, but the lights dimmed and the previews started.

"Leigh, come on and sit," Travis said. "You don't want to miss the movie. Should be good."

Suddenly, delightfully, a thought occurred to Leigh. If Jared had followed her, then he was going to have to sit through this tearfest. She could hardly wait to watch him squirm and sigh for the next almost three hours of tragedy.

Biting back a smile, she sat next to Travis. This

movie would teach Jared to stop butting into her dates.

And during the next hour, she realized this movie was indeed torture. The heroine lost her family in a flood, her best friends in a fire, her fiancé in an earthquake and now her beloved poodle looked like he was about to be history based on the smoke puffing out of the volcano in the background.

Around her, Leigh could hear the sad sniffles of many of the other patrons. Once or twice, she'd even heard a soft sniff from Travis.

But Leigh had spent most of the time wondering why the heroine didn't get off her duff and prevent these problems. She was without a doubt dumber than mud, and Leigh's eyes hurt from rolling them so much.

When the poodle started running up the hill straight toward the lava while the dim-witted heroine talked on her cellular phone, Leigh decided she'd had enough.

"I'm going for a soda," she told Travis. "Do you want anything?"

"No," Travis said vaguely, obviously engrossed in the film.

Right as Leigh stood, Jared said, "I'd like a popcorn. I think I'll come with you."

As if.

"That's okay, I'll get it for you," she told him, then she sprinted toward the lobby before he could argue. She didn't want to have to talk to Jared because if she did, she knew it would end in a fight.

No, she'd simply get Jared's popcorn. And since she didn't know how he liked it, she'd be sure to tell the kid behind the counter to drench it in butter.

It was a silly, juvenile gesture, sure, but it was the best she could come up with at the moment.

After getting a soda and Jared's popcorn, she headed back toward the theater. Partway back to her seat, she literally ran into Travis.

"Hi," she said. "Where are you off to?"

She couldn't make out his expression in the darkened theater, but she clearly heard him sigh.

"I think you're terrific, really. But I can't do this. I realize that Carla is the woman for me. I love her, and I'm going to go call her." He patted her arm. "Jared said he'd give you a ride home. Thanks for understanding, Leigh."

Then he walked away.

Leigh blinked. Hello? Who said she understood? She most definitely didn't understand.

She narrowed her eyes and glanced toward the middle of the theater. Jared. She knew he'd had something to do with Travis's sudden decision to rush home and call Carla.

Determined, she headed over to Jared and slipped into the seat Travis had vacated. Even in the faint light, she could tell Jared had his eyes closed. He wasn't watching the move; he was dozing.

"You're a rat. No, you're worse than a rat.

You're whatever rats hate," she practically hissed at him, not wanting to ruin the movie for the rest of the audience but unable to wait another second to tell him what she thought of his plotting.

He opened his eyes and grinned. "I love it when you whisper sweet nothings to me."

Leigh snorted. "As if."

Jared chuckled. "Seriously, I'm sorry Travis left. The second you walked away, he started talking about his ex-fiancée and how much he missed her. All I said was 'hmmmm.'"

"Why are you doing this to me?" she asked. "You turned me down, so stop ruining my dates. You keep saying we're friends. Why don't you act like one for a change?"

A woman behind them said loudly, "Shhh."

Jared leaned close to Leigh and whispered, "I didn't set out to ruin your date. I didn't do anything."

Leigh sincerely doubted that, although realistically, Travis hadn't seemed in the mood for this date. He should have never asked her out since he was in love with another woman.

Still, all that didn't mean Jared wasn't guilty. Of something.

"I can't figure out why you're doing this," she said as much to herself as to him.

Again the woman behind them said, "Shhh."

Leigh glanced at the screen. The poodle, which as far as she could tell was the smartest thing in the movie, was running away from the lava. But the dumb heroine's heel had gotten stuck and now she was crying as the lava approached.

Boy, this was one stupid movie.

Jared must have agreed, because he snagged her hand and stood. "Come on. Let's get out of here. I can't take this anymore."

Finally there was something they agreed on. She shoved the box of popcorn at him, grabbed her soda and purse and went with him.

"This is the worst movie I've every seen," she muttered as they headed toward the exit. "And for the record, no woman in real life is as dumb as that heroine."

They'd reached the lobby, and she turned to face him. "*I'm* not as dumb as that heroine. I know you're up to something...I know it as sure as I know my shoe size."

She took a couple of steps closer and gave him a narrow-eyed look. "I don't know what it is yet, but I'll figure it out. Trust me. I'll figure it out."

6

HE HADN'T SET OUT TO RUIN her date. He really hadn't. But he knew he had about as much chance of convincing her of that as he had of teaching his cows to knit. All he'd wanted to do was remind Leigh that he was around.

It wasn't his fault her dates were losers. How was he supposed to know that the second Leigh walked away Travis would go on and on about some woman he'd once planned on marrying? And then, with absolutely no encouragement, the guy had decided to go call this love of his life.

Leaving a fit-to-be-tied Leigh behind.

Leigh tossed her soda cup in the trash and headed toward the exit. "Okay, you've ruined my date. Again. Let's go home."

She was out the door and a good way across the parking lot before he knew what was happening. When he caught up with her, he pointed out, "Technically I didn't ruin your date. Your date ruined your date. Travis was the one who decided to leave. I don't think he even planned on telling you he was going. I think he was going to sneak out. If you ask me, that was a crummy thing to do. He should have at least offered to drive you home.''

Leigh looked at him. ''That would have been better? He could have said, 'Thanks for the wonderful date. I had a great time. I'd call you again, but being with you has convinced me I'm in love with another woman.' Jeez, talk about flattering.''

Yeah, she had a point there.

''Well, don't take it personally,'' Jared told her, turning her in the direction of his truck. ''Travis was one confused guy. It sounds like he never should have broken up with this woman in the first place.''

Leigh sighed. ''I guess you're right. But I seem to have the worst luck when it comes to picking dates. And I'm not doing such a hot job picking friends, either.''

Jared laughed. ''Hey!''

She put her hands on her hips. ''Seriously, you're not helping any by showing up.''

''Fine. Here's an idea, why don't I help you pick better dates, and then I won't have to show up?''

Leigh frowned. ''What?''

''I know, let me pick your next date. And I promise, I won't ruin it.''

He could tell Leigh was debating with herself, so he upped his offer. ''It's only fair since I'm letting you pick my next date. And remember, we already agreed—no senior citizens, okay?''

For a second he thought she'd tell him no way,

but suddenly, she relented. "Fine. I guess it can't be any worse that what I've been picking on my own."

They'd reached his new black truck, and he unlocked the passenger door and held it open for her.

"Where's your motor scooter?" she asked as she climbed in the truck. "Amanda said you drove a motor scooter."

"Ha, ha. My motor*cycle* is home. I decided to drive my truck instead."

She studied the truck slowly. "You know, this looks like the Batmobile."

"Har-de-har-har," he said, using one of her favorite lines. After she got in, he closed her door and walked around to the driver's side. Okay, so maybe his truck was a little on the seriously black side, but it was hardly the Batmobile.

When he opened his door, Leigh asked, "What do all these buttons on the ceiling do?"

"Well, the one you're pushing opens my garage door," he said dryly.

"Oooh. The entrance to the Bat Cave. Got it."

Jared climbed in and tossed his leather jacket on the seat between them. "It's just a truck, Leigh."

She rolled her eyes. "Excuse me. Have you looked at this thing? It has more gizmos and gadgetsthan the space shuttle."

He chuckled and started the engine. "You're easily impressed."

She gave him a look that spoke volumes. "Hardly."

"Okay. So if this is the Batmobile, does that make you Catwoman? 'Cause if you're interested in putting on that skintight black outfit, I'm on board with the whole concept."

Leigh snorted. "Dream on."

Yeah, no doubt he would tonight.

"I like this truck," he said, turning on the CD player and heading back to Paxton. "I needed a truck because of the rodeo school, but I also wanted something comfortable. So I bought this."

Of course, that had been in the days when he'd been making good money. Still, he liked his truck and planned on keeping it.

"Well, I think it's practical and yet decadent." She laughed. "Yes, that's you all right."

He loved the sound of her laughter. So beautiful. So sexy. So free.

"I'm not sure whether that's a compliment or an insult," he said.

"Oh, you're sure all right. You always are, Jared."

Yeah, he usually was sure of himself. But Leigh confused the hell out of him. He knew what he wanted. What he wanted her to feel for him. What he wanted them to be together.

But for the first time in his life, he was unsure how to get what he wanted. Sure, his plan seemed to be working so far, but it was like walking through a minefield. One wrong step and *kapow!* That would be that.

For the rest of the drive, he and Leigh discussed the parade. Despite a bumpy start, things were coming along.

"Thanks for letting us use your barn to keep the floats in," Leigh said.

"No problem. I'm sure my horses will find it entertaining. And it will give them a break from trying to learn to dance."

"Any luck with that whole 'Hokey Pokey' thing? Are they taking to it?" she asked with a giggle.

"Oddly enough, no." They reached Paxton, so he headed toward Leigh's house. "And they didn't like the whole potty training idea, either. Sorry."

Leigh giggled again. "Darn. Oh well. At least you tried."

He slowly turned his truck into the driveway of Leigh's house, very reluctant to see the evening end. After shutting off the engine, he glanced at her and felt compelled to say, "I want you to know, I didn't mean to ruin your date. It just happened."

She pushed open her door and light flooded the cab of the truck. For a second, she just looked at him. Then she leaned over and kissed him. Hard.

This was the very last thing he'd expected her to do. But never one to miss an opportunity or to question his good luck, Jared wrapped his arms around Leigh and kissed her back.

Who cared why she'd kissed him? He sure

didn't, especially when she lightly brushed the tip of her tongue across his lips.

Yeow.

Jared spent a long, long time kissing Leigh, and when she finally pulled away from him, he grinned. Man, that had been one hell of a kiss.

"Why'd you kiss me?" he couldn't help asking.

Leigh batted her eyelashes. "Why, gee whiz, I didn't mean to kiss you. It just happened."

Even though she was pretending to be unaffected by the kiss, her voice was warm and raspy. She was every bit as turned on as he was.

Good.

With a flirty wave, she hopped out of his truck and headed toward her house. When she reached the porch, she glanced over her shoulder and said, "Oh, and be careful with that popcorn in your new truck."

Then she unlocked her door and went inside.

For a second, he just looked at the closed door. Then he studied the box of popcorn next to him on the seat. The bottom was gooey. Thankfully it hadn't hurt the upholstery. But his bomber jacket would never be the same.

Neither would he after that kiss.

"I THINK YOU'RE MISSING a golden opportunity," Leigh's sister-in-law Megan said as she took the rolls out of the oven. "If you like Jared, you should let him know."

"I don't like Jared. Not in the way you mean."

Hailey laughed. "Please. I saw the way you acted around him the last time he was in town. You more than like him." She grinned at Erin and Megan. "Do you think there will be another wedding soon?"

Leigh snorted. "As if."

These women were demented. Leigh wouldn't have come to dinner with her family tonight if she'd known they were going to act this way.

Not that they ever behaved themselves. This was the Barrett clan. Even the ladies who were Barretts by marriage seemed to be developing ornery streaks.

Erin still had a golden-peachy tan from her honeymoon, so Leigh wasn't a bit surprised when she said, "You can't stop love."

Leigh groaned. "From this moment on, no more talk about love and marriage or I'm leaving, got it?"

All three of her sisters-in-law looked at her for a moment. Then they smiled. Sweet, smug, annoying-as-all-get-out smiles.

"Fine," Megan said. "We won't discuss love or marriage."

"Can we still talk about Jared?" Hailey asked. "I mean you keep telling us you have no intention of falling in love with him, and you'll never want to marry him, right? So it's still okay to talk about him, isn't it?"

Before Leigh could answer, Trent, the youngest Barrett brother and Erin's husband, entered the kitchen. "What are you ladies talking about?"

"We're not talking about love or marriage," Erin told Trent, leaning up and kissing him. "And we're not sure yet whether we can talk about Jared, either."

Trent grinned. "I'm lost. I haven't a clue what you're talking about, or rather not talking about, but Chase wanted me to let you know the steaks will be ready in a couple of minutes."

On his way out the door to the patio, he grabbed one of the rolls in the bowl near Leigh. "Oh, even if it's not okay to talk about Jared, I sure hope it's okay to talk *to* him since he's joining us for dinner."

Leigh shook her head. She'd planned for this possibility. Since Sunday dinner with her family was a tradition, she knew there was a chance Jared would try to crash it. So she'd made certain he would be busy. "No. No, he isn't. I made certain he couldn't come."

Megan moved forward and gave her a questioning look. "How?"

"He has a date tonight."

Now Hailey walked over to stand by her. "How do you know that?"

"Because I set it up. I'm helping Jared find dates."

Trent laughed. "Well, you're not doing a very

good job, because the lady you set him up with called this afternoon and said she couldn't make it. Something about *one* of her ex-husbands stopping by unexpectedly.''

Now Erin joined the group. ''One of her ex-husbands? Leigh, how many times has the woman been married?''

Leigh sighed. Sheesh. ''I don't know. Two or three times, I guess.''

''Which is it? Two or three?'' Erin asked.

The back door to the kitchen opened and Chase entered, carrying a serving platter piled high with steaks. Behind him came Nathan…talking to Jared.

''This woman's been married six times,'' Chase said, shooting a nasty look at Leigh. ''And I imagine you knew that when you set Jared up.''

Oh, great. Now they were all going to gang up on her. Looking at Jared, she said, ''You told me to find you women who were interested in marriage. Trisha is definitely interested in marriage.''

Jared gave her a lopsided grin. ''I said interested in marriage, not interested in making a career out of marriage. If I didn't know better, I'd start to think you didn't want to help me find my soul mate.''

Like spectators at a tennis match, all of her family's heads swiveled as they turned to look at her. Leigh groaned. ''Hardly. You yourself have pointed out a couple of times that I'm bad at picking dates.

Think about it. If I pick lousy ones for me, why wouldn't I also pick lousy ones for you?''

Without waiting for his answer, she grabbed the bowl of rolls and carried them into the dining room. She knew her response wouldn't slow her family down for long, but at least it would buy her a little time.

Personally she was thrilled Jared hadn't even gone out with Trisha. She'd been a little worried about that. Ever since their kiss on Friday night, she'd decided she wasn't trying hard enough to get him to come around to her way of thinking.

Okay, so he wanted to settle down. But did it really have to be right away? And sure, he said he was done with his wild oats days, but maybe with the right enticement, he might consider spreading around just a few more of those oats.

At least it was worth a try. She'd failed last summer, but that didn't mean she couldn't give it another shot. Since she was stuck working with him anyway, she might as well enjoy herself.

It didn't take long before the rest of the group came out of the kitchen. Thankfully they were carrying food and for a while only talked about dinner and work and nice, normal, nonaggravating subjects.

Until they all sat down.

''So are you going to keep letting Leigh set you up with women?'' Megan asked as she passed the salad to Jared. "I think she has a solid point about her making poor choices."

Jared glanced at Leigh, a definite twinkle in his brown eyes. "I don't know. I have to agree, she isn't very good at it."

Chase laughed. "Excuse me, but she fixed all of us up and did a darn fine job of it." He nailed Leigh with a direct look. "I think she's just not trying hard enough. I wonder why that is."

Leigh looked at Megan. "You have my sympathy. I didn't realize what a doof my brother was when I fixed you up with him."

Megan laughed. "That's okay. I like doofs."

Deciding the best offense was a good defense, Leigh said, "It's not my turn to fix up Jared. It's his turn to fix me up with one of his friends. Let's see if he's any better at this than I am."

Truthfully she didn't want to go out with one of Jared's friends. Deep down, she was hoping he'd get jealous and call the whole thing off.

Instead he nodded. "That's true. So, Leigh, what are you doing Tuesday night?"

That took her by surprise. Apparently he'd already given this some thought. Darn him. "Why so soon? There's no rush."

"We have the parade meeting tomorrow night, and then we need to start building the floats this weekend. Homecoming is the end of next week. We don't have a lot of time," Jared said. "Besides, he's really anxious to go out with you, so Tuesday seems like the best choice.''

Erin was sitting on Leigh's left and she handed her the tossed salad. ''So are you busy? Are you going to go out with this guy?''

''I'm thinking,'' Leigh said.

Wow, Tuesday was so soon. She didn't have time to really think this over, to dangle it in front of Jared and try to make him jealous.

But since her entire blasted family was looking at her, waiting for an answer, she sighed. ''Fine. I'll go out with this guy. But tell him I can't stay out late because Wednesday is a school day.''

''Duly noted,'' Jared said. Then he smiled. One of those I-know-something-you-don't-know smiles.

Leigh started to tell him this better not be a joke when she noticed that Megan was almost as green as the lettuce in the salad. ''Hey, Megan, are you okay? You look odd.''

Megan didn't say a word. Instead she jumped from her chair and sprinted out of the room. Chase was right behind her, leaving the rest of them staring at each other.

Stunned, Leigh spun around to stare at Nathan and Trent. ''She's pregnant?''

''I don't know.'' Nathan looked at Hailey. ''Is she?''

Hailey shrugged. ''Beats me.'' She looked at Erin. ''Have you heard anything?''

Erin shook her head. "Nope." She looked at Trent. "You?"

"Not a word," Trent said.

Something in the way Jared was sitting so silently made Leigh look at him. Unlike the rest of them, he didn't seem a bit surprised. "You know something, don't you?"

Jared merely said, "You should ask Chase and Megan."

Leigh gaped at him. "You *do* know something. How come out of everyone in this room you're the first to know that Megan is pregnant?"

"I didn't say she's pregnant," Jared countered. "You said that."

"But you didn't say she isn't pregnant." Leigh leaned back in her chair. Chase sure had come to like Jared if he'd already told the other man about Megan's pregnancy—even before he'd told his own family.

Chase came back into the room then, and everyone asked almost in unison, "Is Megan pregnant?"

Chase got a dopey grin on his face. "Yep."

Hailey and Erin went after Megan, leaving Leigh alone with her brothers and Jared.

"Wow, a baby," she said as she walked over and hugged Chase. "Congrats."

Chase hugged her back. "Thanks."

Leigh found her gaze drifting to Jared, and found him looking straight at her.

For a split second, she could read it all in his eyes. His desire to be in Chase's place, happily married with a baby on the way.

Understanding hit Leigh like a right hook. Jared was trying to get her to change her mind about falling in love and getting married. Here she was going to all this trouble to get him to change his mind, while at the same time, he was trying to change hers.

And since he was trying to change her mind about dating and having fun, that meant that whoever her blind date was with Tuesday night was probably going to be missing his front teeth and apt to scratch himself while they were being served the entrée.

Leigh bit back a laugh. They were playing a game. Winner takes all.

What Jared hadn't counted on was that she was very, very good at games. And she wasn't about to lose this one.

ON MONDAY NIGHT, JARED had barely entered the gym when Mary Monroe cornered him. "Do you know how to make a giant X on me?"

Okay, he'd come to expect a lot of weird things from this town, but he hadn't expected Mary's question.

"Maybe your husband should do that instead," he said when she kept staring at him, obviously expecting an answer.

"No, he can't. Ted's going to ask Leigh to make a giant *R* on him, and I need someone to make a giant *X* on me or it won't be fair."

Dang. At times like this, he couldn't help thinking his brain had been addled a little too much while on the rodeo circuit.

He raised his hands. "Mary, I give up. I haven't a clue what you're asking me to do or even why you'd want me to do it."

Mary give him a look that made it clear she thought he was denser than a log. "Ted and I are going to walk in the parade, and since we own the drugstore, we thought it would be cute if he had an *R* on him and I had an *X* on me. We thought we'd wear black leotards and have the letters written on us in chalk."

Oh, now it made some sort of twisted sense. "I see," he said, although the thought of Ted and Mary Monroe walking around in leotards was enough to make him shudder.

"I have a thought, rather than having the letters drawn on you, why don't you wear sandwich boards? That way, you'll have signs both on your fronts and your back so people watching the parade can clearly see you. And you won't need anyone to draw letters on you. You can make the signs yourself."

Not to mention, the whole town would be spared the view of the couple barely dressed.

"I don't know." She turned to look at the man who'd wandered over to join them, Earl Guthrie, mayor of Paxton. "What do you think, Earl? Should Ted and I wear a sandwich board?"

Earl took off his glasses and slowly cleaned them on his shirt. He appeared to be giving Mary's question serious consideration, but Jared had a feeling the older man was just stalling for time.

Finally Earl put his glasses back on and then looked at Mary. "I think a sandwich board would be the best approach. It certainly would be easier for people in the crowd to see. The chalk could rub off you."

Apparently since Earl was the one now offering the opinion, Mary decided to accept it.

"Yes, I see what you mean. I don't want everyone confused as to what Ted and I are doing," she said. "Well, let me go tell Ted so he doesn't waste his time asking Leigh to write on him."

As she walked away, Earl said, "I think the entire town owes us a hardy thanks, don't you?"

Jared nodded. "Absolutely."

He watched Mary make her way to the other side of the room, and then his gaze landed on Leigh. She looked so pretty tonight, with her dark hair pulled back from her face with clips. She was laughing at something someone had said, and Jared couldn't help smiling.

Damn, she was beautiful. And that kiss she'd given him had rocked him clear to his soul. Now, more than ever, he was determined to work things out between them.

"I guess I'm standing here talking to myself," Earl noted. "I don't think you've heard a word I've said. You're too busy making cow eyes at Leigh."

"Hey, I'm not making cow eyes," Jared said. "I was just..." He floundered for an excuse. Finally he sighed. "Sorry, Earl, didn't mean to ignore you."

Earl grinned. "That's quite all right. I was young once upon a time. I know how difficult it is for a man to concentrate when a certain woman is around. Why, one time, I was so besotted that I forgot where I parked my car. No matter how hard I tried, I couldn't remember where I'd left the thing."

"What happened?"

"I married her." Earl chuckled at the odd look Jared gave him. "I mean the woman, not the car. I eventually found my car three blocks from my house. Why I left it there I'll never know. Must have been too busy thinking about love."

"Hey, don't you go around town telling stories to everyone that I'm in love and especially not who I was looking at," Jared said. "I'll get in trouble."

"Secrets stay secrets with me," Earl said.

Jared believed that. He'd always liked and admired Earl, and the rest of the town must have, too, because the man kept getting elected mayor.

"I'm having enough trouble getting the people in this town to forgive my past indiscretions," Jared explained. "I keep getting them pointed out to me everywhere I go. Guess I underestimated how long memories last."

Earl scratched his bald head and looked thoughtful. "Well, some folks must be warming up to you a mite. Take Mary Monroe. She just asked you to draw a big *X* on her body. Seems pretty warmed up to me."

Jared laughed. The older man had a point. "Maybe she thought I'd be the only one willing to do something so outrageous."

"Could be. But don't let the gossip get you down. Hang in there. Sooner or later, I'm sure these folks will thaw and stop bringing up every little thing you ever did wrong. You're one of us. You were born here in Paxton. Raised here. And you showed a lot of gumption moving back." He fixed Jared with a steady look. "I admire gumption."

Jared really appreciated the older man's support. "Thanks, Earl."

Earl patted him on the shoulder. "You bet. I'm glad you came home." Then, with a conspiratorial smile and a quick glance at Leigh, he added, "And good luck with all your endeavors. I have a feeling you've chosen a tough goal with that one, but it will be worth it. You'll see. My Fran took some convincing, but we've been together almost fifty years."

With that, Earl wandered off. Jared looked over at Leigh. Yep, he'd chosen a tough goal with her. But as Earl said, it would be worth it, no matter what it took.

That kiss had convinced him he couldn't give up.

7

LEIGH OPENED HER FRONT DOOR and wasn't a bit surprised to see Jared standing on the doorstep.

"I don't believe this. You're my date?" Although she tried to sound disappointed and upset, it wasn't easy. She'd been hoping Jared would come himself instead of sending one of his friends. The more time she spent with Jared, the more she wanted him. So much so that she'd given up the idea of enjoying her freedom with other guys.

For the moment, the only guy she wanted to be with was Jared.

He leaned against the doorjamb, looking too sexy for words in his jeans and T-shirt. A slow, lazy grin crossed his face. "I ran into a little trouble thinking of guys who'd be willing to go out with you."

"Hey!" She shoved his arm. "A lot of men find me very attractive."

Men like him. She could tell from the appreciative way his gaze skimmed her little black dress that he was enjoying the view very much. Yahoo! Looked like seducing Jared wasn't going to be too difficult after all.

"Oh, you won't get any argument from me. You're good-looking, but at times you can be..."

When he didn't continue, she prompted, "Witty? Enticing? Intriguing?"

He chuckled. "Stubborn. So I couldn't fix you up with just anyone. He had to be tough."

Leigh rolled her eyes. "Give me a break. You didn't even try to find me a date, did you?"

"No. I did. But the problem was, how to find you a date that was as...unique as the ones you found for me. Most of the guys I know are fairly normal. Although Barry Olsen can make the exotic dancer tattoo on his belly shimmy like a real woman. I considered setting you up with him, but he's up in Wyoming at the moment. Sorry."

Pretending to be disappointed, she said, "Some friend you are. Well, I guess I'll see you at the parade meeting tomorrow night. Remember, everyone's coming to your place to start assembling the floats. And whatever you do, keep an eye on Tommy and Kate. Those two disappeared twice last night. Who knows what they were up to."

Jared winked. "I have a fairly good idea what they were up to."

"Yeah, well, they need to cut it out, so help me keep tabs on them, okay?"

He nodded. "Fine. But what about tonight? You're not seriously going to stay home. Not when I'm standing here, more than willing to be your date."

Leigh put her hands on her hips and slowly studied his clothes. Although he looked gorgeous in his jeans and T-shirt, he was hardly dressed to match her.

"Gee, as tempting as it sounds to go to the local hamburger joint and have a milkshake, I think I'll pass."

"Whoa. Whoa." Jared stopped the door from closing. "Come on. Change out of that slinky dress and into jeans, and I'll take you for a ride on my Harley."

That made her stop. Slowly she turned back to face him. Now this could definitely work in her favor.

"Will you teach me how to drive it?" she asked.

Jared laughed. "You're kidding, right?"

Leigh reached out and tugged the door free from his grip. "Say good night, Kendrick."

Once again, Jared stopped her from shutting the door. "Fine. Fine. If you're serious about learning to drive one, I'll run you through the basics tonight, then we'll go to dinner. If you still want to learn after that, I'll teach you once we're done with the homecoming parade. Deal?"

Leigh grinned. This was perfect. Absolutely perfect. "Good. And just so you know, I'm holding you to that promise. Learning to ride a motorcycle is one of the three things I most want to do now that I have my freedom."

He gave her a devilish smile. "Of course, I now have to ask what the other two things are."

Leigh didn't plan on telling all of her secrets at once. She had him intrigued. She planned on keeping him that way.

As far as she was concerned, this game they were playing had just started. He might think he could change her mind about settling down, but he was wrong. But that didn't mean she couldn't change his mind about having an affair.

She was very good at getting what she wanted.

"Give me a moment and I'll go change my clothes." Without waiting for his answer, she sprinted toward her bedroom. She knew exactly what to wear that would get Jared's motor racing. Tugging on her favorite snug jeans, she added the new red sweater she'd bought last week. The sweater was a little too short to reach the top of her jeans, so a small strip of her stomach showed between the two.

That ought to get him.

Wandering out a few minutes later, she found Jared prowling her living room like a bored lion. He turned when she entered, then froze.

His gaze was heated as he studied her outfit. "Man, you look…" He blinked. Twice. "Good. You look good."

The way he said the word *good* made it clear he meant she looked hot. "Thanks."

Biting back a smile, she walked over and tugged

her keys out of her purse. Stuffing the key to her
house in the front pocket of her jeans, she then
turned to face him.

"So where are we having dinner?"

Jared's attention was riveted to the small strip of
skin showing between her jeans and her top.

"I can't help wondering if your belly button is
pierced," he murmured.

Since the top of her jeans just covered her navel,
she knew he couldn't see. At first, she started to
tell him no, but then a better idea occurred to her.

"I guess you'll have to find out for yourself,"
she teased, liking the way he looked at her with
such heat and intent in his gaze.

A slow seductive smile crossed his face. "Is that
a challenge?"

She tipped her head and pretended to consider
his question. "Take it any way you want."

Jared chuckled. "Tonight should be interesting."

She couldn't agree more. Wanting to get started,
she reached over and grabbed his hand. "Come on.
I want you to teach me how to drive a motorcycle
before it gets dark."

Jared wrapped his hand around hers, and then to
her surprise, tugged her close. Leigh's breath
caught in her throat and she tipped her head to look
up at him.

"Just a second, okay?" His voice was soft, and
smooth, and deep, and Leigh's heart pounded in her

chest. Ever so slowly, he leaned down until his lips were a whisper away from hers.

"I wonder if anything else on you is pierced," he said softly.

Then he kissed her, his tongue gliding inside her mouth. With an eek, Leigh wrapped her arms around his neck, and kissed him back. Wow. This man could kiss. She couldn't remember ever being kissed so thoroughly.

In fact, she was so busy kissing Jared that it took a minute for her to realize that the hand he had at her waist had dipped beneath the waistband of her jeans and was now exploring her navel. At his touch, the air seemed to catch in Leigh's throat.

As his wandering hand continued to explore, she did the only thing a self-respecting modern female could do. She slipped the fingers of one of her hands under the waistband of his jeans.

Jared broke the kiss and with a chuckle, said, "Guess we both now know the other doesn't have a pierced navel."

She flashed him a grin. "Or a pierced tongue."

FOR THE TENTH OR ELEVENTH time, Jared shook his head. "No, Leigh, that's the brake. You just don't seem to be paying attention."

Man, that was an understatement. No matter how many times he ran her through the parts of the motorcycle, she didn't seem to remember them. Normally he'd think it was because she really wasn't interested in learning.

But tonight, he figured she was as distracted as he was. That kiss had been wild. And they both knew good and well that a kiss like that promised more to come later.

He could hardly wait.

Walking up behind her, he wrapped his arms around her waist. "Tell me another one of those things you've always wanted to do," he whispered in her ear. "Maybe we'll have better luck with it."

She leaned back against him. "Before I do, I want you to know I won't marry you."

He'd expected her to mention this sooner or later. He knew very well how she currently felt about love and marriage. That didn't mean he wasn't sure she'd eventually change her mind.

"Did I ask you to marry me? Seems to me we were talking about something else," he pointed out.

Leigh turned within the circle of his arms until she faced him. "Okay. So we're clear on this. If we're going to do any more of what we were doing earlier, I want it clearly understood that we're just messing around."

Jared leaned down until his forehead rested against hers. "Yes. I agree. We're just messing around. Now tell me another thing on your list."

He must have sounded pretty convincing, because she said, "I want to go to one of those wild, crazy nightclubs in Dallas and dance."

That was something he could easily do. "Fine. Let's go then."

With a squeal, Leigh threw her arms around his neck and kissed him hard. "I like a man who is so agreeable."

Jared got on his motorcycle, and then helped her on as well. Yep, he planned on being agreeable. Very, very agreeable. So agreeable that pretty soon, Leigh would fall in love with him—whether she wanted to or not.

Then they'd talk about that whole getting married thing again.

He handed her one of the helmets, then put on his. "Wear that. You may want to use your brains later on in life."

She laughed but did as he said. "Har-har."

"Now hold on to me," he told her. As soon as she wrapped her arms around his waist, he started the engine. Leigh immediately scooted closer to him and held him tighter. He loved the feeling of her pressed against him. So soft and warm.

"Drive really fast," she said into his left ear.

Jared chuckled. Leave it to Leigh to want to be fast and wild. He headed out of town and more or less did what she asked. It would take them over an hour to get to Dallas if they didn't get stopped for speeding. And he didn't want to get stopped. Not tonight. He had too many things planned.

So he kept Leigh moving. Through dinner at a cozy little Italian restaurant, then club hopping in the West End. When they ended up at a completely insane place in Deep Ellum, he kept her close. Speaking of piercings, he and Leigh seemed to be the only people who didn't have their lips and noses pierced.

"This place makes me feel a hundred years old," Jared yelled to Leigh.

Leigh was standing in the middle of the dance floor, staring at people as they went by. "I know what you mean." When a man danced by with hair spiked so high it looked like spears, she shuddered. "Let's go home."

About time. Jared snagged her hand and pulled her through the crowd. He'd been waiting to head home for the past two hours.

When they reached his Harley, he once again handed her a helmet. She flashed him a sexy grin.

"Thanks for making two of my three wishes come true," she told him. Then she leaned against him and kissed his chin. "I'm really enjoying this date. It's so much more fun when you're part of the date rather than merely ruining it."

He chuckled. "Gee, thanks. I'll keep that in mind."

"Have I told you tonight that I think you're a really nice guy?"

Her compliment caught him by surprise. He hon estly couldn't remember anyone ever calling him nice and sincerely meaning it. "I don't think many people will agree with you on that one."

"They will. Eventually."

Unable to resist, he leaned down and kissed her. He wrapped his arms around her and poured all the love and desire he felt for this woman into his kiss. It must have been pretty good because several people in the parking lot started hooting and hollering at them, cheering him on.

He broke the kiss when a kid with purple and pink hair slapped him on the back and told him to "go for it, dude."

"Um, thanks," Jared told the enthusiastic spectator.

Leigh was laughing as they got on the motorcycle. "This place is insane."

"Many days Paxton doesn't seem much better."

She leaned against him, wrapping her arms around his waist. "So are you going to do what he suggested?"

Jared wanted to think he knew what she was talking about, but he'd learned long ago to never make assumptions when it came to Leigh.

"What would that be?"

"Go for it, dude. I think it sounds like a wonderful idea."

Jared grinned. "Sounds like a plan to me."

THE SECOND JARED TURNED OFF the Harley and helped her down, she wrapped herself around him. No sense giving him the chance to change his mind.

Although from the way he was kissing her back, he wasn't changing his mind anytime soon.

"Where's the key?" he asked between kisses. "I don't want the entire town of Paxton watching us."

"It's almost midnight. Most of Paxton is asleep," she teased, reaching into her pocket to get the key. It wasn't there, so she tried the other front pocket.

"Uh-oh."

Jared had been kissing her neck, but now he leaned back to look at her in the light from her front porch. "Uh-oh, what?"

"Uh-oh, I seem to have lost the key. Must have been when I was dancing at one of those places in Dallas. Well, we won't worry about it. My address isn't on it, so no one will ever know what door it fits. Let's go back to kissing some more."

Jared blew out a deep breath and gently held her away. "Seriously, we can't stand in front of your house doing this. Since you're trying to land a teaching job, I doubt if necking with the town's bad boy will help."

He had to be kidding. "You're not changing your mind, are you? Please tell me you're not changing your mind."

"No. But before we go any further, let's head to my house."

She put her hands on her hips. "That's too far away. Let's just break in."

"I'm not breaking into your house," he said. "Who else has a key?"

She held up one hand and ticked off their options. "My big brother Chase. My other big brother Nathan. And my last big brother Trent, who also happens to be the chief of police. Which one do you think we should call?"

"None of them," Jared muttered. "One look at the two of us, and whichever of your brothers stops by will string me up from the nearest tree."

"You're probably right there. At the least, they'd insist you head on home before they unlock my house." She glanced around. Of all the stupid times to lose her key. She wanted inside this house now.

She knew if she didn't think fast, Jared would change his mind. He'd say it was for the best, and then he'd kiss her and get all noble, call one of her brothers and leave once she was inside her house. All alone. And frustrated.

Not on his life. Even though he was pretending he didn't care that all they were having was a fling, she knew he felt differently. She could feel what he felt in his touch, see it in his gaze.

And sure, she cared for him, too. Not in the "till-death-do-us-part way," but deeply. He probably wouldn't believe her if she told him this, but she wouldn't want to make love with him if she didn't care about him.

But caring and marrying were two *verrrrry* different concepts.

Jared was looking at his watch. "Leigh, it's late. Maybe we should do this some other time. Why don't we call one of your brothers? I'll stick around until they show up and let you in."

Leigh snorted. "As if. You said you'd make love with me, and I'm not letting you off the hook, buddy."

Jared chuckled. "Takes a particular kind of woman to say something like that to a man."

Leigh nudged past him. "Yeah, well, I expect you to honor your promise." She tugged on the doorknob. "Stupid door. Stupid key."

When she glanced back at him, he was studying her. "When exactly did I promise to make love with you?"

He seriously couldn't have changed his mind, could he? She looked him up and down. From what she could see, he still was very interested in the whole making-love idea.

"Hey, you agreed to go for it, dude. If that isn't a promise, I don't know what is." She tugged on the doorknob again. "Besides I bought a brand-new red lace bra today that I'm currently wearing and I'd like your opinion on it."

Jared made a groaning noise and took a step toward her. Leigh laughed and held up one hand. "Down, boy."

Then she quickly amended, "Forget I said that.

But give me a second here. The locks on my house aren't very good. I know you know how to break in.''

He frowned. ''What do you mean the locks aren't very good? Leigh, even though you live in a small town, you have to be careful. First thing tomorrow, I'm changing your locks. You're going to be safe.''

She bobbed her head. ''Good idea. You do that. Right after you break in tonight and check out my red bra.''

Jared glanced around. ''I don't know.''

Oh, for pity sakes. ''Hello,'' she said, then once he was looking at her, pulled aside the neckline of her sweater and flashed him a little peek at her bra. ''Passionate lovemaking awaits inside.''

Jared made another groaning sound, then immediately set about examining the lock. Eureka. Nothing like flashing a man your undies to get him in gear.

''Which door is easier, the front or the back?'' he asked, and she didn't miss that his voice was raspy with desire.

''I guess they're both the same. I've never rated them on an easy-to-jimmy scale so it's hard to say.''

''Very funny.'' He examined the front door. ''Opening this will be a piece of cake. You keep an eye out.''

''You bet.'' Then just to make certain he didn't lose his motivation, she proceeded to whisper naughty suggestions in his ear the entire time he was fiddling with the lock.

"We're going to get caught," he told her, but not with any conviction in his voice.

"I'm breaking into my own house and everyone around here knows it's my house. What's the worst they can do to me?" She leaned forward and nibbled on his earlobe. "Put me under house arrest? I'd welcome it at this moment."

Before Leigh could torment him much more, he threw open her front door and tugged her inside.

"That is the worst excuse for a lock I've ever seen," he told her as he pushed the door closed and relocked it.

Leigh turned on the lamp by the couch, then pulled her red sweater over her head. She stood before him in a skimpy red lace bra and low-riding jeans. "Was it worth it?"

Jared grinned. "In the morning, remind me to write that company and thank them for making such a crummy lock."

She grinned back. Tonight was going to be serious fun.

JARED HAD NEVER BEEN so turned on. Sure, Leigh was gorgeous and sexy and he could hardly wait to make love with her.

But he was also in love with her, which made tonight even more special. He was going to do his best to convey how he felt about her in his lovemaking. That was, of course, if he didn't go insane with lust first.

Any plans he had for taking it slow and easy were being completely undermined by Leigh. Still flashing him a sexy grin, she unzipped her jeans and shimmied out of them.

She had on red lace panties that matched the bra.

Slow and easy was out of the question now. Jared was across the room and had her in his arms before he knew what hit him. He kissed her like a man possessed, unable to get enough of her.

"Which way to your bedroom?" he finally muttered between kisses. "All the blood has left my brain and I've lost my sense of direction."

Leigh giggled and pointed down the hallway. "You poor baby. I'll help you find the way."

Jared followed her, dropping kisses on her bare shoulders as they walked. When they finally reached her bedroom, he yanked his T-shirt over his head and dropped it on the chair by the door.

Leigh ran her fingers down his chest. "Do you know that most of the female population of Paxton rearranged their schedules so they could watch you paint the water tower without your shirt on?"

Yeah, he'd known. Not at first, but then when he'd seen a crowd forming after a couple of days, he'd known he had an audience.

And because he'd enjoyed upsetting the good people of Paxton, he'd played to the crowd. He'd taken off his shirt slowly. Flexed his muscles a lot.

It had been fun. But it would have been more fun if Leigh had been watching, too.

"You were never part of the crowd," he said. "Guess you weren't interested back then."

Leigh rolled her eyes and popped open the top button of his jeans. "I was just more subtle. I worked in the law offices across the street from the water tower the entire summer. I had the best seat in the house, and you put on quite a show."

He liked knowing even then she'd been interested in him. That was a good sign. A very good sign.

And he would have teased her about watching him, except she chose that moment to slide down the zipper on his jeans, caressing him as she went.

He'd died and gone to heaven.

"Leigh, I'm not sure how much longer I can wait," he said, absolutely serious. The sensation of her hands touching him was driving him insane. He wanted her. Right now.

She leaned up and kissed him. "So what are you waiting for?"

Good question. He scooped her up and settled her in the middle of the bed. It didn't take long to pull off her bra and panties. And it took even less time to shuck off his jeans and boxers.

"I can tell this isn't your first rodeo," she teased.

But she was wrong. Sure, he'd had sex before, but until tonight, he'd never made love. He softly kissed her. Even though he knew she might get upset, he had to tell her how he felt.

He held her gaze as he said, "This is different, Leigh."

For a moment, he thought she'd protest. But then she smiled a siren's smile. "Show me how it's different."

So he did. With his hands and his lips, he caressed and loved her soft body. He fanned the flames of her desire until she said, "Enough, enough. Now I can't wait any longer."

He felt exactly the same way. "Works for me." Then suddenly, he remembered. "Damn."

She stared at him. "You'd better explain that comment quickly."

With a sigh, he admitted, "I don't have any condoms with me."

Before he could say another word, she crawled over him and dashed into the bathroom.

"I've got the situation covered," she hollered.

He knew it was stupid and juvenile, but he wasn't thrilled knowing Leigh kept condoms on hand. And what was even more stupid and juvenile was how thrilled he was when she reappeared with a brand-new, completely unopened box.

Rather than patiently opening it, though, she tore it open and quickly did indeed, have things er, um, covered.

"There. We're all set," she announced. Then

with a mischievous grin, she said, "Now where were we?"

Jared was delighted to show her. He quickly joined them and then settled into a rhythm that soon had both of them gasping for breath.

He prolonged the pleasure as long as he could, but all too soon, they both shattered. Once his heart rate had slowed, he opened his eyes and looked down at her. He expected her to make some sort of teasing remark, but instead, she merely touched the side of his face gently.

For one split second as he looked into her eyes, he clearly saw what she felt for him.

Leigh Barrett might not know it yet, but she was in love with him. Now all he had to do was get her to face the truth.

8

"YOU HAVE A HICKEY," Hailey said.

Leigh, Erin and Hailey were helping with last-minute touches on some of the floats. The parade was rapidly approaching, and at the moment, Leigh was painting what she hoped looked like a panther on the side of the float Nathan's business was entering.

Leaning back, she surveyed her handiwork. Yep. It looked like one big, black ferocious…inkblot.

"I have an idea. Let's make Nathan's float a giant Dalmatian. Then my black blobs will make sense," Leigh suggested.

Hailey tapped her on the shoulder. "You're ignoring my comment. Young lady, you have a hickey on your neck. Where in the world would you get something like that?"

"Hickeys Are Us," she said, leaning back and surveying the panthers Erin was painting. They looked like panthers. "I nominate Erin to do all the panther painting from now on. Who seconds my nomination?"

She glanced expectantly at Hailey, who merely gave her a pointed look. This was the problem with being friends with the wives of your brothers. If you told them something, then you were also telling your brothers. And she, for one, did not want her brothers knowing she'd spent the last evening having unbelievable fun with Jared.

"Hailey, if you don't get back to work, I'm going to tell Nathan that you're goofing off and that I need more volunteers from his company to help," Leigh said.

Hailey laughed. "Oh, right. Tell him that. And I'll tell him that you have a big hickey on the side of your neck and a goofy smile on your face. He's a bright man. He'll quickly figure out what's going on."

Leigh snorted. "Pulleese. It took him forever to figure out he was in love with you."

Erin walked over and poured more black paint in her tray. As she was about to walk away, she said, "Hey, Leigh, you have a big red mark on your neck."

"It's a birthmark," Leigh muttered.

"It's a hickey," Hailey corrected.

Erin tipped her head and studied it. "You know, I don't think so. I think it's beard burn." She looked at Hailey. "I think someone who has a beard was kissing Leigh's neck recently."

Hailey leaned over and inspected the mark. "I think you're right. And it seems to disappear beneath the collar of her shirt, which leads me to believe it's on more than just her neck. Now who does

Leigh know who would have a beard and would want to kiss her?''

Erin tipped her head. ''That's a good question, but I have no idea. The last I heard, she wasn't seeing anyone.'' She examined Leigh's neck again. ''But she sure is now. And he certainly is attracted to our Leigh.''

''Cute. Very cute.'' Standing, Leigh brushed off her jeans. ''Since I'm no use at painting the panthers, and I have no intention of telling either of you anything, I think I'll go see if I can help Steve Myerson get his wagon ready to pull Rufus in.''

She was all set to walk away when Hailey said, ''Looks like it won't be long before there's another wedding.''

That stopped her cold. She walked over to where her sisters-in-law were working and said firmly, ''No. Don't even think that. Don't even think about thinking that. In fact, forget you ever knew how to think. There will be no wedding. Got it? I'm just having a little fun. Heck, I haven't even graduated from college yet. I'm not getting married.''

Hailey looked at Erin, who shrugged. ''All I was going to say was that the church books up early. You need to plan these things a long time in advance.''

Grrr. ''Read my lips—there isn't going to be a wedding.''

Once again, she started to walk away when Erin said, ''You know, I didn't want to fall in love. I mean, I really, really didn't. How about you, Hailey?"

Hailey nodded. "Me, neither. I didn't have time to fall in love. I had my life all mapped out. And I was happy. Or at least, I thought I was happy. But then someone convinced me I was being an idiot." She pretended to think. "Now who was that?"

Erin smiled. "I know, it's baffling, isn't it? Who was the person who made certain we all admitted when we'd fallen in love?"

Oh, for pity's sake. "I'm not in love. He's not in love. We're not in love. It's sex. Pure and simple. Now paint some panthers."

Hailey studied Leigh, then finally said, "Okay. If you say this is just about sex, then we'll leave you alone. But remember, life doesn't always work out the way you have planned. You have to be flexible if you don't want happiness to pass you by."

Erin nodded. "I couldn't agree more."

Leigh liked these ladies; she really did. But boy, they were wrong abut her. She was having the time of her life, enjoying her freedom, savoring her independence. She wasn't giving that up for anyone.

Not even for Jared Kendrick.

Deciding the best way to avoid talking about love any more was to, well, avoid it, Leigh headed across the room. Billy had finished his cow car, so she figured she'd go check it out. It wasn't every day you got to see a 1997 sedan decked out like a cow. Udders and all.

Truthfully it had turned out kinda cute. Well, for a cow car. She was all set to walk away when a muted giggle caught her attention. Stopping, she strained to hear over the noise in the barn. Maybe she'd been mistaken.

She took another two steps and heard it again.

Someone was giggling. And they were doing it *inside* the cow.

Oh, for the love of Pete. She needed this aggravation like she needed to go cross-eyed.

Although she didn't want the entire barn to know what was happening, Leigh wanted those two love-struck teenagers out of that car right now. She rapped on the side of the cow. "Get out here."

A couple of "shushes" was all she got in return.

Leigh rapped again. "Tommy and Kate, I know you're in there. Get out now."

She still got no reaction and was about to knock again when Jared wandered over. "You mad at the cow? Maybe I can help improve your mood."

Although she was happy to see him, now was not the time to flirt with Jared. She wanted those kids out of that car right this instant.

"Tommy and Kate are in there." She blew out a breath of disgust. The only saving grace to this mess was that most of the crowd had already left for the evening.

But still, she wasn't in the mood to do this. She glanced at Jared. She was in the mood to do... well, him.

As much as she'd like to, she couldn't think about that right now. She had to do something about Tommy and Kate.

"You can't stay in that cow forever," she pointed out.

With a lot of moaning and groaning, first Tommy, then Kate crawled out from under the tarps covering Billy Joe's car. Predictably the kids looked a mess.

Tommy smoothed his hair away from his face. "Hi, Ms. Barrett. The float looks cool, doesn't it?"

"The only thing that needs to cool around here is you and Kate," Leigh said. "This is crazy. You two need to cut it out." She looked at Kate. "Have you told your father you're seeing Tommy?"

Kate shook her head. "I think he'd have a stroke."

Yes, that was a possibility. "You still have to tell your parents." She looked at Tommy. "You, too."

Tommy groaned and scuffed one sneaker on the ground. "Why? Kate and I are in love. If we tell people, they'll just get all huffy and tell us we're too young to be in love. Then they'll do everything they can to get us to stop seeing each other."

He moved over and draped one arm around Kate's shoulders. "We're old enough to recognize true love when we find it. Not a lot of people can say that, but we can."

Leigh was trying to formulate a response, when Jared jumped in.

"If you're truly in love, you shouldn't be hiding in a cow," Jared told him. "Be proud of what you feel and tell the people in your life. Tommy, your folks love you. So do yours, Kate. I'm sure if you two agree to handle your relationship responsibly, your parents will let you date." He gave Tommy a pointed look. "And responsibly doesn't mean hiding in closets or homecoming floats."

Both Tommy and Kate nodded. "Okay, I'll tell my parents," Kate said. "Dad will have a fit, but he'll probably calm down. Eventually."

Leigh looked at Tommy. "What about you?"

"Yeah, I'll tell them, mostly because then Kate and I can let everyone know we're in love."

In a way, the two of them were really sweet. Of course, Leigh didn't believe for a second what they felt was true love. But they believed it, and she knew no one would be able to change their minds.

"Okay, now that we've settled this, I think both of you need to head home and tell your parents tonight. Frankly I'm tired of hunting you down," Leigh said.

Kate sighed. "Okay. I'll tell Dad. Maybe he won't get so upset if I tell him that one day, Tommy and I are going to get married."

With that, the two teens headed for the door.

"You think ol' Gav is going to be happy to hear

his daughter's planning on marrying Tommy Tate someday?'' Jared asked dryly.

"No. Especially when he figures out that then she'll be Kate Tate."

Jared chuckled. "True. But you can't stop love."

Grrr. Leigh was tired of talking about love. Really tired of it. She glanced around Jared's barn. Her sisters-in-law had obviously been watching the entire confrontation with Tommy and Kate. Oh great. Now they'd quote Jared's comments about love to her.

"I think it's time we sent everyone home," she told him.

Jared nudged her. "Are you going to keep me after, teacher?"

She shouldn't. Considering all the talk about love floating around this barn, she should head on home. But then Jared gave her a slow, sexy grin, and her common sense got vapor-locked by the desire fogging up her brain. Her gaze dropped to his oh-so-delicious mouth.

Yep, there were lots of reasons she should go home alone tonight, but thankfully, not a single one came to mind.

So after Hailey and Erin finally left, laughing and singing "Love is a Many Splendored Thing" off-key, Leigh turned to Jared and said, "Just so you know, I'm not going to fall in love with you."

Jared's expression didn't change a bit. "The thought never crossed my mind."

Oh right, like she believed that. But no matter what he thought, she really wasn't going to fall in love with him.

No matter what he, her family and the population of Paxton thought.

It just wasn't going to happen.

"YOUR PLAN ISN'T WORKING."

Jared had been brushing his favorite horse, Spirit, but now he turned and looked at Trent Barrett. The parade was going to start any second. Leigh's brother should be helping with crowd control.

He glanced at the few folks on the sidewalk and the tons of people lined up in the parade. Okay, so the spectators weren't exactly going to be a problem. But someone had to keep this parade in line so Mary and Ted Monroe walked next to each other and didn't wander off to talk to friends, leaving everyone wondering what the letters on them meant.

And someone needed to tell the band teacher that she could play the "Hokey Pokey" all she wanted, but his horses weren't going to shake it all about.

"What exactly are you talking about?" he asked Trent. "And why aren't you helping Leigh line people up? I'm the end of the parade." He patted Spirit's rump. "Remember?"

"I'll get up there in a second. First, I want to talk to you. Erin told me what you said to Tommy and Kate in the barn. You need to take your own advice. Carpe diem, Jared. Seize the day.''

He'd like to seize the day, but if he did, Leigh would more than likely seize his neck—and squeeze. "Things aren't that simple."

"If you love her, tell her so," Trent said. "That's pretty simple."

"It's not simple at all." Jared brushed Spirit a couple more times. He'd like to tell her, but she kept making it crystal clear that she didn't want to discuss love. Even when they were making mind-blowing love, she didn't want the words.

Getting her to admit she loved him was going to take some doing.

Trent sighed. "You know, I went through the same sort of thing with Erin. I fell for her a long time before she fell for me. It was tough. But I hung in there. I let her know how I felt, and I stood my ground. You need to tell Leigh you love her and that you're going to keep loving her whether she likes it or not."

Jared chuckled. "That ought to show her."

Reaching into his shirt pocket, Trent pulled out a pair of sunglasses. He slipped them on, then said to Jared, "No one ever said love was easy. But it is worth all the trouble. Man, is it ever."

With that, he headed toward the front of the parade. Jared could hear him shouting at the panthers from Bud's Boats and Baits to keep their paws off the panthers from Patty's Powder and Primp.

But at the moment, his mind wasn't on the parade. It was on what Trent had said. Should he stand his ground and confront Leigh about his feelings? Would it do any good or would it make Custer's last stand look successful?

He turned and told the other two riders, Stan and Dwayne, to saddle up. He'd have to think about what to do with Leigh later. Right now, he had a parade to ride in.

Even if his horses still couldn't do the "Hokey Pokey."

"BEFORE WE BEGIN TONIGHT'S halftime show, I'd like to take a minute to recognize some of our volunteers," Gavin said into the microphone.

Leigh rocked her weight from heel to heel as Gavin's speech droned on. She didn't know why she had to be here. She'd already done her part. She'd coordinated the parade yesterday, which if she did say so herself, had turned out great. No one got hurt. Everyone had fun.

What else could you ask from a successful parade?

Tonight was the homecoming game, followed by the student dance. Then tomorrow night, the alumni got their chance to pretend they still were young at their own dance.

But her part was done. And she wanted to go home and be with Jared.

She glanced at the man in question. He looked

as anxious to leave as she was. Good. That meant they'd have another amazing night together.

She could hardly wait.

Unfortunately Gavin had other ideas. He kept talking, and talking, and talking. Sigh. He first explained how important homecoming was to Paxton High. Then he thanked everyone who'd helped make this weekend so exciting. Then he thanked the people of Paxton for supporting the homecoming efforts.

And finally he thanked the Paxton Panthers themselves, who so far were ahead 21 to 3.

Wahoo. Go Panthers.

Finally the speech ended, and Leigh and Jared headed off the platform.

"It didn't take me that long to finish high school," Jared murmured in her ear.

She laughed, and was all set to see if he wanted to cut out and head back to her place when Gavin jogged over. "Glad I caught you two. I want to talk about Kate."

Uh-oh. Leigh shifted until they were off the field and on a fairly deserted walkway. "Look, Gavin, I know you may not approve of Kate seeing Tommy—"

He blinked. "Why wouldn't I approve? The boy's got half the colleges in the country offering him scholarships. I'm sure he'll end up in the NFL."

Wow. That was the last thing Leigh had expected. She glanced at Jared, who seemed equally surprised.

"Glad to hear you feel that way," she said, bemused.

"Oh, don't get me wrong. I still want Kate to go to college and everything, but as long as she and Tommy don't do anything—" He shrugged. "You know. Then it's fine with me."

"Oh." Leigh smiled. "Good."

Gavin nodded. "Yes, it is. Kate's happy, so I'm happy. Love's a great thing."

Ah, crud, here they were with that love stuff again. All Leigh said in response was, "Hmmm."

Jared patted the other man on the shoulder. "Congratulations on homecoming weekend. It seems to be going well."

"It is. It is. Of course naturally, the student dance sold out, but the alumni dance did, too. We really pulled them in this year. People are coming from all around."

"That's great," Leigh said, wishing he'd finish up so she and Jared could leave.

Gavin looked at her. "That's not all that's great. Leigh, I wanted to tell you that a full-time teaching position is waiting for you next year. You've really proven yourself with the parade."

Leigh hadn't been expecting him to offer her a job, well, certainly not so soon. She let out a yelp, then with a self-conscious laugh said, "Thanks. I really appreciate it."

"You earned it," he said. "Well, I've got to go see what my family is up to. And watch the game."

Gavin headed off, and Leigh commented, "Why do I get the feeling Kate will have a terrible time if she ever decides to break up with Tommy?"

"Yeah, it does seem like Gav's got his heart set on having a pro football player as a son-in-law." He nudged her. "Congratulations, teach. Looks like you got what you wanted."

Leigh grinned. "I did, didn't I? I got the job." She shot him a flirty glance. "And I got you. Yep, I'm one happy lady."

For a second she simply enjoyed her feeling of pure bliss, then she noticed the odd look Jared was giving her.

"What?" she asked. "You got what you wanted, too. You have your rodeo school."

"Sort of. Right now I'm entertaining Steve's brother and his family. They're not really the kind of students I had in mind."

"But you're running your own business," she pointed out. "And once you bring in enough money, you can afford to make your school the best around. Then you'll get lots and lots of rodeo students."

"True." Even though he'd agreed with her, he kept giving her that odd look.

"Oh, and let's not forget what else you have," she said, hoping to turn around his mood. "You've got me."

She leaned up, all set to give him a kiss, when he said, ''No, I don't. I don't have you, Leigh.''

Ah, jeez. She knew this was going to happen if everyone insisted on talking about love all the time.

''Jared, we agreed—''

''No, you agreed. And I didn't argue. But here's the thing, Leigh. I love you. And I want to marry you.''

She stared at him. This was much worse than she'd expected. Not only had he used the *L* word, but he'd gone and used the *M* word, too.

''Have you been thinking all along that I'll change my mind and suddenly decide I can't live without you?'' she asked. ''Was all this dating stuff some sort of plan, because if it was, it was a bad plan. And it didn't work.''

Jared didn't seem upset with what she was saying. Just kinda resigned. ''Fine. It may not have worked, but at least I gave it a shot.''

Taking a step closer to her, he added, ''You know, everyone in this town loves to point out to me all the things I've ever done wrong in my life. You'd think I was the only one in this damn town who ever made a mistake. But you know something? Loving you isn't a mistake, and nobody's going to tell me it is. Not even you. If you're too scared to give us a chance, then that's your mistake, not mine.''

Leigh opened her mouth to say something, but he shook his head.

"Let me finish," he said. "I may not have all the answers, but I know one thing—you and I belong together. Not because I'm the bad boy in town and I get your brothers upset. But because I love you more than any man ever will." He drew in a deep breath. "And what's really sad is deep down, you know I'm right. You're just too confused to admit it. Even to yourself."

With that, he turned and walked away from her. Leigh stared after him. Wow. She hadn't really expected that. Okay, that was a lie. She had sort of expected it. But she hadn't expected him to be so…sincere.

Well, he was wrong about her. About them. He might like to think that she loved him, but she didn't. She liked him. She liked him a lot. But that wasn't love.

Love was…a million clichés occurred to her, but that was all. Her mind was drawing a complete blank.

So she wasn't sure what love was, but she knew what it wasn't—it wasn't what she felt for Jared Kendrick.

Not at all.

9

"DON'T YOU KNOW HOW to tell time?" Leigh asked her brother Chase when she found him standing on her doorstep at seven the next morning. "It's Saturday. Some of us like to sleep in."

"Seven is sleeping in," he said. Then he shoved a pastry box at her. "Here. Stop being grumpy. I brought jelly doughnuts. That should keep you from biting my head off."

Leigh yawned—deliberately—and took the box. "Fine. You gave me the doughnuts. Thanks so much. Now can I go back to sleep?"

He chuckled. "To quote you, as if." Without first asking permission, he squeezed past her and headed toward the kitchen. "Got any coffee made?"

She so didn't need this today. The fight with Jared had preyed on her mind, so she'd hardly gotten any sleep at all last night. All she wanted to do was curl up in bed and forget about everything.

"No, I don't have coffee made. Up until a couple of minutes ago, I was *asleep*." When Chase didn't answer, she padded after him. "Go home, Chase. I'm serious."

She found him making coffee. "Don't do that. You won't be here long enough to drink it. Take these doughnuts and go home. I'm sure Megan would like some breakfast, too."

"Megan's still asleep," he commented as he searched the cabinets. "Where do you keep your mugs?"

Grrr. She walked over and grabbed a mug out of the cabinet next to the sink. "How come Megan gets to sleep in and I don't?"

"Megan's pregnant. She needs her rest. You've got love-life trouble, which you need to take care of." He started the coffee and sat at her small kitchen table. "So what are you going to do about Jared?"

She started to tell him it was none of his business, but then he said, "And how can I help?"

Oh, now what was a girl with a broken heart supposed to do when her big brother offered to help? Leigh sat down next to him.

"I guess somehow you know what happened last night at the stadium."

He nodded. "This is Paxton. Everyone knows. A couple of folks overheard you."

Overheard. Spied on them. Same thing in Paxton. With a groan, Leigh ran her hands through her hair. "Then they would have heard the part where I'm not interested in getting married. End of discussion. Jared and I want different things out of life. I thought we'd come to an agreement, but I guess not.''

"I see," Chase said. "Go on."

"Go on? There's nothing more to go on to. We broke up. That's the end of the story.'' Although it bothered her admitting they were through, she'd just have to get used to it. Jared had known how she felt before they'd started dating. As far as she was concerned, it was dirty pool for him to try to change the rules now.

Chase stood and headed over to the coffeepot. Once he'd filled two mugs, he brought them to the table.

He shoved the mug with little hearts on it toward her. "Here."

Leigh shuddered. "It's black. I'd rather drink motor oil."

"Why drink coffee at all if you're going to gunk it up with milk and sugar?" Chase took a big sip from his mug. "Yum."

"One man's yum is this woman's yuck," Leigh informed him. She headed over to the refrigerator and got out the milk. After pouring a healthy dose into her mug, she returned to her seat.

"So how is Megan doing? Still feeling sick?" she asked.

Chase chuckled. "Nice try, kiddo, but you're not changing the subject. Unlike you, Megan is fine."

"You know, I'm getting tired of you saying something is wrong with me. Just because I'm not interested in falling in love and getting married doesn't mean I'm the one who's wrong," she pointed out. Then, hoping if she were eating he'd leave her alone, she snagged a doughnut out of the box and took a big bite.

For a second, Chase just watched her. Then he said, "We boys never meant to make you miserable. Nathan, Trent and I just wanted to take care of you 'cause you're our sister and we love you. I'm sorry if we made you feel stifled."

This couldn't be Chase, the man who had single-handedly broken up most of her dates during high school, and even a couple during college.

She tapped the side of her head. "Excuse me? I must be hearing things. I thought you apologized."

Chase laughed. "Okay, okay. I know. It's not something I've done a lot in my life. Guess being married has mellowed me."

"Mellowed you. Not me. I'm still looking forward to having some fun and excitement in my life," she pointed out.

"You know, love and excitement are compatible, Leigh. You keep acting like if you fall in love, your life becomes dull and boring. That's just not true. Look at me. I'm about to become a dad. I don't think there's anything boring about that."

Leigh wanted to argue with him, but nothing came to mind. "I guess," she relented. "But it's not about that."

"It's about having your own way for once in

your life, isn't it?'' he asked. ''Because you feel
like Nathan, Trent and I pushed you around, you
now want to call the shots. That's understandable.
And I won't lie to you, when you fall in love, you
have to be willing to compromise. Not issue ulti-
matums like you did to Jared.''

''Hey, I didn't issue an ultimatum,'' she maintained.

''The way I understand it, you told him not to
fall in love with you, then got mad at him when he
did. Sounds like an ultimatum to me.''

Well, it wasn't. Not at all. It was…the rules for
their relationship. Okay, okay, her rules. Maybe she
hadn't given him a lot of options. Or any options
for that matter. Maybe she had said how she
thought things should go and had expected that to
be that.

She nibbled on her doughnut, suddenly unsure.
Now that she thought about it, that didn't seem
right. Or fair. Jared was a person, too. Why didn't
he get some say in their relationship?

Grrr. More importantly, why did Chase have to
point all this out to her and muddy waters she
thought were crystal clear?

Chase stood. ''Guess I'd better head on back
home. You seem to be doing okay. I thought you'd
be all weepy because you were never going to see
Jared again. But you're just fine.''

He leaned down and dropped a kiss on the top

of her head. "See ya, kiddo. Don't forget, you're riding to the alumni dance with Megan and me."

Ah, jeez. The dance. She'd completely forgotten about the dance tonight.

"I don't think I'll go," she said.

Chase gave her a pointed look. "Now won't that give the town something to talk about? I can hear it now—Leigh Barrett had a big fight with Jared Kendrick, and now she's too ashamed to even show her face in public."

Leigh was beyond caring what everyone in Paxton thought. But sitting around her house wouldn't do her any good. And besides, she was starting to think she might owe Jared an apology. "Yeah, you're right. I've got no reason not to go."

She glanced at the clock. She'd need to get busy since she was going to the dance tonight. She wanted to be composed, and she didn't feel even remotely composed yet. She felt…sad. She might not be weepy like Chase had expected, but she was hurting. As much as she hated to admit it, she missed Jared. A lot.

And it had only been since yesterday.

She looked up at Chase. She was glad he'd stopped by, glad to know that her doofy brothers were always there for her. "Thanks."

"No thanks necessary. See you later, kiddo."

Leigh nodded, but her mind was already on tonight. She could only hope that Jared intended on coming to the dance because she needed to talk to him.

She needed to talk to him badly.

"BUT YOU HAVE TO COME to the dance," Janet Defries said for about the millionth time.

Jared sighed. Why didn't the woman just take no for an answer and head on home? Her riding lesson had ended twenty minutes ago. It was time for her to leave.

But good manners kept him from kicking her out. Instead he said patiently, "Janet, I'm not coming to the alumni dance. That's that."

"Because of Leigh Barrett? Oh, come on. You have to move on with your life. Get back on the horse."

"Pull myself up by my bootstraps?" he couldn't resist adding.

Janet frowned. "Don't tease. You have to come. The awards committee has something for you." She placed her hands on her hips and tried to look sexy. "Besides, you owe me a dance."

"Since when?" He started leading Spirit toward the barn, figuring Janet might finally get the hint.

Unfortunately she didn't. She simply fell into step next to him. "Since the senior prom. I asked you to dance with me, and you said later. Well, it's later, Jared. You owe me a dance."

There was no way he was dancing with Janet. Or anyone else for that matter. All he wanted to do was stay home and take care of his ranch. He'd had no intention of going into Paxton for a while.

He'd stay out here by himself. Well, by himself with Steve Myerson's brother and his family. And the family from Little Rock who'd heard about the new dude ranch and showed up on his doorstep today with no reservations but high hopes.

Damn. Even his business wasn't working out right. "I'm not going, Janet. Have a good time, though."

They'd reached the barn and he started to head inside when she said, "So, that's it? Leigh says no and you give up? The way I heard it, you told her you loved her and how things were going to be. But she threw your love back in your face. You can't hide out now. People will think you're a coward."

Jared considered what she said. He didn't really care what the people of Paxton said. What bothered him was Janet's interpretation of what had happened. Had he really told Leigh how things were going to be?

Now that he thought about it, maybe he had. He hadn't said it would be okay for them to still be together even if she didn't want to get married. He hadn't said that he understood that she'd need time to think about what she wanted from their relationship.

He'd told her.

No wonder she'd told him no.

He missed her so much. He couldn't help thinking his plan had been dumb. He should have known better than to try to force her to fall in love with him.

He should have let her make her own decisions.

"I'll be at the dance," he said, his mind made up. Behind him, Janet started talking about all the things they could do once he showed up at the dance, but he wasn't really listening.

All he could think about was seeing Leigh tonight.

"THIS ISN'T WORKING," Jared said to Trent. He glanced at his watch. The dance had started twenty minutes ago and she still wasn't here. It looked like Leigh was going to skip the dance just so she didn't have to see him.

"You worry too much. She'll come around. Just you wait," Trent said, getting a couple of glasses of punch.

"I agree. It's early," Erin said, taking one of the glasses of punch from her husband. "Wait and see what happens tonight."

Based on what had happened last night, he wasn't sure she'd even give him the chance to apologize. He figured one of two things would happen: either Leigh wouldn't show up or she'd show up, take one look at him and walk the other way.

He hated both scenarios.

"Maybe I should head on home," he said.

Trent slapped him on the back. "Don't give up yet. The night's young. Lots of things can happen."

Jared watched as Trent and Erin set down their glasses, and then headed onto the dance floor. Yeah, lots of things could happen. Lots of bad things.

He glanced at his watch yet again. Maybe he could wait another fifteen minutes. But after that, he really was going to head home. He'd try to call her in a few days and see if she'd talk to him. Maybe if she cooled down, she'd give him a second chance.

Almost as if his mind were playing tricks on him, he heard her laughter floating down the hallway leading to the gym. She had come to the dance after all.

For a split second, he felt like he was seventeen again, waiting for the most popular girl in town to notice him. Except now, the stakes were much, much higher. He wanted the woman he loved to forgive him.

And he figured he had about as much chance of that happening as he did of flying by flapping his arms. Still, he tensely waited for Leigh to appear in the doorway.

When she did enter, she looked amazing. She had on a long black dress that shimmered when she walked. The dress hugged her figure, draping over her curves and skimming down her long legs.

Desire hit him hard, followed by longing. Damn, he missed her.

After staring at Leigh for a long, long time, he

finally noticed that Chase and Megan were with her. Focusing on Leigh, he waited for her to spot him. When she did, he expected her to immediately look away. But she didn't. Her gaze stayed locked with his, and he couldn't help hoping that was a good sign.

At this point, he'd pretty much take anything he could get. He started to cross the room to talk to her, but the song ended and then Janet, Tammy and Caitlin gathered around the microphone.

"This year, we have a lot of great awards to give out, so let's get started," Janet said.

Jared didn't care about the awards. He only wanted to make his way through this crowd so he could talk to Leigh. It wasn't easy, especially once they started announcing the winners. Who had traveled the farthest to come to homecoming, who had traveled the least. Yeah. Yeah. He tried to see Leigh, but he could no longer make her out in the crowd.

Why didn't they hurry up and finish these blasted awards?

"And for the most likely to eventually employ all of us, Nathan Barrett," Caitlin announced.

Jared stopped and watched Nathan climb the steps to accept his award, which was actually a stuffed panther toy.

"Gee, thanks," he said.

Poor guy. Jared really felt for Nathan. But true to form, Nathan was taking it with good humor.

They continued to give out awards, but rather than thinning the crowd, it seemed to actually make the people push closer to the stage. Finally there was a small break, so he cut through.

And Leigh was standing there, not three feet from him.

"Hi," he said, coming over to her.

"Hi."

For a moment, they just looked at each other.

"I'm sorry about—"

"I feel badly about—"

They both laughed. "You go first," she said.

"Okay. Leigh, I was wrong to push you the way I did. You don't have to fall in love with me, and we certainly don't have to get married. All I'm asking is to be with you, and that you don't mind if I'm in love with you."

She was grinning at him. "That's so sweet. But I shouldn't have backed you into a corner, either."

Jared was leaning down to kiss her when he heard Janet say, "And the award for the person most likely to get arrested, Jared Kendrick."

Ah, hell.

He lifted his head, but before he could say anything, Leigh made a growling sound and stormed the stage. Baffled, he watched her take the stairs in a bound. Then, she grabbed the microphone out of Janet's hand and faced the crowd.

"What's wrong with you people? Jared was a kid when he did all those things. You need to let it go and get on with your lives. You can't tell me each and every one of you doesn't have things in your past that the rest of us could rub in your face.''

Janet started to take the microphone back, but Leigh glared at her. ''Janet, you of all people shouldn't want someone's past thrown in their face.''

With a gurgling noise, Janet moved away. Jared's attention shifted back to Leigh. She looked magnificent up there, defending him.

Man, he loved her.

''And for the record, you should thank your lucky stars we had Jared. He made this town interesting. He kept things lively. But that was a long time ago, and by dwelling on it, you're missing out on what a wonderful man he's become. He's kind and generous and...''

Her voice grew soft. He could clearly see tears in her eyes. Crying? He didn't think Leigh ever cried. But she was now. He watched a tear trail down one cheek. ''And Jared is truly, truly the best man I've ever known. The best man I'll ever know. I'm so lucky to have him in my life.''

Amazed at what she was saying, especially in front of this crowd, Jared slowly started walking toward the stage. His gaze locked with Leigh's and she smiled.

''You know, sometimes you don't realize what someone means to you until someone else says something bad about them. I have to thank Janet for her nasty comments. They've made me face what I've felt for a long time but didn't want to admit—I love you, Jared.''

A gasp went through the crowd, and Jared felt his heart thump wildly. She'd said she loved him. And in front of a lot of people.

''I love you, too,'' he told her. ''And thanks for standing up for me.''

She grinned and came over to the edge of the stage. Kneeling, she leaned over and kissed him. Jared couldn't believe how wonderful, terrific, amazing this woman was.

And he was lucky enough to have her love him. Life didn't get any better than this.

When the kiss ended, Leigh leaned back and whispered, ''Marry me?''

Since she still had the microphone in her hands, that whisper echoed around the gym. Jared laughed. ''I will if you will.''

By now, the crowd was clapping and cheering them on. When Leigh yelled, ''Yes'' the entire room broke into applause.

After Leigh set the microphone down, Jared reached out and lifted her into his arms.

''I really do love you,'' she said, caressing the side of his face. ''I can't believe how stupid I was not to realize it sooner.''

''That's okay. I'm just glad you finally realized.''

Then he kissed her.

Yeah, life didn't get any better than this.

Epilogue

SOMETIMES LIFE WAS SIMPLY too good to believe, Leigh Barrett-Kendrick decided as she slipped into the arms of her new husband for their first dance as a married couple.

"Did I tell you yet today that I love you?" Jared tugged her even closer. "That I adore you? That I'm absolutely crazy about you?"

Leigh pretended to think. "Um, well there was that one time in front of the minister. No, wait. Then all you said was 'I do.' I don't remember anything about you loving, adoring or being crazy about me."

He chuckled and feathered kisses down the side of her neck. Slowly the band started to play something completely unrecognizable but romantic all the same. Jared glided her around the dance floor inside the reception hall.

"Then let me rectify that right now. I, Jared Kendrick, do love, adore, and am certifiably crazy about you, Leigh Barrett-Kendrick. I promise to treat you like a goddess—"

Leigh laughed and wrapped her arms around his neck. "Which, of course, I am."

"To me you are," Jared said.

Oh, well, there was no way a woman could let a man say something that romantic without rewarding him, so Leigh kissed him long and deep. She couldn't believe how lucky she was to have this man love her so. Her life was perfect. Absolutely perfect. She had a wonderful man who loved her, and whose rodeo school was finally taking off. She also had a new job teaching math at the high school. And a family who was too precious for words.

Yes, her life was perfect.

And the wedding today had been perfect, too. That, of course, was thanks to the excellent planning she and Jared had done for the past ten months. They'd made all of the decisions themselves, and even though she'd never thought it was possible, they'd had no problem reaching compromises whenever they'd had different opinions.

Now, looking back on the wedding, she had to admit that every detail had been flawless. Not a single thing had gone wrong.

Well, not many things anyway. Sure, her brother Trent's dog, Brutus, had taken a big chomp out of the wedding cake. And Chase and Megan's new son, Kyle, had spit up all over Megan's matron-of-honor dress. And Hailey, who was about to give birth any day now to a little boy, had started feeling oddly, so no one knew for certain if she'd make it through the reception or not. Then the smell of that spit-up had made Erin, who'd only recently announced she was pregnant and no doubt also was going to have a boy, to have to race off to the ladies' room seconds before the wedding was to start.

But still, the wedding had been perfect for Leigh because she'd been with her crazy, wild, meddlesome family while she'd married the man she positively adored.

If that wasn't perfect, she didn't know what was.

When they finally ended the kiss, Leigh grinned at her new husband and flicked open the top two buttons on his vest. "Got any plans for later this evening?" she teased.

She felt his hands on the back of her dress, and she knew for a fact he'd slid down the zipper. She'd deliberately bought this dress because it had a zipper on the back.

"I don't know. Let's see, I may take out the trash. Watch a little TV. Why, you have anything special in mind?"

Leigh giggled. "Um, let me think. How about making insane, unpredictable love to your new wife?"

"Sounds like a plan to me." He kissed her again.

While they were kissing, Leigh flicked open another button on his vest. She wasn't going to be the only one standing on this dance floor half-dressed when this song ended.

And speaking of this song, it was so familiar yet she couldn't place it. Drat. It was driving her crazy.

She tried mentally humming the tune softly, but still had no idea.

Where'd she know it from? Unable to think of the title after a couple of seconds, she broke off the kiss and looked at Jared. "What is this song they're playing? I know I know it, but I can't think of what it is."

He grinned. "It's our song, darlin'. Don't tell me you don't remember it."

Their song? They didn't have a song. Did they? Had she forgotten something? "What are you—"

Suddenly it hit her and her mouth dropped open. She stared at Jared, then started to laugh. "You've got to be kidding me."

Jared twirled her once again to the music, which was kinda difficult considering the band was playing a slow, mushy rendition of the "Hokey Pokey." "What else would I have them play?"

"What am I going to do with you?" she teased.

"Love me forever?" he suggested.

Leigh smiled. "Sounds like a plan to me."

* * * * *

If you missed the first volume of
HOMETOWN HEARTTHROBS—
*Chase's story and Nathan's—
check out Duets #71
published in March 2002!*

A visit to Cooper's Corner offers the chance for a new beginning...

COOPER'S CORNER

Coming in December 2002
DANCING IN THE DARK
by Sandra Marton

Check-in: When Wendy Monroe left Cooper's Corner, she was an Olympic hopeful in skiing...and madly in love with Seth Castleman. But an accident on the slopes shattered her dreams, and rather than tell Seth the painful secret behind her injuries, Wendy leaves him.

Checkout: A renowned surgeon staying at Twin Oaks can mend Wendy's leg. But only facing Seth again—and the truth—can mend her broken heart.

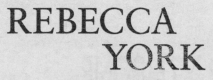

$ **Saving Money** $
Has Never Been
This Easy!

Just fill out and send in this form from any
October, November and December 2002 books
and we will send you a coupon booklet worth a
total savings of $20.00 off future purchases of
Harlequin and Silhouette books in 2003.

Yes! It's that easy!

Please send this form to:
   In the U.S.: Harlequin Books, P.O. Box 9071, Buffalo, NY 14269-9071
   In Canada: Harlequin Books, P.O. Box 609, Fort Erie, Ontario L2A 5X3

Allow 4-6 weeks for delivery. Limit one coupon booklet per household. Must be
postmarked no later than January 15, 2003.

HARLEQUIN®
Makes any time special ®

Silhouette ®
Where love comes alive™